DYKEWORDS

An Anthology of Lesbian Writing

EDITED BY

*The Lesbian Writing
and Publishing Collective*

women's
PRESS

CANADIAN CATALOGUING IN PUBLICATION DATA
Dykewords: an anthology of lesbian writing
ISBN 0-88961-149-1

1. Lesbians' writings, Canadian (English).* 2. Short stories, Canadian (English)
— Women's authors.* 3. Canadian fiction (English) — 20th century.* 4. Canadian
poetry (English) — Women authors.* 5. Canadian poetry (English)
— 20th century.* 6. Lesbianism — Fiction. 7. Lebianism — Poetry.
I. Lesbian Writing and Publishing Collective.

PS8287.L47D9 1990   C811'.5408'0353
PR9195.85.L47D9 1990   C90-094721-7

Women's Press gratefully acknowledges permission to reprint the following song
lyrics.

From "Birds Of A Feather" © 1980 Mummy Dust Music Limited. Words aand
music by Carole Pope and Kevan Staples. Taken from the True North album
"Rough Trade's Greatest Hits / Birds Of A Feather." Reprinted with permission.

From "I Got The Will" © 1982 Irving Music, Inc. (BMI).Words and music by Otis
Redding. All rights reserved. International Copyright secured.

From "Breakin' Up Somebody's Home" © 1988 Intersong U.S.A. Inc. and Chap-
pell and Co. Inc. All rights reserved. Used by permission Warner/Chappell Music
Canada Ltd.

Cover art: Grace Channer.   Cover design: Kim McNeilly.
Editing and copy editing: Ellen Quigley.
Proofreading: Pinelopi Gramatikopoulos.

Published by Women's Press, 517 College Street, Suite 233,
Toronto, Ontario, Canada M6G 4A2.

This book was produced by the collective effort of Women's Press and is a project
of the Lesbian Manuscript Group.

Women's Press gratefully acknowledges financial support from the Canada
Council, the Ontario Arts Council, and the Lesbian and Gay Community Appeal,
Toronto.

Printed and bound in Canada by union labour.
1 2 3 4 1994 1993 1992 1991 1990

Contents

Introduction

Dykewords: An Anthology of Lesbian Writing is a collection of short fiction, poetry, texts, and drama. The mixture of genres alone suggests the wide scope that The Lesbian Writing and Publishing Collective hopes to span. Eroticism and humour combine with issues of language, pregnancy, alcoholism, abuse, rehabilitation, military control, homophobia, and racism. Totally unselfconscious narrative is included alongside texts in which the writer, the reader, and the mediums of creation are visible objects.

There are contributions by Native women, women of Colour, and white women; contributions by working-class women and middle-class women. Geographically, the contributors cover much the same range as the last anthology. While this anthology has gained representation from women in some of the smaller cities in Ontario, it has lost representation from the Prairies. Still, there is nothing from the Atlantic Provinces, the North, and little from rural lesbians. Why? How can we write from a lesbian voice and still keep a safety net of invisibility around our lives? (Will I be alienated from my support community? Who will get custody of the children? What about job security? Will my mailbox be smashed on Hallowe'en, or will the young punks be waiting for me?) Is the effort of developing a culture — of standing strong and proud where we've been repressed for so long — too difficult to achieve in isolation from community and without the anonymity of a city? Are we just too busy trying to survive? Or do some lesbian writers still feel excluded?

The process of editing an anthology of lesbian voices is an awesome task given the lack of many previous examples.

Who are we? How and what do we write? Where do our voices come from? Given this set of unknowns, the tasks of networking and selecting become daunting. How do we choose but not restrict? This is the second of a series of books, and what we have chosen here does not represent all that we want or all that can be, only the best of what we received. We are still searching for more voices, alternate writing styles. The only concepts of writing that we are committed to are feminism, anti-racism, and social responsibility.

We hope that anthologies that we have published will encourage growth in the field of lesbian writing. And the writers do seem to be getting stronger, more self-assured. More of the contributors explore the lesbian body, erotic desire, suggesting a comfort in our right to build a self-defined niche in the literary world. More of the writers include serious issues that often plague people shoved to the fringe of a society controlled by white, heterosexual men. This suggests a need to move beyond simplistic celebration of our love for women and dig deep into the dirt — the layers of scars that affect some of our lives. Sometimes a writer tackles these issues head-on; other times they are just another part of a lesbian's struggle to survive or be accepted.

Dykewords offers works by women who have never previously published, women who have often published, and the whole gamut between. It is refreshing and challenging to listen to new voices emerge and sometimes suprising to see new twists in writers we are already familiar with. Different aspects in this collection have enticed me with each reading. It's been exciting working with other lesbians writing ourselves.

Ellen Quigley

untitled

Dionne Brand

this is you girl, this cut of road up
to blanchecheuse, this every turn a piece
of blue and earth carrying on, beating, rock and ocean
this wearing away, smoothing the insides pearl
of shell and coral

this is you girl, this is you all sides of me
hill road and dip through the coconut at manzanilla
this sea breeze shaped forest of sand and lanky palm
this wanting to fall, hanging, greening
quenching the road

this is you girl, even though you never see it
the drop before timberline, that daub of black shine
sea on bush smoke land, that pulse of the heart
that stretches up to maracas, la fillete bay never know you
but you make it wash up from the rocks

this is you girl, that bit of lagoon, alligator
long abandoned, this stone of my youngness
hesitating to walk right, turning to schoener's road
turning to duenne and spirit, to the sea wall and sea
breaking hard against things, turning to burning reason

this is you girl, this is the poem no woman
ever write for a woman because she 'fraid to touch
this river boiling like a woman in she sleep
that smell of fresh thighs and warm sweat
sheets of her like the mitan rolling into the atlantic

this is you girl, something never waning or forgetting
something hard against the soul
this is where you make sense, that the sight becomes tender
the night air human, the dull silence full chattering, volcanoes
cease, and to be awake is more lovely than dreams

Pumping Light

Beth Follett

The damn' dishwasher bust, and I'm standing here sudsing up this pile of bowls like a bloody idiot. Seems like I'm forever standing in front of this sink. I'm too nice for my own good. I say, "Sure! I'll do them," all sweet and smiling to that sly staff member Helen, 'cause I figure she'll boot me outside if I don't, and it's pissing out, and I left my raincoat at the workshop yesterday, and I ain't got nowhere to go, besides. And doesn't Helen know all this, anyway, and isn't that exactly why she bothered me when I was getting nice and cozy with my coffee and cigarettes and the paper? Anyway, why don't the others clean their own breakfast dishes before they run off to wherever the fuck they have to go each day? Damn' idiots. Lazy bunch o' bitches. How did I end up living with this bunch of stupid cunts?

Whoa, pony! Do as the good staff tell you. Count to ten. Count to twenty. Count to whatever goddamn' number you have to if it keeps you from putting your fist through the wall and getting kicked out of here for good.

Ah, they can all go to hell!

"Now Sylvia, we don't have too many rules in this house, but we have some expectations."

That was Helen, in my interview. I remember her sitting on the swivel chair by the desk with her one leg tucked up

11

under her fat ass, smoking, and swiveling slightly, and bouncing her sandal off the toes of her other foot. They all wear those same dumb sandals that look like boats. THEIR uniform.

By signing the paper that explained the so-called expectations, I was agreeing to be a bloody mindreader. If only I'd known. The expectations grow like cancer in the staff's heads. Coming to live in this house was like agreeing to go for a walk in a jungle set with a million bouncing Betty booby traps.

But I agreed to go out every day for a least four hours, and if Helen finds me hiding out here in my room, the shit's gonna fly. And what am I gonna do when I get a nicotine fit? I could maybe sneak one in the laundry room, if that Helen didn't have a nose as big as a fire extinguisher.

It's as cold as Hades down here. Those cheap bitches must close the vents into the basement. Sure as anything, I'm gonna have my piles acting up, sitting on this dryer. I wonder. If I turned it on for a minute, would Ms Snoop be alerted? Who else is in the house? Well, Doreen, but she NEVER does her laundry — fuck, that's a laugh — what laundry? She's only got one dress, and I swear she sleeps in that!

Shit! Who's that coming? Out through the window I go!

I'm about as pathetic as a body can be. Now look at me, out here on the driveway in the pouring rain, no jacket, no cigarettes. Sylvia, you're losing your touch. Just walk in the front door, real cool like, as if nothing could be more regular than a walk in the spring rain on a Thursday morning. Ain't no expectation that says a woman can't get soaking wet if she feels like it.

"Hey, Helen, how's it hangin'?"

Now that was very fine! She hardly looked up from her desk. What do these staff write in that daybook that keeps them glued in that damn' office, anyway? Far as I can see, we're ten mental women sitting around on our butts watching TV, or listening to records, most nights, and complaining about having to go to stupid hospital programs and shrinks most days.

So if Helen's been sitting in the office all this time, who was that in the laundry room? Waste of a good cigarette....

Only five more hours, and I can turn on the TV. Only three more hours, and I can legitimately show my face around the staff-room door.

Wonder which staff comes on at one? Hope it's Dorothy. Then I can get away with murder.

"Sylvia! Can I speak with you in the staff room for a minute?"

Oh-oh.

"Hey, Helen, it's a pleasure! How can I help you?"

"Very cute, Sylvia. Since you're obviously forgetting some of the house agreements, how would you like to review your contract, maybe go over some of your goals while we're at it?"

I've been able to squeeze out of the last three months' worth of contract reviews. No staff full of the power of irony is gonna get the better of me now.

"Gee, Helen, could we just talk? I've got something that's troubling me, and I'd be really happy if I could get it off my mind" — and load it on yours, honey!

She puts her cigarette out and gets up to close the door. Great. She's mine, all mine. These staff just melt at the words, "Can we talk?" They like talking almost as much as writing.

Of course, since they write about what we talk about, the time for talking is only as long as they have time left to write about it. Helen goes off shift at one, it's now eleven. Relax, Sylvia, you've got one whole hour!

"… you know, and if I had the power to do it, I'd put all men so far away, they'd have to pump light to them."

"Well, Sylvia, I'm sorry you've got to put up with these men at the workshop, but a woman like yourself should be able to put them in their place, hmm?"

"But Helen, these guys are animals! I mean regular Tarzan weirdos. And if they think I'm into their games, they're even crazier than me!"

"Sylvia, you're not crazy…."

"Was I in the nut house or not?"

"It's not a 'nut house,' Sylvia…."

"No, it's a bloody prison. This is a palace in comparison to Whitby. But you can lose a lot of spunk in prison, Helen. You know, I might have had a soul if not for Whitby."

"Okay, Sylvia, we're getting off track here. Look, I'm sure the workshop could be more exciting for a woman with your smarts, but you know, until you work on that anger of yours within a community setting, you're not ready for anything more independent. You know what happens to you when you try to be a lone wolf."

"Yeah, okay, you've got a point, Helen. But today I just had to take a break from the cretins. You know, get grounded."

It's great to use their words on them. They think they've really influenced some big changes in you. They can envision you striding further and further away from hospital. At this point, I'm making strides to put Paul Bunyun to shame.

"So, what exactly are you going to do to ground yourself?"

"Thought I'd write in my journal this afternoon, maybe pound a few pillows."

"Sounds good, Sylvia."

Here it comes. We sit here eye-balling one another, and I can hear the words as if I was gonna say them myself.

"Well, Sylvia, if you'll excuse me. I've got a little writing to do before I leave."

"Sure thing, Helen. And thanks for listening."

Scored! It's noon, and Helen's got her work cut out for her. Then there's shift change at one, that'll last for about twenty minutes, then whoever comes on will have to read the log — another twenty minutes — la-te-dah! I've got one hundred free minutes to do a big, glorious nothing.

What the hell am I gonna do?

"HEY, WHY DON'T I JUST CUT MY WRISTS AND BLEED ALL OVER THE SUPPER TABLE! OR BETTER YET, WHY DON'T YOU JUST SMASH MY HEAD OPEN AND SPILL OUT EVERYTHING? WHAT'S THE USE OF HAVING A FUCKIN' ROOM OF YOUR OWN IF A BLOODY FREEWAY RUNS THROUGH IT! I THOUGHT THIS WAS SUPPOSED TO BE A PLACE WHERE I COULD GET MYSELF BACK ON MY FEET. IT'S A JOKE, IT'S A GODDAMN' JOKE!!!"

Lianne and Helen are behind me, and the three of us are staring at the shattered glass of my bedroom window. Then they see my hand, and Helen is running for the first-aid kit, and Lianne is beside me, not looking at all afraid that I might plow her one. I like this woman. She's got her shit together.

"Someone wrote LESBIAN in my journal."

I'm turning my hand around, checking out the pretty good job Helen did on the bandaging. It hurts like a bugger. I'm out of here for sure, once all the staff find out about this.

Lianne takes a cigarette, then offers me one.

"I have some of my own, it's okay."

"These are yours, Sylvia. I brought them along from your room. You don't mind, do you?"

God, I like this woman!

"Any idea who might have done it?"

"Could be anyone here. They all know I'm a dyke. They all hate me because they're scared of me."

"Well, you know, Sylvia, when you go around putting your fist through things, you do nothing to endear yourself to people."

"I don't give a shit for anyone here, except you, maybe. How would you like your privacy invaded? What have any of them done to endear themselves to me?"

Lianne is quiet, and I feel real dumb for that last statement. I sound like a bitter victim. I don't want to equate being gay with being a victim. Too pedestrian.

"Sylvia, I agree that you've been treated unfairly. No one has the right to be in your room uninvited, never mind your journal. Your anger is legitimate. But does it have to be so expensive to the house? The plaster over last week's hole is still wet."

"I'll pay for the window."

"Your welfare cheque doesn't even keep you in cigarettes. How are you going to pay for the window?"

"I'll smoke less."

She and I both know what a lie that is.

"Sylvia, I'm not in a position to bargain with you. The collective has to decide what course of action to take. I can tell you that you have our empathy when it comes to being out in the world — I for one have a lot of respect for you — but the safety of the other women in this house is of primary consideration, and explosions like yours just don't make people feel safe."

"I suppose I'm supposed to feel safe knowing people are reading my journal, writing hate literature in it."

"You know you aren't the enemy. You know other women in this house are more frightened by your anger than by your choice to love women."

"And you know it's not fear of my anger that motivates them — it's envy."

"Sylvia, I want you to hear this. It IS your anger that frightens them, because you express your anger like a man."

"FUCK YOU, LIANNE."

I hope that staff door handle is right through the wall.

I'm gonna walk to Mississauga. I could walk to Detroit, with the adrenaline I've got feeding into me. Walk to bloody New Mexico, maybe. I'm gonna pump these legs so hard, maybe I could be my dream-self and fly.

Five o'clock. Shift change. Wonder who's come on. Wonder who else now knows about big bad Sylvia.

Sure isn't summer yet — shit, it's cold! I'm hungry. Two lousy dollars. What'll it be, Sylvia? Cigarettes? A beer? Or a bus ride home after coffee?

"Hey man, can you spare some change?"

"How much you charging, honey?"

"Oh, piss off!"

Christ! Bloody buffoons. Thought for sure a three-piece suit would have some class. Nah, a dink's a dink.

So, Sylvia, my dear, now what? You've bought your precious cigarettes, leaving you with about an eight-mile walk back to your funeral. Face it, girl, you've screwed up for the last time.

"'Scuse me, can I borrow your phone for a minute? ... No, it's not long-distance.... C'mon, it's kinda an emergency.... Look, it'll only take a minute.... That's none of your goddamn' business! ... Asshole." Should call that place Donuts and Dimwits.

Hey, self-pity, what took you so long? I was expecting you hours ago.

Okay, let's count up the reasons why I'm walking along Lower Sherbourne at ten at night, freezing my ass off, talking to myself, smoking myself to death, when I could be warm and cozy in front of the TV, bugging Doreen at commercials. Must be 'cause I'm a dyke. Must be. Must be 'cause I spent time in Whitby getting my brains cooked. Must be 'cause my mom's a fuckin' alcoholic.

Poor, poor Sylvia. Couldn't be because she's got about as much self-control as the Three Stooges on acid. Nah.

Kinda a good night for suicide, eh Sylvia? Too bad you can't afford the ride up the CN tower. Too bad you argued so much against taking meds. Too bad you're a chicken shit.

Go on home, Sylvia. Go receive your sentence like a man. Ah, shit! Like a man.

"Sylvia, is that you?"
"Yeah."
"Wanna come into the staff room for a minute?"
"Nah, what's there to say?"
"Did you have any supper? ... C'mon, I'll warm you up some macaroni and cheese."
"Nah, it's okay, I'm not hungry."
What do I need Lianne's pity for?
"Hey Doreen, how ya doing? Nice dress."
The day that woman answers me is the day I believe in miracles. Hell, I'd believe if she'd just look me in the eyes.

Think I'll make me a nice cup of Nescafé and settle into the news. My legs feel like planks. I'm sure gangrene's already taken over my hand.

Damn. No instant left. "Mary, do you know how to use this machine?"
"LEAVE ME ALONE!"
"Nice to see you, too, toots." What a nut case. I'm surrounded by idiots.

"Lianne?"
"Mmm...?"
Look at me! Please look up from your writing.
"Lianne, will you show me how to use the drip coffee machine? I've really got a taste for some strong coffee, lots of sugar."
"Sounds healthy on an empty stomach."

"Lianne — " please look at me!! — "I want some coffee, not a lecture."

"Okay, I'll be right there."

What does it matter if I ask her not to lecture, when I can hear it anyway? Granny, Lianne, Dr. Borowski — their words are inkblots in my head. But what do I really see, beyond their expectations of me? One sorry excuse for a twenty-eight-year-old dyke? One twenty-eight-year-old woman who still uses "Sorry" as an excuse.... Grow up, Sylvia.

"Is there something else, Sylvia?"

NOW she sees me!

"Look, Lianne, I'm sorry about the window. I'm not sorry about my anger, but I'm sorry about the window."

"Helen and I decided not to clean up the mess in your room. Want to do that while I make coffee? Then we can talk if you want."

"You'd make a damn' good mother, Lianne."

"Thanks. You've taught me everything I know."

A million dollar smirk has this woman. If I didn't know better, I'd let myself fall in love with her right here and now. Would. Except she scares the piss outta me.

"Can I have another cigarette, Sylvia?"

"Thought you were quitting."

"That's another thing I learned around the women in this house.... Smoke other people's cigarettes! Almost sabotages guilt."

How I'd love to be that cigarette between her lips! How I'd love to figure out why I'm ogling this woman who, not more than ten hours ago, I told to fuck off!!

"Am I gonna get kicked out of here, Lianne?"

Damn. She just turned to ice in front of me.

"That's for the staff to decide collectively."

"Do you want me to go, Lianne?"

"That's not the question, Sylvia."

"But that's my question. Do you?"

"I want a lot of things for you. But who cares? What matters is what you want for yourself."

Now she's skating away on her own icy pond. Power. When you have it, who can't you fly by?

"In that case, I want all the authority that the staff is currently holding in their collective hands."

"We never wanted it. You gave it to us today, shards of glass and all."

"Well ... I want it back."

"What are you going to do with it?"

"Walk right across all the wet paint on the floor of this square room I'm cornered in, and try again."

"I like your spirit, Sylvia. But your timing needs a lot of work."

We're looking at one another, she in the swivel chair, me on this couch. Those damn' sandals point their accusing toes at me. I feel cold. Did I just land on a booby trap?

"So, Doreen, off to bed? Me too. It's been one long day. I'm gonna sleep so deep and dream so hard, morning is gonna have to slap me in the face to get me going. Gotta go off to the workshop, you know. Busy, busy. Well, have a good sleep, Doreen."

Move Quickly

Nalini Singh

move quickly now let me pull away and regroup move now
go far where I won't be able to see you it's not sight I want I
know when I close my eyes I can see just as well it's better left
in the dark where I find my way by instinct

window's framing something underneath there in between
lineless space look the transparency of the glass is behind you
your hair has fallen left a little curl in one of my creases which
I save for later then watch it melt next time you come by

following where your tongue has been I touch a trail of tiny
bubbles crumbs of air to find where you are now giggling a
triangle of subtle movement that saves its effects for later tell
me something tell me something tell me

soft focus sensing a greenish flavour is filling the room my
hips have come to life they're drifting orange near the ceiling
a sharp shadow lying back on the bed you're heating up now
aren't you whirling away in a dance of your own

that's right find my rhythm and go slow tease me with tension
you know where I want you next but you're not going you
can't see my face in the darkness twisting with effort to suck
your fingers into my ache you're a clever one I could play like
this for hours

you've got my arms held behind my head pressing hard while you rake your teeth way past my limits but I'm far from complaining my skin has a bite of its own becoming blurry can't tell who's doing what and now I want to sink my teeth into you push back roll you over and we tumble right off the end coming to a stop in the doorway

flickers of light where have I seen this before? blue flash grey flash blue flash steady shaking but it's not either of us yet it could have been in my dream of the village whore laughing at me when I opened her legs to find out something about her

black and white dreams I close my eyes expecting colour but not this time baby this time the nuances are all in sheer texture held in by the cold rigidity of glass all around

lying right here one morning in silence then she says what are you doing I'm smiling but then I realize she didn't hear me I'm playing I say now she is watching me and I laugh you can lull yourself into a trance like this I tell her ear which has come closer lazily she stretches out pinches a piece of me into a tingling point her timing is just right

wiggles her fingers in my hair coming close almost touching her proximity is pleasing faster closer the beginning of those waves coming but quick as a wink she grabs my hand flings it into the air you're losing your trance she says with a wicked grin makes me want to lick around it swallow it but her mouth is not open to me she'd closed that part off long ago

she's greedy now guiding my hand to where she is surprisingly slippery how lovely I think she's turned it all around turns on her side wraps her legs around my cooling skin rides

my hand quickly cries her sharp throat deep coming recovers
with the same speed

bring her hand back it's distracted now that she's done make
it squeeze my left breast flick my nipple stiff she's impatient
wants to go never has time for my pleasure anymore if I want
to swim I've got to hurry so I do and the force of those damn'
waves hits me so strong it gives me a headache and I'm so
grateful for this intensity because it's her in my mind time to
get up move quickly let me pull away without ripping

ask which feels better anyway doing this with her or doing it
on my own time at my own leisure there isn't an answer

but you're not her are you you're different you're my fantasy
woman I've thought of you many times before ever since I
saw you across the room and now you're not a fantasy you're
in my bed in me and so much better than how I imagined you

move quickly the light is hitting you in the best possible way
shining off the other colours here tell me something

watched you dancing the other night and my skin broke out
in bumps danced with you the other night and it was such a
relief to see that same smile on your face to feel your leg
between my sweaty thighs your hands stroking my back
smelling the heat rising off your neck remembering what you
sounded like

I know you have a steady lover but I'm brimming over with
lust it's not often you know with me that it is attached to
someone I don't know well

it's not caretaking I want if I close my eyes I can see you just as well if I close my eyes I'd have you back here with me for many more nights next time it became dark and I was glowing green and orange I missed the feel of your body

don't want to sit here imagining what we'd do next time want it to be then I wouldn't talk so much

things are dimming now slowing down the shadows have risen to shower leaves are wilting in the window but that doesn't phase me because I'm a magician I'm an archivist I'm a strongbox of memory watch me at work

candle's burning out my fingers are heavy tired of thinking of the right word the perfect encapsulation of every shade of manipulated meaning filtering everything down through layers and layers of interpretation

fast forward rewind and cycle all around I shut down and close up and when I stand something warm leaks down my thigh next time I wouldn't talk so much

February 1987

Michigan

Kathryn Ann

Coincidence is a hard thing to figure. It's as exhilarating as winging upwards on a ferris wheel at a carnival: part of it is the motion, part of it is the view. It was one of those flukes, I guess. A woman comes along and she's a light socket, and, wham! you're plugged into the universe again. It's pure magic when it happens, and all my attempts to pin it down with a grid of words seem futile and lame when the actual event takes place.

I was in the sober-support tent because I needed to be. The woman with the cap and sunglasses was there because she was lost. It was the first of five days at the annual Michigan Womyn's Music Festival. She was looking for the Cuntree Store, and she happened to wander into the tent to ask for directions. She asked me.

I could hardly see her face, or those most crucial conveyors of the soul's substance, her eyes. Her sunglasses were enormous — purple-rimmed, as I recall — and between them and the peaked cap I could discern her cheeks (soft, dusky with sun) and the strong line of her jaw. Her lips were curled into a mischievous smile and her eyebrows arched above her sunglasses. A shock of hair had escaped from her cap and splayed across her forehead. The overall effect made me think of a female version of Dennis the Menace.

There was a note of self-conscious humour in her voice when she asked me if I knew where the Cuntree Store was.

"Cunt" — the word echoed charmingly in my mind, alongside a few other words, such as warm, wet, soft, and I had to clear my throat twice before I was able to impart directions. Luckily, I'd already been there to replenish my supply of diet gingerale.

She looked my way for several seconds before she turned and walked, with what I later learned was a characteristically bouncing gait, out of the tent. It was impossible to tell whether she'd actually been staring at me, because of the sunglasses, but I had, at the time, the most exquisitely painful sensation that her eyes were burning holes in my skin. I don't have much truck with the notion of fate, but somehow the effect she had on me prompted me to put my limited understanding of the universe on hold. Whatever had just transpired here was bigger than one woman, even if she was a dyke. While part of me believed that I'd never see her again — after all, there would be thousands of women circulating through the grounds during the next few days — another part of me was saying, almost singing, that lightning was going to strike in the same place twice.

I traced a convoluted route back to my campsite, but our paths didn't cross. When I got back, Annie was heating coffee on the Coleman, and Kate was struggling to erect a tarp beside the tent. I lent a hand with the tarp, and then we sat in companionable silence as the sky darkened, and the tree toads started to chirrup. We gazed contentedly around our cluttered campsite .

It was the first time here for each of us. The whole gamut of american dykedom was gathered in one place at one time. And a reassuring sight it was. We'd loaded our copious gear into the shuttle and headed for a site in the Jupiter Jumpoff area, which was, as well as being for quiet campers, reasonably close to the sober-support tent and the various stages. The first thing I'd done after helping the others erect the tent was bone up my supply of soda pop, then visit the sober-support tent to get my bearings, in case I was tempted at any point to smoke up or accept a beer from a well-intentioned stranger.

Fifteen minutes before the evening's concerts were scheduled to begin, we packed up a tarp, a thermos of coffee, mosquito coils and three pillows, and headed for the commons where the Night Stage was located. There were throngs of women walking all around us, loaded up with blankets and lawnchairs and what-not. A few were whooping and whistling and talking animatedly; most were, like us, walking quietly with bowed, smiling faces.

Oh, what a wild and fine feeling enveloped us all. We were an integral part of something great, something magnificent. The wind whipped up and shredded the clouds, and the sky was studded with stars, and the loons hooted their mournful cries from the nearby lake. We spread our tarp as close to the stage as we could find room to and craned our womanly necks and locked eyes and smiled at each other. A safe and nurturing womb — that place, those women. We created a paradigm for a supportive and peaceful community. Inwardly we rocked as we hadn't been rocked since our mothers had expelled us from their arms and set about instructing us how to survive.

A few techies were still fussing about on the stage. An aspirate and impertinent voice sounded over and over again through the P.A. system: "Tasting. Tasting. One-two-three, tasting." I poured myself a mug of coffee and stretched out my legs, content to wait.

It was August the twelfth, and the Plesieds meteor shower was beginning. Each configuration of stars blazed brightly in its place, exactly as it was portrayed in Annie's star book. Kate used a flashlight as a pointer, and I heard her soft voice saying,

"That's Orion's Belt," as the flashlight traced a figure in the sky.

Did I feel her eyes on me? The air that night seemed alive with the gentle feelings conveyed upon our warm, exhaled breath and became a medium of communication. It spoke to me as I breathed in the pine-needle scent, and it told me to turn around, which I did, and in the spin-off from the stage lights I saw her not ten feet from me, perched on the edge of a lawnchair, her elbow resting upon her bare knee and her fist propping up her chin. The cap and sunglasses were gone, but I recognized her by the puckish smile on her face and the simple directness of her posture, which told me she certainly recognized me. She sat there, looking into my eyes as if she'd been anticipating this, this response to the air's invitation, and, having initiated it, she posed unmoving, expectant. I glanced at the wisps of grey-brown hair peaking up from her forehead, at the eyes that might have been any colour in that dim light, at the skin stretched around her smiling lips, at the sinewy throat disappearing into the collar of her white shirt, and I climbed to my feet.

My body was abuzz with an adrenal discharge I'd never experienced the likes of. It swamped my vocal chords, played tiddlywinks with my heart, left me ready for the fight of my life but with no capacity whatsoever to speak a word on my own behalf. I was beside her in a few strides, looking down as she lifted her head from her fist and looked up, and I was speechless. I tried to smile, but my lips quivered, and I abandoned the attempt. Mute, expressionless, almost blind with the tears that had risen unexpectedly to my eyes, I would have backed away — back to my safe friends and my normal pulse rate — but before I could place one foot behind the other, I felt her hand, thumb and forefinger circling my wrist.

She couldn't have rooted me to the spot any more effectively if she'd tied me to a stake. Her hand opened and slid palm-first into mine, then, cool as water, she slipped her fingers out of mine and returned her hand to her chin.

I tried to imagine what was going on in her mind. Couldn't. Generally speaking, I'm an apologetic sort of person, humble. Anger frightens me, particularly my own, and I'm happier walking away from anything resembling confrontation than I am turning to face it. But there was something about her boldness that fired my own modest cache of courage, and, without considering the matter further, I dropped to one knee and rested my palm lightly on her thigh, which was bare beneath the hem of her long shirt. Startled, she glanced down. I expected her to balk at this forwardness, but instead she seemed to trace the raised, bluish veins with her eyes and outline each finger with a feather-light, ocular caress before she returned her attention — a soupçon of a smile playing over her lips — to the stage. Her response might have meant, "Hello," or, "Where have you been all my life?" — who knows? But it certainly meant, "Yes, this is allowed."

I knelt in the dampening grass, on the edge of a precipice and for the moment dared nothing more. Everything, the trees, the stage, the women, seemed to have faded from the foreground and left only the two of us greeting one another in this most peculiar way. Somewhere in the background I heard the rising of applause as Lucie Blue mounted the stage, resplendent in *bleu céleste*, and the first notes from her guitar glimmered like silver drops in the air.

The whistling and clapping subsided, voices hushed, and the woman on the stage gently, almost humbly, gathered our attention as she gave voice to what, until now, had lain wordless and tuneless in our hearts. She sang, "Mademoiselle, mademoiselle, can't you see? Would you come home with me to Québec Citee?" and the Yankees laughed, warmly, eager to oblige.

I knelt there, propless, afraid to shift my position and lose our tenuous contact, already wondering if she wished I'd go away. In spite of the cool night air, my palm felt hot and damp against her thigh; but I didn't dare let go, in case I never found my way back there again. I had to do something, preferably something to bring us closer, but before my benumbed mind could study the situation and stumble towards a solution, her hand — in one smooth motion — separated from her chin and swooped down to her leg, the little finger extended slightly, crossing mine. I felt the shock of that in my lower regions and closed my eyes for a moment. What is it about women that imbues the most innocuous gesture with eroticism? As if the mere image of one woman moving purposefully towards another is charged with more sexual energy than you can pack into a multiple orgasm. I gazed at her as she continued to stare over the heads of the women clumped around the stage, at her eyes — an almost indistinguishable shade of green — the slight slope of her nose, the upward tilt of her lips, and the silver earring she'd clipped to the cartilage of one ear. She sat perfectly still, seemingly entranced, except for her hand, which edged sideways, humping mine finger by finger until I was covered, subdued, my palm pressed firmly into her thigh by a pressure she exerted.

"Oh, it's just so womanly," Lucie Blue crooned, her sweet vibrato softening the contours of my confusion as the heat of this woman's body crept up my arm. And I was confused. Seriously. The tips of my ears, like Piglet's in *Winnie-the-Pooh*, were flushed. The skin covering my chest and throat burned the way it does just before I reach orgasm. I knelt on the wet grass and welcomed the cool breeze ruffling my hair and wondered whether there was steam coming off my skin.

Surely she could feel it, the heat radiating out of my body. The time for talking, for exchanging names and pleasantries, had come and gone, if it had even been there at all. There was nothing for it but to forge ahead in the direction that regardless of our wills, or at least without my informed consent, we had been propelled.

I'd never become intimate with a woman before weeks, months, of courtship, whether or not I might have wanted to. By the time I was almost too debilitated by sleepless nights and malnutrition to summon the energy to pucker my lips, I'd ask considerately if she'd mind very much if I kissed her. This was the only model I understood, felt at all comfortable with, even if it didn't correspond with my raunchy and free-wheeling fantasies. I didn't know this woman's name; I had no idea whether she shared my enthusiasm for classical music or preferred Joan Jett and Blackhearts, if she had cultivated a taste for tofu or consumed blood-rare beef seven days a week. Nor did I care. I wanted her. And I wanted her to want me back.

My attention momentarily shifted to Lucie Blue as she sang, "I'm losing all that I had for something physical, so physical," and then I forgot about the singer and the song because a fingertip drifted lightly up my forearm, dipped into the wedge at the inside of my elbow, and circled there for a moment before it retraced its route back to my hand.

It's not as if I'm a neophyte. I've been with a few women. Quite a few. Enough to consider that whatever was happening here between myself and this lovely stranger ought to be highly suspect. What I couldn't understand, although I have a reasonably well-developed intuitive sense, was the utter faith I had in this attraction. It carried with it a certain sense of inevitability, much as one season follows upon another. And if this was a matter of seasons, which was I entering?

I'd been alone, well, single, for almost two years. I'd been lonely, but it wasn't a no-name brand loneliness that just anyone could alleviate. In fact, I hadn't even bothered trying. I'd derived what solace I could from my friends and accepted that the underbelly of my pain would simply have to be endured as a fact of my life. I had learned, I thought, that the kinks in my character did not lend themselves to happy twosomes, and with campy lesbian bravada had, at least in my imagination, committed myself to a life of singularity. But suddenly I was wondering if it had been, simply, a period of contraction, of gestation, readying my heart for this moment of rebirth.

And what about her? What might account for this word-less willingness to connect in such an impetuous fashion with a complete stranger? Maybe she did this sort of thing every other day, preying on the naïveté of lonely women, smiling at them behind the dark, cool orbs of her sunglasses, inviting them to use her as the means of their own seduction.

Lucie Blue was taking a bow, muttering "thank you"s and "merci"s into the microphone as the applause thundered, and voices whooped, and women cried out for more. I momentarily reclaimed my hand and clapped enthusiastically for I'm not sure what, since I'd been mostly oblivious to the goings-on on the stage. I clapped as long as I decently could, but finally the applause died down, and a few tremulous notes from Lucie Blue's guitar thrummed through the air as she launched into *For Those Eyes*, and the wistful melody tugged at my attention, and I let my arms fall to my sides, helpless, somehow, to reestablish contact with the woman who sat, hands folded in her lap, beside me. Lucie Blue's voice wavered through the clear air: "There are times when I look through my window and I see your eyes / I imagine you waking me up to look at the sunrise."

Everything it occurred to me to say echoed like a cliché in the confines of my mind; I wished I was a wordsmith of Lucie Blue's caliber. I was afraid to say anything. Afraid to break the gossamer threads that had, thus far, connected us. Afraid to infect the magical with the mundane.

If Kate hadn't chosen that moment to intrude, I don't know whether either of us could have brought ourselves to initiate the next act in our drama. A few women had climbed to their feet and were swaying and bobbing to the music. Kate turned her head, spotted me and scrambled over.

"Feel like dancing?" she said.

"Not yet," I said.

She looked down uncertainly at the woman who sat looking up at her and said to me, "Who's your friend?"

What could I say? You tell me? I don't know who she is; I've just spent the last half-hour holding her hand? Whoever you are, this is my friend Kate? My head swiveled from one to the other until the matter was taken from my hands.

"Hi," the woman said. "I'm Joan."

"Pleased to meet you. I'm Kate."

I grabbed my cue, my voice coming out in a rush.

"And I'm Chris," I said, reaching out to shake her hand.

"It's nice to know that," Joan said, and she grinned so widely that I could see one of her right molars was missing, and she'd foregone a cap. Bemused as I was, I thought it was charming.

Kate left to find someone more receptive to dance with, and Joan, who'd released my hand after a formal shake, glanced at me with a wry smile, leaned over the arm of her chair and spoke in an undertone, close to my ear.

"I'm going for a walk," she said. "Want to come?"

I was on my feet before she was. We turned and walked into the shadows. As the darkness engulfed us, my courage returned, and I reached out and found her hand. We followed the main road for a way, then turned right onto Trail Mix and headed towards the Twilight Zone, an area set aside for loud and rowdy campers.

"Is it all right if we go back to my tent?"she asked. "I need a sweater, or pants, or something."

I'd never been so inarticulate in my life, and that's saying quite a lot. I didn't know what to say, or even if it was necessary to speak. I let her lead me through the softly lit trail and breathed the pungent scent of decom posing pine needles. When we arrived at her campsite Joan let go of my hand and lighted a kerosene lamp. Then she opened the flap of an octangular tent and crawled inside.

I stood within the ochroid glow of the lamp, my arms folded protectively around my torso, and gazed around the campsite, while a few errant mosquitoes whined around my face and jabbed at my arms. There was no doubt about it, I was searching for a clue to her partnership status. There was a single lawnchair beside the tent, but she'd left another at the Night Stage, so that didn't tell me anything I wanted to know. A small styrofoam cooler poked out of the grass beside a two-cup Melitta coffee pot, half-empty; excellent signs, both. In the distance I heard waves of applause as Lucie Blue was flattered into an encore. The applause waned, and all I could hear was the rustle of flesh against canvas and then the swift zip of a gym bag being closed, or opened.

As I waited, I considered why it was that our ability to camouflage the naked truth was so commonly interpreted as a sign of character; all I wanted to do was climb into the tent, find Joan in the dark and continue what we'd started out there on the commons. I longed to feel that forefinger trace my arm past the elbow, all the way to my throat, and then down. To feel her lips in the hollow of my neck and shoulder. To lie back and give the woman her head. But how could I do that without betraying the extent of my desire? And, if I posed no resistance, would she want me after all?

Her face appeared suddenly through the opening in the tent, wisps of greying hair, celadon eyes luminous, lips crooked into a self-depreciating smile. She was clutching something in one hand. I couldn't see what it was. She looked up at me.

"Am I being presumptuous," she said, "or would you like to join me in here?"

The crickets and the tree toads chirruped; a loon let loose its haunting cry; Lucie Blue's audience rose on a crescendo of applause; then all melted back into silence — the perfect, unfettered country silence that frees your ears and sends your other senses reeling into weightlessness.

The flickering light from the kerosene lamp glowed through the half-open tent flap. A strand of saliva glittered and stretched between our lips as we rebounded from the first tentative kiss. I thought of a spider's web in the sunlight, after rain, and brushed my mouth across hers again and again, careful not to break the delicate net that held to every point of my body.

We knelt on her sleeping bag, her legs separated, mine tucked between her thighs. She raised her hands to my shoulders and a tube slipped from her fingers and plokked onto the canvas floor. Mine cupped her face, my fingers moved over her downy cheeks, her earlobes, my thumbs caressing the corners of her lips. I pressed them lightly back and ran the tip of my tongue over her teeth, then backed away again. We were speaking, in a way, with this tensile coming and going, this pausing to look at each other's faces in the fluttering light, to discern and decide what would be the best way to proceed to ensure our merging.

Questions flared and died in my mind, just as the meteors crashed through the stratosphere and dissolved in seconds of brilliance as the earth spun on its unbalanced orbit through the Plesieds. The old questions, cautions, concerns, doubts and scepticism couldn't survive for long in this atmosphere.

She was smiling. I kissed her again, this time delving to the roots of her tongue, and a moan escaped from deep in her throat. Suddenly she was up on her knees pushing me back onto my elbows, and she shifted her body forward and moved her crotch over and over my belly, moaning again and again, her mouth still on mine. I breathed with her; her hips spun in small circles, and then she said my name, thrust hard against my abdomen and cried out that she was coming. And she came. Or it came; a nine-pound blockbuster baby of an orgasm, all shoulders and swagger and strut, erupting from that frenzied body.

I watched her shoulder blades rise and fall as she caught her breath, her greying hair soft and damp. I needed to uncontort myself; my bent knees were taut cogs of pain by this time. I lifted my lower body under her, unwilling to dislodge her, and she came a little away from the floor of the tent as I uncurled my legs, carrying her like a rider upon my belly, and stretched out flat. She eased her body over mine, straddling my legs, her breasts pressing under mine, her face couched in my neck and the tip of her nose nuzzling the lobe of my ear.

I wanted to say something, but again I couldn't find the words. Oh, there were plenty of stock phrases that alluded to the situation while bypassing the gist, the heart of it, by a mile, so I flipped through them and discarded them and lay there, the skin on my back imprinted with the creases in the sleeping bag, unwilling to intrude upon this quietude that I felt might be more meaningful, more promising, than any attempt at articulation, and gradually her breathing slowed and she took a deep, shuddering breath and rolled off me.

"That was nice," she said, patting around the floor of the tent for the tube she'd dropped at some earlier point in the proceedings.

"Nice"? My whole body and being had just been sucked into the maw of her passion, chewed up and regurgitated, had lain beneath the comforting bantamweight of her body and was no longer the same body and being it had been a few minutes before, and that was "nice"? What was this for her —recreation? A dive and a couple of laps in the pool? An hour under the summer sun and an icy tumbler of lemonade?

I was drenched in sweat where our bodies had rubbed together, and now the cool air chilled me, and I began to shiver.

"You need some serious warming up," she said, climbing on board again and moving her hips with excruciatingly slow torque over mine.

Like hell I did. What I needed was a serious talking-to. With the exception of my last lover, I'd shown a lamentable tendency to involve myself with women who had other things to do. Like pursue their careers. Or Have Fun. Or enjoy themselves with whole bunches of lovers; if one is nice, three or four must be nicer, right? One had actually told me I ought to feel flattered that she was attracted to other women since it was our own intensely sexual interaction that had fired up this non-particularized libidinal energy in her. Well, I thought, as she put her mouth against my ear and whispered something unintelligible, there must be a locatable median between viewing her as a good time, or, conversely, the love of my life. I heard a dull roaring as if a seashell had clamped itself against my ear, and she slid her tongue in as far as it would go and started probing it around in there.

Where some women's nipples seem to have a hotline to their cunts, mine link up directly with my ears. Any audial stimulation, whether it's the right words delivered in the right tone of voice or something more corporeal — say, a tongue cruising around — has the effect of rousing me to an almost violent passion in mere seconds. Involuntarily, I jerked my head away. She laughed softly.

"I've found a spot," she said, leaning back on one elbow to uncap the tube of KY jelly.

She squeezed a daub onto each of my nipples then bent over me, the soft cones of her breasts brushing my belly, and spread the cool jelly around with her lips and tongue while, with a forefinger, she dallied at the outer edge of my ear. I wondered if that was Lucie Blue I could hear singing, "Guava jelly all over my belly," and then I couldn't hear anything except the hot blood pounding through my temples because I felt the heel of her free hand glide across my abdomen and her fingers — lubricated with two substances — open me like a diver breaching the water. She moved her mouth to my ear again and rolled around the grooves with her tongue while I rocked my head on the pillow, and she pursued me relentlessly, until somewhere very far away I heard another roar of applause and whistles keening in the cold air as my vagina contracted like a loving hand around those slippery fingers, and I was absorbed into the spastic rhythm of my own orgasm.

She moved to my side, slipped an arm under my neck and the other over my waist, and we lay there in a gentle, amicable silence. The residual sexual flush on my skin warmed us both, and when she suggested we climb into the sleeping bag I knew it wasn't for need of heat, but an invitation to stay the night.

It occurred to me, very momentarily, that my friends

might be wondering what had become of me, but surely they would know no harm could come to me here, among these women, and would form their own prurient conclusions. At any rate, I forgot them almost immediately because Joan zipped the bag around us, and there was only enough room if we lay in one another's arms, and I floated, rather than lay, in this warm, sexually charged cocoon. She draped a leg over mine, and then, with the soft curls of her pubis nestled against my thigh, she fell instantly asleep.

I was already in the nebulous landscape between waking and dreaming, and my thoughts roamed, unhindered by reason or the real world, and at one point I found myself murmuring, "It's impossible," and suddenly I was wide awake.

I turned my head and saw that her eyes were closed, and she hadn't stirred at the sound of my voice. Her breathing was light and even. All the warm vitality seemed to have drained from her features. She looked like a serious child, and I thought that this must be the woman exposed, and at the core of her self-possession was this child, solemn and alone. I knew little about the essential woman, and this mattered to me. What had started so simply, so easily, had become a puzzle, a maze; I was finding my way into something, and I no longer knew the way out.

There is always a discernible moment in a developing relationship when you can opt out, spare yourself the repercussions of caring too much and short-circuit the whole process. This was my moment. I could disentangle myself from her sleep-heavy limbs, stealthily undo the zipper on the bag and join the stream of women returning to their campsites. I could slip in beside Annie and Kate, my tried and true and more-or-less predictable friends, and they would ask no questions, and I would ask myself none, and Joan would wake in the morning and assume of me what I was now beginning to assume — that we'd shared a purely sexual encounter, and it had been nice, ah, so nice, and all the baggage we carried away from it was a sense of physical well-being.

I began, very slowly, to unzip the bag.

But, before I could complete the process, one of my irrepressible theories bobbed up, and I found myself treading water as I considered the nature of our encounter. We fit together in some way; some mechanism operated between us to circumvent the social proprieties, so that we were lovers, really, before we had even exchanged names or telephone numbers. It was — and here a chill swept over my exposed shoulders and scuttled down my spine — as if we had known each other before. And this, I saw in retrospect, had been evident between us since the first moment she had looked into my eyes, and I had looked into the eyes of my own reflection in her sunglasses. There had been such a surcharge of energy between us that it had demanded release here, like this, before we had even established the possibility of being safe with one another, or had discovered whether we might have something substantial to offer each other, or would be gentle with one another come morning. It had, in fact, amounted to an extraordinary act of faith.

I slipped the zipper back to its starting point, lay down and stared at the canvas roof, which appeared to quiver in the flickering light until the kerosene lamp consumed all its fuel and sputtered out. I made a mental note to check in at the sober-support tent the next day; I felt as if I'd swallowed a pint of bourbon and was being swept away into a lunatic joyfulness on updrafts of sheer exuberance.

Joan shifted to her side, her back to me. I cupped the top of her head with my chin, tucked my legs in behind hers and said, so softly that she couldn't have heard me even if she'd been awake, "I'm falling in love with you."

And then I stopped struggling and let the current take me.

As I lay there, dimly aware of the sounds of women settling into their tents, chatting softly — and someone was strumming a guitar some distance away — the question of love went round and round in my head like a whirlpool, sucking me in dizzying circles ever downward.

Then I was sitting up. There were no sounds now, and the silence seemed hastily imposed and out of place. The first thing I became aware of was the hammering of my heart. The next, that there was a hand clutching my wrist.

"Are you all right?"

"Yes," I said. "What's wrong?"

"You tell me. You were yelling in your sleep."

Oh Isis, not again. I'd spent the final six months of my last relationship yelling in my sleep and thrashing about and mistaking the innocent woman at my side for one of my night-terror nemeses. Once, I'd even woken up in the midst of shaking her hard, by both shoulders. She'd cried, that time, and I'd held her and kissed her and whispered over and over, "I'm sorry. I'm so sorry." But this had stopped after we'd separated. Until now.

"You sounded angry," Joan went on.

I took this in, then asked what I'd been yelling.

"I didn't hear it all. You said 'No' over and over. Are you okay, lover?"

That little tag on the sentence, that innuendo of good intent, went straight to the heart of me. I lay back down and rested my head in the crook of her shoulder. She sighed. How could I tell her whether I was okay? I didn't know myself, anymore. Whatever had erupted from the subterranean depths was beyond my powers of waking comprehension.

What had I been saying "No" to? What had my subliminal mind apprehended and let percolate almost to the surface while I slept?

I woke up shortly after dawn to the sound of a steady patter on the roof of the tent. A pool of water had collected on the floor just inside the half-open flap and was inching its way towards the sleeping bag. I heard a roll of thunder in the distance and seconds later, another, closer.

Electrical storms frighten me. When I was a kid, I used to hide in the basement during thunder storms so that I wouldn't have to see the lightning flare in the windows and anticipate the next bolt fingering its way through the ether to me. Perhaps I believed, in my kidlike egocentric way, that I was responsible for the squalor and tumult on the home front and that nature, if not God, had my number. Well, whatever the childish rationale had been for this electrophobia, it had burrowed in deep, deep, scuttling just out of reach of the pointed, reasoning snout of my mind.

I began to ease myself out of the bag. The storm might still skirt us, but if it didn't, the less I could see of it the better. Besides, if I didn't close the flap, we'd soon be swimming.

"Where are you going?" Her voice held no trace of sleepiness. I leaned over her — she was lying on her side — and saw that her eyes were open, unblinking, alert.

"To batten down the hatches," I said. "We'll drown."

"Not yet," she said, and then, as if she'd been planning her strategy as she waited for me to wake up, she rolled over, flipped the cover back and foraged for a space between my legs, butting my thighs apart like an affectionate calf.

As the next surge of lightning illuminated the walls of the tent, I felt her tongue, warm and rough, licking in the crevice she'd made. I began to pant in an unholy joining of lust and fear as the ensuing peal of thunder roared in my ears.

"Joan, wait," I said. "I have to close the ..." and then I couldn't say anything else because she eased at least two fingers into me and dilated me all the way back to my cervix.

My arms gave way. The back of my head thudded lightly against the canvas floor. Behind my clenched eyelids, I saw a tremendous fountain of light, followed by an ear-splitting, tent-rattling peal of thunder, and forgot for once in my life to be afraid. I arched my back and met her thrusts, climaxing. There was another perilously close crack of thunder, and the patter of rain geared up into a steady drumming. I reached down and touched her wrist, and she collapsed, breathing as hard as me, onto my heaving stomach.

Thunder rumbled faintly from the south. The sun steamed through the receding clouds and glittered on the soaked grass. The air was dense and humid. Joan climbed to her feet, pulled on a short kimono-style robe and went outside to boil water on the Coleman while I lazed luxuriantly on my back and tried to decide whether or not to dress. I would've been content to lie there with her all day, indulging in desultory getting-to-know-you type conversations, interspersed with rounds of lovemaking and perhaps the odd cup of coffee, but already the air in the tent was becoming uncomfortably warm, and by noon, I knew, it would be unbearable. I slipped into my clothes and stepped out of the tent. We could always go for an aimless walk along the trails and exchange herstories. We could check out the crafts displays and attend a workshop together. Endless possibilities.

I watched Joan's back while she measured hot water into the filter cone. The woman was a caffeine connoisseur. She squatted on her haunches, the tail of her cream-coloured kimono brushing the wet grass. Her sleeves were rolled back to the elbow, exposing her tanned, muscled forearms. The boughs of a large oak tree swayed over her in the bluster of the passing storm. Shadows of leaves dappled the grass and played over her crouching body. When she rose to her feet and swiveled around to face me, I don't know what I expected; perhaps anything except what actually happened.

She smiled at me, rather wanly, I thought, and said, "How about a cup of coffee before you leave?"

Without waiting for my reply she walked with bouncing steps to a nearby carton and, dropping to one knee, began to rummage through it while she muttered something about an extra cup.

There is a sensation that borders upon humiliation, but surpasses it, that sidles up to shame, but exceeds it. I can only describe it as something akin to being emotionally skinned alive. It tends to happen when you realize, jarringly and sickeningly, that you've been operating on an assumption that hasn't been shared. There was no basis for mutuality between us, and I'd been foolishly naïve to expect anything else or to believe that anything faintly resembling my own eruption of roseate hopes might have suffused her mind, or heart.

She poured coffee into two cups and handed one to me.

"Thanks," I said, taking the cup as she extended it, handle-first.

She carried her cup to the one lawnchair and sat down, her back to me. I couldn't tell whether she was waiting for me to join her, or waiting for me to leave. And it never occurred to me to ask.

If I chose to join her, I would have to sit at her feet, a position that would only serve to enhance my already consuming sense of inferiority. But I couldn't just stand here, stupidly holding my cup, tongue-tied. I lifted the cup to my lips, took a reckless gulp of coffee and parboiled the inside of my mouth.

Only half an hour earlier we'd been engaged in a fierce exchange of sexual energy; now she sat, massively self-contained, her small, strong back turned squarely towards me. I felt sure that if I'd only cared less, not been so hopelessly hopeful and easily taken advantage of, I would've found the wit to offer a remark that might at least evoke a smile from her, or a moment's attention, something for her to remember me fondly by. Ah, Sappho, I had it bad. Real bad.

I dumped the remains of my coffee into the grass and stole around to the rear of the tent. Luckily, there was a small footpath leading into the woods. The path was bound, at some point, to tie into one of the main trails. I walked almost on my tiptoes, careful to make no sound, only wanting to get away before she could notice my abject retreat.

I'd been told once, by a friend, that I had no street smarts, that there were women one had to encounter with caution, and, since I'd been crying the blues over the fact that I'd just been given the emotional one-two by a lover, it was critical for me to learn how to survive in the anarchy that is lesbian love. She insisted that this was especially important for me because, being an adult child of alcoholics (ACA), I have a reckless tendency to bond almost instantly with a woman I'm strongly attracted to. By the time I figure out who this person really is, the glue has set, and I'm in for the long-haul, like it or not. "You have to learn to take your time," my friend had said, and I reheard her advice filtering through the raucous cries of the crows as I beat my way through the ever-narrowing trail and swatted at the black flies that travelled in flying-formation alongside my head, one or two breaking free every few seconds to kamikaze my face. Finally I broke through the bush and emerged onto Easy Street.

Once I had my bearings, I continued on slowly, my eyes stuck to the ground, pursued by an unfortunately familiar sense of having blown it. I'm a mistress of the art of making a scene without raising my voice; without, in fact, saying a single word. I sum up a situation — consulting no one in the process — jump to refractory conclusions and usually land on my ass. And look like one.

I felt as if I was swinging wildly between two poles. I knew this was a perilous state for me to be in, and, when I reached the main road, I hung a right and headed for the sober-support tent. Just then I spotted Kate across the road waving a plastic soap case over her head to catch my attention. She had knotted a towel over her hips. Her long brown hair was slicked back and hung stringily over her shoulders. She looked like heaven to me.

"Cold water showers," she said with unfeigned enthusiasm, skipping across the road. "You should try one. Beats a cup of coffee for getting your heart going."

"Probably," I said.

She came to a halt in front of me, peered at me, removed her glasses and peered again.

"What's up?" she said.

"Oh, nothing. I fell in love last night, spent hours having passionate sex, then left without saying goodbye because ... because I'm not sure why. And I feel like having a drink. Several drinks."

"Want to talk to a stranger," Kate asked, nodding towards the sober-support tent, "or a friend?"

I stared at the muddy toes of my sneakers. Kate took my arm and guided me towards the Jupiter Jumpoff area. I relaxed in her grip and allowed myself to be led through the high grass and into the cluttered campsite. Kate filled two mugs with coffee and sat down beside me, cross-legged in the grass.

"This'll help," she said, handing over one of the mugs. "You could stand a spoon in it."

My stomach turned at the smell, and my tongue still burned from this morning.

"She practically asked me to leave, or I thought she did. And now I've made an ass of myself."

"Hey, you'll see her again. Maybe you can straighten things out."

"I don't want to see her again."

"Right. That's why you look like you just got run over by the shuttle. Look, here we are in the lesbian capital of the country, with five thousand like-minded women. Even if you're right about Joan, there are dozens of women out there who'd love to get to know you — in spite of your neuroses."

My heart was fine-tuned to Joan's. I couldn't attune myself to anyone else's wavelength, and knew I wouldn't try. My sullen mood darkened and spread a bruise over the Festival.

Annie crawled out of the tent, her glasses teetering on the verge of her nose, and asked chirpily whether anyone wanted to join her for leftover tofu stew with poached eggs on top. Kate and I declined to partake of the tofu portion.

After breakfast, Kate handed me a cup of lukewarm coffee then went off to wash our dishes in the paltry stream of water that issued shakily forth from our five-gallon plastic holder, and I was left alone with my reflections. I watched Kate's hands slide over the soapy dishes and thought of Joan's fingers sliding into me. I could almost feel the soft down fuzzing her cheeks as my lips travelled lightly over her face, the blunt fleshy tangents of her earlobes and the firm delineation of her jaw. Each of her features was like a point on a roadmap that led me, finally and fulfillingly, to her lips, which opened and took me in like a weary traveller on a highway, accelerating towards a destination that promised bed and breakfast.

Kate lifted the pot we'd poached the eggs in from the stove and whipped off the lid. The diluted scent of vinegar wafted to my nostrils, and I almost moaned out loud. That's what she'd smelled like, there, between her legs: mildly acetic and ciderlike, with a hint of woodsmoke. I reeled from the olfactory input.

Suddenly, Kate was standing over me asking if I wanted to explore the crafts displays. I followed her, zombie-like, along the trail, and, as we walked, Joan's disembodied spirit assailed my senses and penetrated me in every imaginable way. She wound tendrils lithely through my brain, and every synapse in my body held a trace of her and exploded with each turn of thought or exertion of muscle until I felt like a walking minefield of desire. I was consumed with a hunger for her that obliterated my ability to focus upon anything else. I hurried Kate at top-speed through the crafts displays, then along the trails, my legs long and insatiable, striding towards a future that had not yet formed itself. Kate kept pace and soon abandoned any attempt at conversation. She glanced sideways at me from time to time, and only once left my side to pick her way, graceful as a deer, into the underbrush to retrieve a discarded pop can. She tucked it into her pack, then ran to catch up with me.

When we trekked down to the commons that evening, we were among the last to arrive. We couldn't get within fifty yards of the stage, so we shook out our tarp and settled in the shadows beyond the stage lights. I scanned the sea of heads in front of me, but they all looked identical from behind with the spotlights silhouetting them into anonymity.

I hardly noticed the hours pass, or who the performers were, or what they sang. I squinted at the dark heads, searching for the almost-familiar curve of her jaw, or the peaks of her greying hair, but the evening passed, and I never spotted her. I wanted, at least, to have a chance to observe her from a safe distance and decide whether I might chance approaching her. I would be able, I thought, to calculate the risk from any number of minute clues: whether or not she was looking around (presumably for me), whether she appeared to be totally preoccupied with the music, whether she was with someone else.

But the night went by and suddenly Kate and Annie were on their feet gathering up our paraphernalia, and I took one long, last look around before I turned away and joined the streams of women, faceless in the dark, drifting back to their campsites. It crossed my mind that at this time last night Joan and I had been wrapped cozily in one another's arms, and I had been deliberating whether or not to leave.

Back at the site, I brewed a pot of coffee while the other two prepared for bed. Neither of them wanted a cup, so I was soon left to my own sorry devices. Kate bent over me and kissed my cheek before she crawled into the tent to join Annie, and they were soon lost in a contrapuntal stream of zeds that wafted through the walls of the tent. I slouched in a lawnchair and sipped my coffee and brooded. I was too tired to make much sense, even to myself. My thoughts seemed to circle endlessly and tiredly over the same points and impressions — eagles hunting carrion. I tracked and retracked; I wondered whether I ought to have left her last night, or not left this morning; I rode up-currents of warm air as I considered the sweetness of making love at dawn while the thunder broiled around us, and then, as a shaft of cold air sent me plummeting, how vulnerable I'd felt with her afterwards. None of it made any sense. I barely had the energy to recall the ACA pattern about love being a force fraught with danger, and how, typically, old habits kick in when one begins to approach love, best short-handed as "I love you/go away." It was just more trouble than it was worth; but oh, such desirable trouble.

When the pot was empty, I struggled into my pyjamas, picked my way over Annie and Kate and lay down, exhausted but doomed to wakefulness for the remainder of the night as the caffeine batted my eyelids up and down and turned my body like a rotating planet.

"You look wonderful," Kate said as I emerged, wan and groggy, into the full sunlight.

"Didn't sleep too well," I muttered, and went in search of soap and towel. Clean, but unrefreshed, I joined the others who were energetically scarfing down bowls of sliced bananas and yogurt. I poured coffee into a mug, which jittered in my trembling hand. We had no mirror, so I was spared the sight of the smudges beneath my eyes and the pallor of my skin, which I guessed must have shone like albumen beneath the paint on an artist's canvas. I knew my eyes must have that staring, crazed look that only febrile blue eyes can have.

I half-listened to the other two yakking, but couldn't think of anything to contribute to the conversation. Obviously, I wasn't going to be any good to anyone, let alone myself. I got up and went for a walk, following the trails as they unfolded before me, wandering more or less aimlessly. I was, despite my general dazedness, scrupulously avoiding the Twilight Zone. Even if I did want to see Joan, I certainly didn't want her seeing me, not like this. At best, I wasn't sure I could handle a confrontation with her; at worst, she would probably make some derogatory sound at the sight of me and ... but my imagination was overworked. I resolved not to think at all, shoved my hands into my pockets and walked on, staring doggedly at the ground and sometimes at the varied footwear of the women who passed me.

Shortly after noon I returned to the campsite and, not finding Annie and Kate, crawled into the stifling tent for a brief nap. The heat was pushing down on my body, pursuing me through every twist and turn, until I fell into a fitful and suffocating sleep. I slept until twilight, and probably would have slept longer if a sound, which I dazedly sensed didn't belong, hadn't roused me.

I opened the tent flap, wondering if my friends had returned. Her eyes gazed down at me, unblinking, and it was hard to tell in that dimming light, but I thought I noticed a shadow of uncertainty cross them; but if her gaze wavered for an instant, it recovered quickly. Mostly, her eyes were concerned and grave; whether for herself or for me I could not tell.

My mind scurried around in a reflexive attempt to unearth some witticism that might take the edge off the moment and relieve the gravid atmosphere, as only humour can. But my thoughts were an expanse of fog, with half-formed shapes cluttering the landscape, and I soon gave up the quest and my eyes slid down to her knee caps.

"Your friend told me where you were camped," she said in response to the obvious, unasked question. "We wound up in a workshop together. So I asked — Kate, is it? — how you were. She said you weren't so great. How come?"

I couldn't think of a thing to say. I had a strangled sensation, as if the only phrases my mind would allow me to think, and my tongue to speak, were those that reflected the truth; they were collaborating in a conspiracy to force me towards honesty. Christess, I thought; I'm not even on my own side.

I've had, since I can remember, the illogical sense that the surest way to lose someone you want desperately to keep is to tell the unmitigated truth. It's no accident that language lends itself more adeptly to covering up meaning than to extending and elucidating it. It follows some general pattern of human need. People usually prefer not to know what's really going on. It's too dangerous.

"And how come you left yesterday? Like that?"

"I left because I was seriously scared," I said.

"Scared of what?"

"That I was on my own. You see, I could fall for you like a ton of bricks." A little more prosaic than I would have liked, but true, nonetheless. A bell, lucid and rich as an Oriental gong, sounded in my mind. Suddenly, I could see again. The interior landscape resolved itself into a forest of trees, each leaf clearly outlined in the sunlight, with sparrows perched in the branches and the piercing birdsound slicing the keen air. It was a nice place. If she didn't want to inhabit it with me, it might be my loss, but it would be hers, too.

"That's mutual, Chris."

She spoke with an inflectionless voice, and at first I didn't grasp the meaning of her words. I'd taken the leap off the high-dive and felt almost smug as I arced through the air filled with an ineffable sense of freedom. I was prepared to dare a double-twist or even a back-flip; it was immaterial to me whether I succeeded or failed, since I was bound to crash anyway. My fate sealed, I concentrated solely upon the picture I presented. But suddenly the sense of her words penetrated, and I found myself thrashing helplessly towards the water. I entered with a perfectly executed bellyflop.

"It is?" My voice, rather than being awash with wonder, cracked dryly over the two syllables.

She didn't answer. After a minute, I felt her fingers lightly kneading the hair at the top of my head. I let my face fall into the pillow. She gathered the blonde strands that draped over my forehead and wove them gently behind my ears. And now, the mutually acknowledged feelings had crept into the gesture and imbued her caress with an undertone, low as a loving voice, and in my mind I heard the words, "Tell me" and "Let's share this" and almost tentatively, like a query, "Mother, daughter, lover...."

She could've done that to me for the rest of the night if she'd wanted to, run her short deft fingers through my hair, and I would've lain there, suspended in disbelief, willing to let this dream — if that's what it was — blot out reality. But there were voices nearby, and the whoosh-whoosh of the Coleman being pumped up, and suddenly the tent flap split open.

"Oh. Oh, excuse me." The voice was Kate's, and it didn't sound a bit apologetic.

A small sigh escaped from Joan.

"Anyone for five-bean stew?" Kate enquired.

I dragged my eyelids up over my eyes and saw, in the sienna light of the setting sun, Kate's face split wide in a grin.

We went, the four of us, to the commons that evening, and I kept my gaze to the ground as we walked, smiling secretly, nestling Joan's hand in my larger one. I quailed at the realization that she might not have come to me — as I wouldn't have gone to her — and I might've been one sad, singular woman moping towards the Night Stage. It struck me what an act of faith and courage her seeking me out must have been, and I squeezed her hand hard before I let it go and draped an arm around her shoulders, pulling her in close to me. She slid an arm around my waist, and, in that tender configuration, we arrived on the commons.

It wasn't until later, after the evening's concert, that we made an attempt to map out the paths we'd taken and consider what had propelled us together and apart. And it wasn't easy to do, in part because we could hardly keep our hands off each other. Her voice was something deliciously tactile, much like the soft swipe of her tongue across my ear. Nonetheless, I tried diligently to keep to the task at hand. We discussed our earlier failure of communication, our mutual contributions to that and considered possible strategies with which we might forestall such misunderstanding in the future, if we decided to have one together. Here I shuddered to think how close I'd come to forfeiting the possibility.

One auspicious fact that emerged from our discussion was that Joan lived in Cornwall, a scant hundred miles from Kingston. I mean, she could have come from Tallahassee.

It was Joan, finally, who disrupted my logical processes by asking if we had to figure everything out this minute, then rudely, lasciviously, she zapped my libidinal circuitry by bending over me and resting an elbow on either side of my head. She looked down at me with one of her warm, self-assured gazes, then dove in for a long, endless, deep roiling kiss. Finally we subsided, laughing, onto our backs.

After our panting had ceased, and we were again ensconced in each other's arms, Joan said, contemplatively, "It's so refreshing to be with someone who talks back."

"Talks back?" I said, uncertain whether she was referring to reciprocation or impertinence.

"Who holds up their end of the conversation," she added, settling her head more comfortably in the crook of my shoulder.

"Ah, " I said; and after a long pause, "You had a relationship with a deaf-mute?"

"An alcoholic."

"Practicing?"

"Recovering."

Between one beat and the next my heart took a vertical

lunge and seemed to wedge itself in my thorax. I couldn't have requested further information if I'd wanted to, which I didn't.

"She expected me to be psychic," Joan went on, happily unaware of the panic-sweat that was beginning to trickle from my armpits. "She rarely told me what she wanted or needed. She made me guess. And when I didn't, she took it as proof that I didn't care about her. And after awhile, I didn't."

I said nothing.

"Pretty heartless, huh?" she added.

I knew the question was intended to be rhetorical, but I found myself saying, in a voice as small as a shy child's, "Did you love her?"

"I don't know what love is, Chris. Do you?"

"Maybe not. But I always know when it isn't there."

"Well, it was wonderful in the beginning. She was wonderful. I just didn't bargain for what came next."

I didn't want to know what had come next. Perhaps I was already too familiar with the pith of the story, and a resurrection of the bones and decomposing flesh would be too distressing. If I had been a stranger to this I might have felt otherwise — aloof, perhaps, calmly attentive to Joan's need to split open and examine this unhappy (or merely unpleasant?) pod of her past. But whatever, whoever, lay biodegrading in that pod was too familiar to be borne.

My last partner of four years had accused me of being uncommunicative, dishonest, unreasonable in my expectations; but at least I had felt, beneath her anger and angst, the force of love. Hers and mine. Still, I'd sensed some solid block of disharmony between us, which left us incapable, like fire and water, of providing some essential element to keep the other intact. We'd struggled, perhaps too hard, to preserve the relationship; and there was, even now, an echo of comfort in that, as if we had assigned some absolute — if unattainable — value to each other.

My perception, horrible as it seemed, was that Joan would recoil from any perceived likeness between myself and her last lover.

Again, my mind swirled with cumulus as the inevitable white-out descended and hid me from myself. This time, I really didn't want to find or give voice to the truth.

It's none of her business, I told myself. I don't owe her this particular confidence. At least, not yet. And with that, the fog rolled in and my body contracted with an internally generated chill, and I shrank a little away from her.

"Of course, it wasn't her fault," Joan went on, serenely unaware of my shirking, shrinking psyche. "Her father was an alcoholic, and her mother committed suicide. Great role models, huh?" She turned her head and planted an affectionate kiss on my throat. "Do you know the term ACA? Adult child of...."

"Alcoholics," I interrupted. "Yes, I know the term. It means you have a hole in your heart as big as the void and a built-in excuse for every execrable thing you do to someone who cares about you." There was more fervour, and perhaps bitterness, in my voice than I'd intended.

I felt Joan's head shift again. "Whew!" she said softly.

We didn't speak for a few minutes, then, as I knew it would — but hoped it wouldn't — her curiosity formed into a question.

"You've been involved with one, too?"

"Intimately, " I said, not missing a beat.

"Maybe that's why I feel so connected to you. We have something significant in common. A couple of things, actually," she added with a warm undertone of laughter in her voice.

Deliberate ambiguity. I am, of course, good at it. Once,

long, long ago, when I was a skinny-legged kid in fat-legged canary-coloured shorts, trying to make sense of and survive in the atmosphere of sheer arbitrariness that my own alcoholic family spawned, I learned all about disguising the unvarnished truth, which more often than not reflected their own failures. I was a smart kid; no, let me rephrase that, a superbly gifted kid with a mind well-able to grapple with the stochastic behaviour of my often besotted parent and his enabler, my mother. Outright lying was too clumsy a survival tool for me; instead, I learned the fine craft of invention, of withholding crucial bits of information, of ambiguity. I became pretty skilled at changing the subject, too. I hadn't had the luxury of developing an acceptable system of values, a decent code of ethics. Besides, who was there to serve as a role model?

Joan and I had something in common, all right. Just not what she thought. I was her ACA revisited; wonderful to begin with, a catastrophe somewhere down the line. The fragile threads that had connected us thus far were strands of hope — frail, illusory, easily snapped. This single, jarring truth could smash all our dreams like a fist through a spider's web; and yet, did I want to entrap her, us, in that web? I knew from experience how the strands grew, clung, until in breaking free a woman left pieces of herself behind and escaped only if she was willing to endure the pain and bleed.

If I didn't yet love Joan, I certainly cared about her, and my concern for her tugged like plumb-bobs on the strings connecting us each to the other, straightening out the moral slack of my desire, reimposing the real and the true. If together we were to build a structure that would withstand the vicissitudes of the weather and our own growing, changing selves, it would have to be founded upon solid ground, and the foundation would have to be true.

There was nothing else for it. This time, as I prodded myself towards the bull's-eye of honesty, it wasn't at all like it had been earlier in the day; I no longer felt as if I was leaping off a highdive and plunging wingless but exhilarated towards the inevitable. There was no freeing recklessness in me when I dislodged her head, gently, and sat up in the sleeping bag.

"It's not what you think, Joan. I was never involved with an alcoholic."

The fog rolled back like a film in reverse, but there were no trilling birds or clearly etched leaves in its wake this time. No sunlight. Only the gnarled, stunted growths of the seeds I'd sewn elsewhere at another time.

I waited, hoping she'd guess the rest and spare me the humiliation of further self-disclosure. She lay stock-still, waiting, it seemed to me, with all her might. I could almost hear the delicate threads snapping, like the crack of frost beneath heavy boots.

"That's what I am," I went on, dully. "I'm an alcoholic. In remission, if you like. And an adult child of same."

There wasn't much light, only the swaying, buttery glow from the kerosene lamp outside the tent. I glanced down hoping to read something, anything, in her face. Her eyes were closed. She'd folded her hands over her chest, and she lay there, the only signal of life being the barely perceptible rise and fall of the cover over her stomach.

She looked utterly self-contained, like a long package about to slide down a chute, and out of my life. What was going through her mind?

I had no idea what to do, or say, next. We'd come full circle, arriving at the same precarious position we'd been in two mornings before when I'd stared at her back as she sipped her morning coffee and decided to slip out the back door. And that's exactly what I wanted to do now. No fanfare. No trumpets. No display of injured feelings or recriminations. I just wanted to get up and steal away into the night, like a shaken dog with her tail curled up between her legs.

That's another thing I hadn't learned much about — the ability to speak on my own behalf. When I tried, once every five years or so, the shock was so great that I generally quit, dead in the water, midway through an eloquent outburst. Although my last lover hadn't much minded my silence (it had, after all, contributed to the longevity of our relationship) I sensed that Joan might view it as a handicap. A lack of spunk, perhaps, bordering on a dangerous impassivity. Hell, we were hopelessly mismatched.

The only thing that held me there was the realization that the other morning, I'd been wrong. She hadn't wanted me to go. She simply hadn't known whether I wanted to stay. She had a fair measure of the insensate pride that plagued me, and when the sheer force of our lust wasn't pulling us together, we were straight-arming each other with our determination to retain our autonomous, independent status. We were afraid, both of us, of sinking roots into anyone; it'd been too awful yanking up the last ones. Here we were looking full into the face of a major crisis of faith, and we'd only had about forty-five minutes to discuss possible strategies for circumventing such catastrophes. Talk is, indeed, cheap.

She unfolded her hands and stretched her arms out at her sides, then opened her eyes. I still couldn't read them, because she was looking down at some lower part of her anatomy. Thus shielded, she spoke.

"I won't go through that again, Chris."

"No," I said. "Neither will I."

Her eyes flicked up to mine and then — was I imagining it or was there a glimmer of respect in that quick glance?

I endured another minute of charged silence, until suddenly she started to laugh. Well, I couldn't really call it laughter. It was a sort of low-toned, rhythmic exhalation, like sobs, escaping from deep in her chest. I'd heard that sound before, and it still called up the same sympathy, hot and keen-edged as a knife in my heart.

"I don't want to hurt you," I said. The words caught in my throat. I ferreted around for something, any damned thing, to add to that; something that might lend credence to my intention, but I couldn't find the right words. Perhaps there weren't any.

"After all," she said, "I met you in the sober-support tent. What did I suppose you were doing there — sightseeing?"

At that moment, the kerosene lamp flared up in a final feverish spasm and sputtered out. The walls of the tent appeared to shudder, and then there was only the blank blackness alternating with crimson flashes as I continued to stare, tiredly, straight ahead.

Something, something just beyond my peripheral vision seemed to be padding about, lightly, persistently, prompting my attention. There was something insidious and thin about this shadow, as if it had adjusted to being elbowed and edged into the background and had grown wily and wild over the years.

If the will to honest outrage is repeatedly violated, is this what it becomes, a fox flitting through thickets of lies and pretence, only discernible by the quiver of a leaf or a faint downwind scent? Elusive, shy, it survives, yet begs to be attended to and tamed.

When I spoke next, I had the dissonant sense that I didn't know who I was addressing, this vulpine presence, or the woman who lay mute and motionless by my side.

"I've had to fight harder than you could imagine to pull myself together," I said, with the keen edge of indignation honing my voice. "I'd like to see you do half as well in my place. You think I'm trouble? You think your last lover was trouble? Why don't you consider what you were to her? Or what you might be to me? Do you have any idea how ... how terrifying it is for someone like me to open up to someone I love?"

My mouth began to stumble over the words, like a sprinter overrunning her legs, and for an instant I was in danger of wiping out. I slowed down and took a couple of deep breaths.

"Alcoholics have about the same wonderful prognosis as people with cancer, you know. You go into remission. It's like living with a dormant monster in your blood. You get to wonder when it's going to wake up and eat you alive. Damn it, Joan, it's not my fault that I wound up with a greater tendency towards entropy than eighty percent of the population."

Was that the husk of a laugh I felt brushing my ears?

"Consider this," I went on, trailing the rank spoor of the beast, thrusting foliage from my face, peering ahead. "A couple of years ago, I left a woman I loved. But not before I'd tried twisting myself into every shape imaginable, hoping she'd mistake me for the woman she *really* wanted to be with. She wasn't crazy about living with a marginal type like me, but she couldn't bring herself to leave me, either. But there was too much baggage from my drinking years, two of which we endured together. I, we, carried that damned baggage through the sober years, and we never got past resenting the weight of it. So finally I jettisoned it, and her in the process. Someone had to do it. Pretty heartless, huh, Joan?"

Oops. I hadn't meant to mimic her. I drew my legs up and

rested my forehead against my knees. Minutes passed. And then, like a glimpse of grace in purgatory, I heard her voice.

"How long have you been sober?"

Six little words. Links on a chain cast out for me to grasp and haul myself up with.

"Four years."

"Oh. She'd only been dry for a few months when I left."

"Yeah, well, it gets worse before it gets better."

"Are you saying I should've hung in there?"

"Everyone gets a second chance," I said. "And maybe I'm yours."

"Well," she murmured, moving her palm lightly, lightly, up the inside of my thigh, "we'll see, won't we?"

Sex Is a Verb

Pinelopi Gramatikopoulos

I'm thinking I'm not thinking about it yet when I look at you I feel as though I am rolling down a steep hill with my eyes open and my body dampening from the friction and the moisture in the grass.

I hum a tune inside to keep you at a distance so that when you ask me if I am a perfectionist or not I am genuinely distracted and have interrupted my singing to wonder how and when it is conversation began.

"In the past," I say, "I have executed the perfect seduction."

Laying down my crochet hook, I looked across the table at your breasts. They were sharply pointed, as if in response to my gaze. I watched you raise an arm to rest your hand on your neck. You were hiding from my arousal. I stitched another loop thinking not so much about sucking your nipples but about whether or not perfectionism has simply to do with my relationship to my mother, or whether it's complicated by the kind of bread I like to eat.

"I'd like to know what's going on," you stared.
"I've been sexing you."
"You can't sex someone!"

"Then how can you unsex someone?"
"Smart ass!"

And the story started with a sigh. Two sighs. And a sign between two women who at first had sat in a room across from each other and later had walked out to the yellow grass to see about talking, though either one could have been thinking more about what she would be feeling.

This is the story of two women being teased and tickled by verbs and nouns and by a particular pronoun: "We" "We" gets all over them like gootchey-gootchey-koo and the palm of a hand. This is the story of two women who went outside and played games with each other, chasing their sensuality round and round the tree — We? We. We? We — until they drove it smack into each other and were forced to stand silent for a moment while its perfume slowly diffused and plied its way like tender-stemmed flowers, into their hair.

The enthusiasm that finally buoys these two women up and around the treetops had to be carefully carved and sanded by secret stares and internal sighs, and a good deal of abstraction:

Though she had been stared at earlier from across a table, it was not as an act of charity that she now harnessed the flaps of her skirt to her waist and stuffed the cloth, like menstrual rags, firmly between her thighs. Nor was it any more charitable when she drew a knife from the entrails of her bag to slice the rough lattice casing of the cantaloupe and lay sections raw and exposed, fleshy and full, onto the mat of dried grasses. Instead there was something uncompromising in her gestures, something pragmatic, some present thing that discouraged romanticism. The crescents themselves, starting from amongst the bristling yellow fingers of grass, mirrored this glaring orange of indomitable presence. Here at last, they seemed to say, is a woman who could easily bend an arm across her chest to obscure the sight of her erect nipples.

It was clear to both, from the first taste of that succulent fruit that they were participants in a coarse grainy game of contrasts. It was so obviously manifest in the cache of husks — piling higher and higher and more and more translucent — that they tried to lay the mass discreetly beneath a hedge, as though they carried with them some former innocence that now, in the face of fresh culpability, had to be buried or deliberately misplaced before they could set out again. And for a brief moment as they raised faces from footsteps to look at one another, each was deciding the extent of her complicity in uncovering this thing. Each was trying to prefigure the moment when everything would become the responsibility or fault of the hot sun, the jacked-up skirt, the knife in the grass.

This is the story of sexing.

"I've been sexing you." "You can't sex someone!" "Then how can you unsex someone?" It often happens between people who have never sexed together before. It cannot be willed, deliberated, hunted. "When I look at you I feel." As it happens, you have a choice to make: to sex or not to sex. You cannot crucify sex and hang it on your wall for adoration, contemplation, abstraction. You cannot sacrifice yourself to it. At least not beforehand. Sexing has no past and no future.

It is, then is not and will never provide a lifetime of illusions or sustenance for long boring train rides or arduous tasks in the kitchen, or a terrible love affair. It is boundless and happens here or there.

There are proponents, opponents, adherents, fearents of sexing. Like perfectionism it is simple and complex. Either you enjoy it because as a child you used water brought from home to make your mud pies in the street, or else you don't because rain puddles were always good enough for you. Or vice-versa.

The worrisome part of sexing is the staring that's involved. It is highly possible that you will forget the sexant's name, hair colour, etc., as you stare intently at her earlobe or her front teeth, or whatever aspect has absorbed your attention. This is the worrisome part for some, forgetting the subject in the object. But what sex fearents themselves forget is the conned-text:

> Unsexing is an act of misogyny that demands a definite size and shape. Unsexing is always an act of objectification affecting the female form. Misogynists have the form pegged down.
>
> Misogynists unsex sexing women. A sexing woman does not comply with misogynist acts. A sexing woman can act upon another woman. She can be the subject of her own action. She is not defined by black-and-white characters in a misogynist text.

Sex is a verb. "I sex you." A woman who sexes is not easily character-ized. A sexing woman sees and chooses: to sex or not to sex. A woman sexing activates her world. Some women forget they can be active verbs and believe they are nouns. A noun is always an object subject to someone else's standard of naming.   A verb decides what to say about a subject; a verb chooses its subject and object, deciding whether the hands will jack up the skirt or tickle the fancy.   A woman sexing defines her own subject.

Sexing sees the erect nipples. Sexing invulves. It is not some thing that lies in a hot bed of sand waiting to be taken. Sexing trips you up and leaves you standing clear-eyed and naked, licking the salty taste from your lips.

Blue Video Night

Marusia Bociurkiw

The TV monitor hovers in blue semi-darkness, my eyes trans-fixed by its flicker. Sixty different light patterns per second, each image lingering on my retina to merge into the other. The woman's body I'm looking at is nothing but illusion: willing collaboration between the visual system and the brain. (The product, really, of desire.)

It's 3:00 a.m. I've got to get out of this edit room. This is the time of night I make cuts I'll later regret: sudden, acciden-tal colour shifts that result in green skin; twists in the narrative that result in tragedy. I don't feel in control.

I close my eyes and see the outline of her body.

It's early in the morning that my yearning for her rises from my skin, the salty smell, the tautness/wetness that happens when I think of how she pulled me toward herself, my wanting reaching down into my bones until I ache.

I put a different videotape into the deck. A closeup of waves — parody of B-grade romanticism — and then the camera pulls back ever so slowly to reveal a woman lying on the sand. The camera-woman walks over to where she is, so there are bumpy shots of sand and tilted horizon. An anti-romantic shot of her feet, and then the camera pans across her body, mainstream-cinema-style.

When the camera gets to her face, I pause the machine. Her eyes are closed, her lips are trying not to smile. Some-times, all I can remember is those lips, the sensuous mobility of her mouth, the way it couldn't decide if she was serious or not, widening with pleasure, or tightening with intensity. Which would then lead me to contemplate her mouth sucking at my nipples, so serious and childlike, then looking up at me and breaking into one of her enormous womanly smiles. Or her mouth swallowing mine. Or her tongue in my cunt.

But in the video image her mouth is closed. I take my finger off the pause button. The camera goes wide, to reveal her starting to peel off her T-shirt.

It was just an experiment in home video porn, a joke, really.

Or, it was an acting-out of the conditions under which we met. My desire to objectify her. Her pleasure at being objectified. The way it happens all the time in the bars, at the dances, all that looking and being looked at.

But she was, is, an active subject, too.

The camera wavers as the T-shirt hits the sand. There's no script, there are only so many times you can pan back and forth, back and forth, along a body. Then she starts to caress her own breasts, pulling at her nipples. The camera zooms jerkily into extreme close-up, focuses on the network of wrinkles forming around her nipple as it becomes hard. None too steadily, the camera follows her hand down to her crotch; she slips her hand into her wetness, then pulls it out and licks it very slowly. She smacks her lips, grins. The framing gets shaky here, from laughter or nervousness, I can't remember which. The horizon disappears. The sequence ends abruptly.

This isn't in the video: she pulls me down with her onto the sand; suddenly, fiercely. Holds my arms down with one hand, explores my cunt with the other, her legs roughly pushing my thighs apart, her tongue loud around the contours of my ear, breathing into it until I'm dizzy. Her fingers persisting into my cunt until her hand is inside of me, and I cry out, her body hard and tough against me all the while.

And this isn't in it, either: how I fell, with such relief, headlong into her strength, me, a strong woman too; how I surrendered.

And there is no way of depicting this: her mind and body confronting my mind and body. The urgent pulse of her ideas. The heat.

Maybe I imagined it, this familiarity after years of otherness. She, like me, is an activist. She, like me, loves sex. The two have been so separate. The struggle had negated pleasure, and pleasure had never seemed worth fighting for.

I frame her with my desire. I slow the image and examine her movements second-by-second, her lips time-lapsing into a smile. I manipulate her body. I have this power. I try to look at it, the hot centre of my attraction. But it's nowhere in these images, exists only in my body. My cunt shudders when I think of her. There is no picture for this.

No, it's simply that we share the same political beliefs. She's against free trade, too. She 's a feminist, too.

She's a woman, too. The edges of our bodies cup each other. Recognition made our eyes water, the first time we touched.

And difference vibrates between us when we make love.

I'm sitting in this darkened edit room, looking at her electronically reproduced image. She's running toward the camera now in fake slow-motion — we're drawing heavily on melodrama here — but her face is illumined with a real happiness. I rewind the tape, she's getting further and further away. I close my eyes for a moment. The flickering image of her body, imprinted on my vision. They call that visual persistence. Or memory, so fragile it's hardly there at all.

The sequence ends. Snow (that's what they call it) fills the screen. Electronic snow, sizzling through blue video night.

The story waits for me to finish it. There isn't much time left, the net is closing in. I want to depict this: a whole body, inscribed with my/her/our political and erotic meaning.

This body that exists only in fragments. This story that survives, waiting for you/me to construct the ending I/we desire.

Primrose Path

Candis J. Graham

Alice pounds on the door, beating her fist against the wood in a desperate pattern of noise. With each harsh sound, she wills the door to open. Someone must be home. She had noticed a light on upstairs as she walked in from the highway. Open the door! She shivers.

A tall, broad-shouldered woman opens the door and shoves her hands deep into jean pockets. The light from the room behind her is bright.

Alice's whole body trembles. "Accident." She lowers her eyes and leans against the door frame. "My bike went off the road."

The woman looks at the helmet dangling from Alice's hand and steps back. "You're sopping wet. Are you hurt?"

She shakes her head and turns back to the dark night. "My bike...."

"It'll wait. You've got to get out of those wet clothes," she says, taking Alice's arm and pulling her into the bright room. "I'll get you a brandy."

Alice sat at the kitchen table, staring into space and listening to the sensual singing voice of Carole Pope. Her teeth pulled at the left corner of her bottom lip. It was a habit, an automatic motion, two rows of teeth grabbing and holding, then releasing.

Should she tell Marie-Therese? She had been thinking about it all week. All week? It had been in the back of her mind for many weeks. She believed Marie-Therese deserved to know. What was their relationship, how close would they ever be if Alice couldn't reveal herself to Marie-Therese? She would. Yes. She wouldn't wait another day. She would tell her as soon as they were alone, tonight, after the game, while they walked home. She wouldn't wait until they were home, sitting face-to-face in the closed privacy of the living room.

Alice realized her lip was sore and probed it gently with her forefinger.

The woman closes the door and leads her to a sofa. Alice feels a tightness in her throat, and she wants to swallow but can't. She watches the woman's face.

"Sit here. I'll get the brandy."

She returns with a large terry-cloth bathrobe. "There's the bathroom." She nods at an open door across the room. "Get out of those wet clothes and put this on."

Alice closes the bathroom door and removes her clothes. She starts to shake again, and drops of water fall from her hair. Her fingers are cold and numb. She fumbles with the buttons and drags wet clothes away from her clammy skin, thinking about the tall woman. Does she live all alone out here? She has a kind face. How old is she? Mid-twenties or so? Alice looks down at the water stains on the wooden floor and sees her own hard nipples. She pulls on the bathrobe and wraps it around herself. The thick robe feels good against her body.

When she returns to the sofa, the woman is waiting with a snifter of brandy. "You're shaking," she says. "Drink this down, Sweetie."

Alice held a bit of bottom lip between her teeth, forgetting the soreness. She loved the ways her body felt when she lived the daydream in her mind. It never failed to excite her. It was her favourite fantasy, had been for years. She changed it, from time to time. Small changes. Sometimes she collapsed when the woman opened the door, and the tall stranger had to catch Alice and carry her inside. Other times the woman removed the wet clothes, because Alice was trembling too violently to do it herself, and wrapped her in a large quilt. Sometimes the woman made Alice bend over the cold kitchen counter. Other times they stayed on the sofa in the living room.

Why did she want to tell Marie-Therese? To stop the secrecy? To erase the guilt? Guiltguiltguiltguilt. How could she call herself a revolutionary lesbian? A feminist lesbian wouldn't take a passive role. Alice fingered her tender lip. The other woman was a nameless stranger, nothing more than a powerful voice and a pair of strong hands. She was an object, created only to help Alice feel sexual. That felt worst of all.

Surely Marie-Therese would not judge her. Marie-Therese would understand that Alice tried, but she was not a radical lesbian. She was a lesbian with strengths and weaknesses. So why did the weaknesses feel like defects? Because she enjoyed the fantasy. Because she did not struggle to overcome her flaws.

Alice stood up, moving slowly and humming to the music. She knew, but it did not reassure her, that no one would judge her as harshly as she judged herself. What would Marie-Therese think? She said the name again, out loud this time, "Marie-Therese."

Alice loved the name, liked the feel of it in her mind and the sound of it in her mouth. It was one of the first things she had learned about Marie-Therese, the herstory of the name. The women of her family had preserved Marie-Therese's name, although it had been anglicized from Marie-Thérèse as it was handed down. The language had been lost entirely three generations ago. Intermarriage with English men and living in English-speaking communities had erased it in one generation.

Marie-Therese mourned her loss. She said everything had

been different in the past, but it couldn't happen so easily now. People were fighting to preserve the French language and culture. Back then, they didn't have pride and determination. And they didn't have the law that said French was an Official Language.

When she was in a certain playful mood, Marie-Therese would say "oui" rather than "yes," sliding the word through the corner of her mouth in imitation of Ottawa Valley patois. It was the only French she knew, that and "Bonjour" and "Comment ça va."

Alice leaned against the kitchen counter, staring into the pot of warming milk and fingering her tender lip. All these months together they had never talked about sexual fantasies. Did Marie-Therese have fantasies? She glanced at the clock. Time was running out. She must concentrate on getting ready. She had to get to the ball park, had to be there soon. The game would start at eight and Marie-Therese was expecting her.

She crushed a cardamom seed between two spoons and scattered the sweet-smelling fragments over the surface of the milk. She used the handle of one spoon in a lever-like motion to lift the lid from the cocoa tin. Brushing her hips and stomach against the oven door in time to the music, she stirred a heaping spoonful of brown cocoa into the milk. She threw back her head and sang with Carole as she stirred.

> If the pleasures of the flesh could transcend
> Then ecstasy would be my end
> Don't be contrite
> Let's take flight
> I might not feel this open again
> Strutting peacock with azure blue

Come into my cage
I mean my room

The milk started to boil. Alice laughed at herself and removed the pot from the stove. Pouring hot chocolate into a thermos, screwing on the lid, putting the thermos into a large canvas bag, all the while she danced to the rhythm.

She walked into the bedroom, holding the canvas bag in one hand. Moving with the grace of a woman infinitely pleased with her body, Alice sat on the bed. She took the blanket from the foot of the bed, folded it carefully into a small parcel, and then sat back against the headboard, stroking the soft wool fibres of the blanket and singing along with Carole's throaty voice.

Birds of a feather flock together
Yes they do, yes
Birds of a feather flock together
Yes they do, yes
It's intoxicating for me to fantasize like this

She closed her eyes, hugging the cream-coloured blanket against her chest.

"*My bike, it's, I have to....*"

"*There's nothing we can do tonight. It's pouring out there, and it's pitch black. You'll catch your death of cold. Have another brandy.*"

Alice holds the snifter with both hands and concentrates on calming her calming herself.

"*Here,*" *the woman says,* "*drink up and lean against me. I'll rub your arms and legs and get the circulation going.*"

She puts the snifter on the coffee table and sits close to the woman. She closes her eyes and waits.

"Don't fall asleep, Sweetie. I have plans for us." The woman holds out her hands. "Look at these hands. They'll give you more pleasure than you've ever known. You'll forget everything else, and you'll want more. I promise you. And I'll give you more." She laughs and laughs.

Alice stares at the hands, mesmerized. They are long and broad. Still laughing, the woman takes Alice's wrists. Her grip is hard. Alice wants to pull away but she does not dare try.

The song ended. Time to leave. To see Marie-Therese. Alice opened her eyes and tucked the blanket into her canvas bag, shoving it gently around the thermos of hot chocolate.

Another song started. She slung the bag over her shoulder, cradling it against her body with her elbow, and reached over to turn off the cassette player. The sudden silence stopped her movements. What if Marie-Therese was disgusted? They shared this bed, had done every night since they'd met eight months ago. What would Marie-Therese say when she knew Alice aroused herself with a fantasy? With this fantasy. Not always, but often. Images that made Alice wet and restless. Not always, but usually.

She stood up and adjusted the bag on her shoulder. She wanted to see Marie-Therese. She took a quick look around the silent room and closed the door.

It was early evening, still bright. The warm spring air had brought her neighbours out of their apartments and houses. People sat on verandas and front steps. Some people strolled along the street. Others chatted in small groups on the sidewalk. She looked into their eyes and nodded slightly in greeting as she passed. Walking briskly, she shifted the weight of her canvas bag from shoulder to shoulder every so often and hummed as she walked.

Would it be better to wait until they were home, in bed? Two naked women, vulnerable and trusting? She imagined

Marie-Therese stretched out beside her on the bed. She adored Marie-Therese's body, adored her sloping shoulders and her breasts, breasts that fit perfectly into Alice's open hands. Small drooping breasts that fit into a 34A sports bra.

Marie-Therese had taken the bra with her that morning. She had tucked it in her red bag, saying she hated to wear it but her breasts hurt when she ran without the stupid thing. Alice had laughed as Marie-Therese put her hands under her breasts and jiggled them. She was still laughing when Marie-Therese leaned across the table to kiss her goodbye.

For a moment Alice forgot where she was, forgot to look both ways before stepping off the curb. The earsplitting sound of an angry driver's car horn brought her back. She stopped, looked up, and hurried to the safety of the opposite sidewalk.

The driver poked his head out the open window and yelled, "Why don't ya watch where you're going, bitch!"

She looked at him over her shoulder and beat the air sideways with her hand, dismissing him. Without breaking her stride, she moved the bag to her other shoulder.

Soon she would see Marie-Therese. She took a deep breath of air and looked around at the city. She loved Marie-Therese, loved her shapely body, her playful sense of humour, her slender hands. She adored the uplifting sound of her laughter. She had waited years to meet someone like Marie-Therese, had been waiting since she came out when she was twenty-one. Fifteen years of waiting. And here they were, after eight months, still deeply in love. It would work this time. She would tell Marie-Therese about the fantasy. That's what she decided as she stood at a busy corner, waiting eagerly for the light to turn green.

A minute later she approached the park. The ball diamond was on the far side of the park, a city-block of grass away. She headed in that direction, past women in green-and-white uniforms doing warm-up exercises. The grass and earth cushioned her movements with an ease quite foreign on pavement, and she slowed to a strolling pace.

She had learned of Marie-Therese's love for softball many weeks after they met, and last week, at the first game of the season, she discovered that Marie-Therese's teammates called her M.T. Alice liked the nickname. But she preferred the long, rolling name in its entirety. Ma-rie-The-rese.

She eased the canvas bag off her shoulder and carried it in her left hand. Women in blue-and-grey uniforms threw balls to one another on the other side of the diamond. Spectators stood in clusters along the fence and a few were already seated in the stands. She nodded at some women and smiled. She said hello to others, those she knew. Then she saw Marie-Therese.

Alice increased her walking speed, heading directly toward Marie-Therese. She wanted to run but she controlled the urge and walked, like a sensible woman. She watched Marie-Therese as she walked.

Marie-Therese was facing away from Alice, talking with a teammate. Both women wore green-and-white uniforms. Marie-Therese moved her hands in the air to guide her words as she talked. Her fingers linked together in mid-air, fitting around one another in a gesture that was familiar to Alice. It meant Marie-Therese was talking about working together. She pulled her fingers apart with an easy downward movement and stuffed one fist into the pocket of her trousers. The green pocket stretched over the ridges of Marie-Therese's knuckles.

Marie-Therese turned when Alice was two steps away, as if she sensed Alice's presence. Alice looked into her warm brown eyes and smiled. Marie-Therese smiled in return, spreading the tiny lines at the outer corners of her eyes. Alice shivered slightly.

Marie-Therese bent forward, and Alice felt a gentle breath brush against her skin before Marie-Therese's soft lips touched her cheek. They moved apart. Alice watched the strands of dark hair that curled around Marie-Therese's ear. She looked into Marie-Therese's eyes and, in response to another shiver, reached out to touch the fist within the green pocket. Marie-Therese's hand relaxed and stretched, pressing against the material and Alice's hand.

Alice turned slightly and smiled at Marie-Therese's teammate. "Hi Marnie."

"Hi. How are you?"

"I'm fine, thanks. And you?"

"I can't complain. It looks like it's going to be a good season. We're off to a good start. M.T.'s playing well, isn't she?"

"Yes, she is. So are you." Alice grinned and turned back to Marie-Therese. She could still feel the imprint of Marie-Therese's lips on her cheek. "Hello M.T."

Marie-Therese nodded in the direction of the ball diamond. "The game's going to start. See you after?"

"I'll be here." Alice leaned forward to kiss Marie-Therese's ear. "I'm wet," she whispered.

Marie-Therese laughed and shook her head. "Tell me about it later."

Alice turned. "Have a good game, Marnie."

"Sure thing."

Alice walked away, moving slowly toward the stands. She hoped Marie-Therese would play well and that her team would win. She sat on the grass, leaning back against the fence. She wanted Marie-Therese to be in a good mood tonight.

Alice opened the thermos and poured steamy hot chocolate into the cup. Marie-Therese listened to her, really listened. They talked constantly, long conversations about everything under the sun and moon. The pressure of the cup against her lip reminded her of the sore spot. It was not perfect, not without problems, but nothing was ever perfectly perfect. This was more perfect than she had learned to expect after years of imperfect relationships. The first tentative sip of chocolate scalded her tongue.

Like last Saturday, when Marie-Therese left their bed early to make bread, because the evening before Alice said she had been craving homemade bread for days. No one had ever done anything like that before for Alice. She sat on the kitchen counter watching Marie-Therese's hands kneading the dough and was so happy she wanted to cry. She knew if she cried Marie-Therese would put her arms around her. That made her want to cry all the more. And the bread, when it was ready to eat, was the most delicious bread Alice had ever tasted.

She took a careful sip of hot chocolate. It was the little things, the small moments of affection with Marie-Therese, that made her rejoice. If they were like this after eight months, it would last. If she had faith, surely their love would endure.

The game started. Marie-Therese's team was first at bat. Sometimes Alice focused on Marie-Therese, sometimes on the ever-changing centre of interest in the game. She was fascinated by the intense activity generated by the two teams. There was constant chatter from the field, as players yelled encouragement to one another. Alice often yelled, without thinking, in response to the players. Her voice was loudest when Marie-Therese was at bat.

In the seventh inning, Alice turned her head to watch the flight of a foul ball and noticed the sun setting behind her.

Plump raspberry pink clouds rested in the sky, just above the horizon. Behind her, the game continued.

"Close your eyes. Don't open them. Turn away from me and don't say a word."

Alice obeys, closes her eyes, turns away, and wonders if her motorcycle is damaged. Wonders what will happen next. Wonders what this woman....

"Keep your eyes closed and don't disappoint me. I want to hear you. No words, not one word. I want sounds. As loud as you like. No one will hear except me. Scream your heart out, Sweetie. Your pleasure is mine."

Alice feels a flutter in her stomach and tightness in her throat. She wants to swallow but can't. The robe is dragged away from her and then she feels a mouth on the back of her neck. Hot mouth. Wide and hot and

The first slap surprises Alice, bringing tears to her eyes. She clenches her teeth. One strong hand holds her wrists behind her back. The hot mouth is on her neck, her shoulder, the soft spot under her arm, beside her breast.

The second slap makes her bite her lip. Tasting blood, she cries out.

"That's the stuff Helen, that's the stuff, come on Helen, like you do, just takes one Helen, just takes one, you can do her Helen, let's go, come on now, come on, that's it, come on now, good one Helen!"

Alice missed a home run while she enjoyed the magnificent sunset, and she missed Marie-Therese's hit to right field. She heard the sound of the bat hitting the ball and turned back to the game in time to see Marie-Therese slide into second base. Behind Alice, women in the stands shouted and clapped. Marie-Therese stood up, grinning and brushing dirt from her ass and thighs with her palms. Then she crouched, ready to race to third.

"Looking good now Marnie, looking good, be boss in there, make her work for it, we need you now, we need you Marnie, that's the stuff, you can do it Marnie, be boss in there, you're the best Marnie, come on, come on now!"

Marie-Therese was left standing at third base when the batter struck out. The teams changed sides.

When the game was over, Alice sipped the lukewarm chocolate and watched each team file across the diamond. Women of various shapes and sizes in green-and-white uniforms and blue-and-grey uniforms moved in orderly fashion. Starting from opposite corners and meeting in the middle, each woman briefly grasped the hand of every player from the other team. Occasionally they spoke to one another.

Alice waved goodbye as women left the park, singly, in pairs, and in chattering groups. The bright overhead lights went out, one by one. The two teams gathered around their benches in the darkness, forming separate huddles to replay the game with words.

Alice hummed to herself, in tune to Carole's voice singing the words in her head, as she pulled the cream-coloured blanket from the canvas bag and draped it around her shoulders.

"I've always loved rainy evenings," the woman says, laughing. "The sound of rain and the sound of a satisfied woman. Are you ready for more?" She picks Alice up and carries her upstairs to a loft. She lowers her to the bed and releases her. "I'll get another brandy."

The mattress is hard beneath Alice's body. She turns over slowly, holding the sheet tightly with one hand, wondering how long she'll have to wait. Her toes curl and stretch.

The woman undresses slowly, grinning at Alice and watching her sip the brandy. Her denim shirt lands in a heap on the floor. She tugs on the zipper of her jeans and slides the trousers down past her hips. She is not wearing underwear.

"You look better now than you did at my door." She sits beside Alice on the bed.

Alice almost laughs. "I feel better."

"No words. Don't forget. Only sounds. Turn on your stomach." The woman reaches for the snifter and tips her head back to take the last mouthful of brandy. "Close your eyes, Sweetie, and get ready. You're going to remember me forever."

Alice opened her eyes. The players were beginning to leave, yelling goodbyes to each other as they headed toward the parking lot. Marie-Therese was walking in Alice's direction, carrying the large red sports bag with her right hand.

Alice grinned. "Sit down, here," she said as Marie-Therese approached her, "between my legs. The blanket will keep us warm."

Marie-Therese came down from her standing height and crouched before Alice. Alice held the folds of the blanket open, and Marie-Therese sat down. She folded the blanket around her. They sat, wrapped in the tent-like blanket, Alice holding Marie-Therese securely in her arms.

"Did you see that sunset?"

Marie-Therese nodded.

Alice's nose brushed lightly across the back of Marie-Therese's dark head, poking through her hair, pressing against her skull, everywhere the smell of damp hair as Alice's nose swept back and forth.

"I want to kiss you."

Alice opened her eyes. "Where?"

Marie-Therese laughed, causing her body to tremble against Alice. "Anywhere you want."

"I like you kissing all of me." Her arms tightened around

Marie-Therese. "That was a good game. Do you mind losing?"

"I like to win."

Alice laughed. "Don't we all. Games. Someone wins. Someone loses." She kissed the back of Marie-Therese's neck. "Do you mind losing?" Her mouth gathered up some tiny hairs and tugged.

"I'm playing to win."

Alice's fingers played with the little hairs on Marie-Therese's neck. "It must be a challenge...."

"A challenge!" Marie-Therese shifted restlessly.

"... to work as a team. It's like socialism. You deny your own needs. And you've got to compete against the other team, but not among your own team."

"It's only a softball game, Alice."

"But it's an...."

"Don't. Don't bring politics into it. You bring politics into everything. It's only a game!"

"You don't mean that. Every single thing is political."

"Sure. The perfect world of the future. Spare me the feminist rhetoric. Let's have fun, too."

Alice laughed. "I had fun watching your team play."

"And me?"

"You best of all."

"What did you like best?"

"When you said you wanted to kiss me."

They both laughed. Alice bent forward, and their lips met. Alice watching Marie-Therese, and Marie-Therese watching Alice. Their lips opened for moist kisses, warm kisses, lips and tongues touching. Alice felt wet. The muscles in her thighs tightened around Marie-Therese's hips. Her fingers caressed Marie-Therese's arms, shoulders to wrists. She held both wrists, massaging, encircling the narrow wrists with her hands, squeezing, feeling bone beneath the soft skin.

Marie-Therese moaned. Her hands held Alice's thighs, slowly stroking downward in circular motions, then sliding back along the insides.

Alice pulled the T-shirt away from Marie-Therese's neck and, with closed eyes, her mouth tasted the sloping shoulder. She opened her eyes to study the skin, minute interconnecting lines, fine hairs, and assorted freckles. Her teeth touched skin, gently, then fiercely, biting with satisfaction.

"Oouch!"

"Did I hurt you?"

"Yes. No. It wasn't pain. You surprised me." Marie-Therese stretched. "Let's go home."

"I thought you liked the great outdoors?"

"I do." She laughed. "But I'm a closet lover. Let's go. Come on. I want to take this stupid bra off." She stood up.

"I have something to tell you." Alice's teeth pulled at the corner of her lip.

"You're wet."

Alice stood up. "Yes, but something else."

"What?"

"Do you want to hear my fantasy?"

"A fantasy about sex?"

Alice nodded, turning her face slightly and looking sideways at Marie-Therese.

"Come on, give me the blanket and take my arm. Tell me as we walk home."

A Stray Sock

A. Parpillée

If I were a man, I would lie with my cock stiff and hard just at the entrance to her moribund cunt, and I would not move until she begged me for it. If I were a man, I would think of a million things other than her soft wet walls; I would empty my mind of every stray sock until she needed me, and even then I would brace myself so as to be lean and hard for her to move herself against me until at last the need arose in me to move on in a bit at a time, always waiting for the next sudden swooping falling away making me follow her, tailing her, catching every sweep until we had it. Then I would fuck her wildly until I came, and she would hate me for it. I am not a man. I am the woman who washes her dishes and cleans her house. At home I wear dark leather wristbands, T-shirts with the sleeves torn out. She likes to think she has me on a chain. She likes to order me to bring her something from the kitchen. When it pleases her, she calls me into bed at night when she is lonely or needs someone to hold her, or when she wants to come and doesn't want to do it for herself. She lets me touch her with her legs wide apart, lets me trace her magenta folds. Then aroused and wanting more, abruptly she mounts and rides me furiously, always afraid she will lose it. I know this, and I am not disturbed by her greediness. It has always been like this, and we have never discussed it. On Tuesdays and Thursdays, I play pool at a downtown tavern. Almost always I leave the bar with a woman, Yvonne, who goes there especially to meet up with me. She knows I have other women, and she knows there is nothing she can hope to do about this, so she teases me that I don't know who she's with on the weekends as she puts on her coat to take me home to her one-room apartment. I have only to lay myself down on her; she is suddenly hot. I begin to move in a slow caramel sweep that waves itself into her until, voilà, dazed and sweating, we swim in each other's milk. I couldn't consider making a life with her though. Intellectually, we haven't anything to talk about. There is one other woman I see occasionally. She is Christina, and Christina would have me believe in the possibility of a working romantic relationship. She would have me live with her in a monogamous set-up, something like wife and wife, or rather, husband and husband, but there is something decidedly missing. Sex with Christina is utilitarian. It happens, but has the texture of a passing thought, something unimportant you remember briefly then forget. She claims to be intensely satisfied. She rarely achieves orgasm, and she thanks me for having the decency not to plague her about this. She is, in a certain way, stiff, until we turn out the lights and even then she will not let me touch her with anything like a stroke or caress — I am to lie on top of her and do what I will until I come. If she makes it with me great. If not, she cuddles and squeezes and plants wet kisses, which usually I do not want, but to which I seldom object, not knowing how I could possibly. She pushes me down so that I flood the warm basin of her belly with my breasts, but she would never dream of having me go down on her, and not once have I dared to put fingertip to mons. She steps into the shower after we've made love. She is saving to buy a house out on the West Coast, where she is from, and she hopes to live there one day — happily — with me. I see her only on Friday or Saturday night, and inevitably we go to a club, or a movie, or visit with lesbian friends of hers. I feel I should take leave of her but, whenever I've tried to bring this up, she waves me off claiming a headache or that the night is too hot for discussions, the wine too sweet. She knows I share a house with a woman named Sandra, and she knows too that I frequent a tavern where I play pool until all hours during the week, but basically she doesn't know about my other women because she doesn't want to. She insists that if we are to go any distance as a couple that I must have time to myself and that what I do when I am not with her is not her business.   Sandra, the woman I live with, knows about the other two, but she doesn't concern herself. As long as I stay living with her and give her the love she wants when she wants it, she is content to let me find my happiness elsewhere. If suddenly she were to become jealous, I would know to look for a break-up between her and one of her incessant boyfriends — which happens quite regularly for they inevitably find her a cold and shallow bitch. Sandra doesn't want me or any woman really. She only keeps me around as a back-up. She likes to have someone bring her cocoa on a cold November night. I know this, and I am not disturbed. She confides to me the details of her relationship with one man after the other, right down to how they make love, which sooner or later turns into her coaxing reluctant me into bed where very soon I am instructed to lie silent and still beneath her, which I do with concentrated diffidence knowing my very failure to engage is what excites her terribly. How she swoops and dives. I sometimes take my own pleasure quietly beneath her, but she would never know this, and I would

never tell.   It
is almost a year that I have lived like this, and I think I can
say quite frankly that if anything I am strangely hopeful. I
have found here a certain stability, though I will admit to
brief stabbing anxiety when this woman I live with threatens
to marry yet another man. Alas, even this becomes predictable and can be borne. At the same time she buys new
curtains for my bedroom, and I know not to take the whole
thing seriously.   I
once worked with a married woman in an office. She had
felt parcelled out to her husband and two children in a way
that roughly parallels how I am parcelled out to these three,
only she took the office job to get away. I at least am alone
in the house during the day, and, when the housework is
done, I have the time to play my clarinet. I would ask only
for the afternoon sun.... if it could be made to fall directly
across this part of the room, right here where I sit to play....
but to bring that about we would have to tear down a wall
and rebuild it, and I know for sure we won't have the money
this year.

Casselberry Harvest

Leleti Tamu Bigwomon

for J. with kisses and revolution

We embraced and your arms slipped slowly around me
like limbs and branches of the
casselberry tree
that grows from the dark moist earth of ashanti soil
your locks brown and delicious carry the fragrance from the
blossoms of that tree
in the language of our foremothers casselberry must mean
sunkissed days blanketing a soft orchard, with the indigo
sweetness of you
I anticipate the familiar flavour of your casselberries at
harvest.

Catherine, Catherine

Ingrid E. MacDonald

As you leave London and travel to the south, you pass a marvellous field, a field so large and plain and empty, without so much as a soccer post erected upon it, that it is astonishing to look across, to find, on the outskirts of a sprawling, ancient, crowded city, a blank space, an empty page of intense green. Walking people diminish to specks of bright colours in the distance, like balloons that have been let fly from the hands of children. It is called the Acre but it is much more than one acre — perhaps it is ten — ten acres of green grass criss-crossed only by paths that cut diagonal wedges through the huge green plates, scoring the ground geometrically like the radial lines on a sundial. The Acre is so large and so empty in a country that is not at all large and never empty that it inspires lofty thoughts and kite flying.

What can't be seen, either on a clear day or on a typical drizzling English day, is the secret of the Acre, the reason for its emptiness, why no one dares to put up even a soccer post on these expansive fields. Had you come here some three hundred and fifty years ago, and then again, perhaps you did, you would have known only too well the reason for the Acre.

For it is here, under the great green flats of grass, that thousands of corpses were brought, carried by horses or pushed in carts up the long steep incline, on a cobbled path, to be buried after the plagues had had their way with the living. It is on the Acre that we meet the subject of this tale, a brawny twenty-four-year-old woman left orphaned by the contagious bites of fleas and left alive, overlooked by a ravaging disease that killed 35,000 Londoners in one year alone.

She was ferrying the last of her family up to the Acre; her father lay in a crude box that rattled in the cart that she hired. She left her father deliberately to the last for she needed to collect her inheritance, and as he had nothing to give her she took what she had wanted the most of him for all her young life and undressed him down to his leggings and put his doublet and breeches on her figure and doffed his sugarloaf hat onto her own head and covered the old man with her rag of a dress, which settled in his stiff hands like a small blanket that he caressed on his last journey. Then she nailed his coffin crudely with the wooden sole of her shoe and brought the box out of the house to the cart.

Once on the Acre, she lowered his box in a newly dug part of the ground and settled her owings with the driver of the cart, a nervous fellow who held a rag up to his nose against the stench. The ground was a fierce sight, churned and steaming, like when the butcher throws a pail of offal into the ditch. For the sake of waving goodbye to someone, she waved heartily to the cart driver, though she did not know him at all. Then she continued walking in the direction south, away from London, for she is leaving it behind, it and all its sooty corridors and crowded streets where a million citizens are swarming like dedicated wasps in a grey paper nest that has been set afire. As she stopped to ladle water for herself from a cattle trough she looked back on the Acre and imagines how each coffin is a brick and how so many bricks make a wall and how so many walls make a pavillion and how a great pavillion is being built underground, a huge fantastic building where half of London now lives. She was thinking of something else, but she can't remember what it is for a moment, then, oh yes, a name, the name, the right new name for herself.

Nightfall had come on by the time I had walked near seven miles, and I was ailing for I had been putting up the boxes since dawn and taken but a mouthful of alesop in the midday. Yet I feared the thought of going to houses abegging for it is known how hostile men can be to strangers, especially to us from the city for they have it that they will catch sickness from the mere sight of us. Afar in a field I saw the lamps of ramblers and reckoned they'd be kinder than settled folk and went to ask for comfort from them even if it would be only to sleep near them and not be afeared of the night.

Coming near them I found them not ramblers at all but a group of religious inspirants. They parleyed among themselves with great vigour about the intentions of God and the defiant ways of men. Chief among them was a woman, and she gave me first a stew of boiled roots and a rasher of pig and then a learning in the Puritan way. She told me her name was Eva and asked me mine, but I said I have no name at all, for what is it to be named by those who never saw thee as thyself. And Eva thinks there is wisdom in that and declares that I should have a new name, but first she concerned herself with the more urgent task of purifying me and described how she saw in me a multitude of demons that must be banished. Thus she learned me the utterances of holy words spake directly to God himself without the nuisance of the vicar in between. Just as if God sat in the chair near yours was how I learned to speak, and, although I could not discern whether this religion or bewitching be, on account of my soul's salvation I followed her ways and most powerfully her blessing appeared to me. 'Twas then I first heard voices liberated in my ears. Once I had learnt the prayer rightly Eva took me away from the others, to the middle of the harvested oat field, and there among the stubble and stem she lifted up her kirtle and peed into a small cup and took the warm yellow drink and blessed me by pouring it into my hair. "Out, out all besetting demons," she called afore me and then gave me the name by which she always called me, Peter.

My tung was freed for prophecy, and I travelled with these inspirants by day and slept on the blanket beside Eva at night. I pined for her although she would have none of me as she would have none of any man. Coming into towns and hamlets we met always with hostility, for the folk were routinely savage and called us scourge. Yet among the people there were those blessed by the Lord, and 'twas my task to seek these out, a task that was simple to perform for I always saw angels perched on the shoulders of the chosen ones. To these ones with angels I declared publickly how they were named by God, and 'twas them who provided us with our suppers and gave generously of their larders. For my deeds in procuring food through prophecy I was greatly favoured by Eva and remained her special companion until one Percy joined our ways.

Percy came wanting the Puritan way but he was treacherous for he had no angels perched on him that I could see, only demons that covered him pestilent as fleas. Eva's prophetic sight must have failed her for she saw not a single demon upon him and took Percy aside and freely kissed him as she pleased. When I protested she only laughed and called me jealousy and kissed me on my lips to tease me. Forever I rued that moment, for 'twas then that Percy's infestation spread, and a demon jumped inside me.

Soon we went to Beatrixbourne where I saw angels on the head of one rat-catcher named Charles, and this Charles had great wealth in the town for his business had prospered during the plagues while all others ailed, and I prophesied that this Charles could walk on the water as the Lord had. Only Percy spoke ill of me and spoilt the rat-catcher's faith so that when he went to step on the river he sank directly and nearly drown'd and had to be hauled up on ropes.

This rat-catcher was a braggart too and had invited all the town to come watch his miraculous feat, but when he floundered the crowd saw me as evil and turned against me and set upon me. I ran like a fleeing rabbit, and they hunted me with their dogs and took me intending to kill me with hasty justice for endangering the rat-catcher's life. In sport they cut my father's clothes from me and when they saw my original nature all the louder did they call for my neck to be hung from a tree. Until one among them saw shadows in me and reckoned I was pregnant with evil seed and proposed to the others that the demon child be cut out of me and spilled on the ground for a demon child not properly killed is quick to return to haunt the lives of his assailants. Away I was taken to a leather-aproned blacksmith who sharpened his axe against a stone.

Hand and foot they threw me into the smith's hut, and as he sharpened they shouted "Cut the devil from her" in terrible voices out front only he never raised his eyes to meet mine, so shamed I think he was of my nakedness. I feard for my life, and the pain of a knife terrified me until I heard a woman's voice. There was no woman to see but an evanescence lit the air around the smith's shoulders. "Take yourself through the small door out to the back," she said, and then with force, "run child." Only my feet wouldn't obey, and I tottered there. I felt a firm push from behind and in that second I thrust myself through a small door, through a passageway and away.

Tired and wretched though I was I did not dare to stop until I had run for some hours and hidden myself in a dark woods. I was so tired I could have slept where I fell on the ground but the murmurings of wild beasts gave me fear — for what is it to escape the blacksmith's knife only to be devoured by an animal's tooth. I devised that I would have to beg for mercy from some person and approached a cottage where I wailed in a low voice and hid myself so that my nakedness could not be seen.

A man came quickly to the door, and in the light of his lamp I saw how his whiskers stuck out of his face the way hairs poke from the crackled rind of a roasting pork back. I marvelled how his doorway suited him as much as a pulpit for he hardly had the door open before he began to preach. He described only the evil of the poor who know not how to work and call damnation upon themselves with their stink and poverty, for no one in his esteem could be poor or ill without the Lord having assigned misery unto them, and what is misery if not payment for sins. So he preached, stoking the hot hell fires of his mouth until he had expended all the miserable creatures of the world with his perceptions, and then he shut his door again leaving not a scrap for me to put in my belly nor a rag for me to wear on my naked back.

I was in greater misery than when I had first cried out, and tears came quick for I hated my wretchedness. I tried to quell my tears as soft footsteps came near me, and amazed I was to see a woman whose countenance I had never before seen for she was dark brown in her whole figure, with broad features for her face and hair that softly shaped around her head. I hid my naked person in the hedge regarding not the pain of the brambles. She spoke with a tung as fine as any good lady ever possess, and I took her as the mistress of the property come to expel me, until she described herself, and then I realised that she was one who laboured for this preaching man. Sharp words had she for his miserly ways, "What nature of man is this who spouts pious concern and then breaks the Lord's first rule with his very sermon. Come near, Poor Tom, whoever thou be."

"I cannot come near for I am naked," I cried and hid myself further from her.

"Then you shall have clothes," and she went away to bring breeches and doublet well used although finer in their aged state than my father's had ever been and a bowl of warm groats that she set down where I might take it. "When God asks of you, report that it was Sabina's kindness you received tonight. I shall pray for the relief of your misery as well." I gladly took what she left for me and slept that night secretly behind her small cottage, able at last to sleep in the comfort of one so merciful.

From there I took to wandering in lanes and streets and would have made a career of begging had the parliamentary forces not come that way out of London with their grievances against the infydelle King. I had no grief against his majesty but the purse they offered an able man to join their side suited my needs, and along I went to conquer hamlets and towns with every rabbler and buffoon and nobleman who could carry a stick. A force is training ground enough for one like me who aspired to become a man and not a wife, for the manners of men with their lewdness and shit-stained breeches are not difficult to emulate, and among them I called myself Matthew. Our duties were arduous with great distances to walk but never so foul as the time we enforced the ban against Christmas — it is known as a pagan and superstitious affair — and took our bats against the citizens. 'Tis the smallest of things, that cause the common man to rise up, and Christmas proved too difficult to take from them. The streets were full of riotous persons, and the fishwifes and religious women the worst among them, shouting names at us that would give a harpie the blushes. And we soldiers had to hit them, men and women alike, and break the glass in the cathedral windows, and show nothing in our eyes.

All the while I was among the men I concealed my person carefully and was reputed to be shy for I held my piss and shit until I could dump it in private, although shyness among men is fecklessness, as far as they were concerned. While I had none of the membrum of men, I did have the hands of a woman and clever hands too for I took some leather and sewed a long sausage of it and filled it with dried peas and to it added the bladder of a sheep that hung from the bottom of the sausage and fastened the piece onto me with a leather strap. To this I added a sheep horn, born through with a hole that allowed me to piss from a height as my fellows do, and my membrum virile woggled proudly in my breeches as a clanger dangles in a bell.

Soon I wearied of the force, for the battle of Naseby left the muddy ground a sight to sicken the strongest. There trampled underfoot lay the parts of men as squished as berries. From that moment on I plotted my desertion and could care no more about the parliamentary victory. One night when the others were sleeping, I stayed awake and made my way in a direction contrary to theirs and walked to a remote hamlet. Hoping she would not inquire too shrewdly of my past, I approached a young maid as she tended an orchard. She was Catherine, and she lived in humble cottage with her mother, her father having long since died. I gave my name as Cornelius, thinking it an attractive name, and amused her with tales I had learned from soldiers. Perhaps I deceived her, although without unkind intentions, when I told her my father was a wealthy weaver in Essex. I never intended to ail her when I described myself as one who imports fabric from the new east for it interested her so much and I could not foresee how it would bring grief. In turn she delighted me, and we went into a cow bairth together, and I tickled her with my substitute, and this she greatly fancied.

Presently we went to her mother to have her agree and then to the parish for the askings. All the while her mother looked at me askance. I knew she took Catherine aside and instructed her how she must touch me just so, here and here, and report precisely what she feels. But no amount of touching would come to any advantage, for I have never had much of a woman's chest, and whenever Catherine stroked my pants my membrum would be there in full virility, erect with its bulge underneath, such that Catherine would have had to blush to describe to her mother how the manness of me held constant vigilance. The mother had little case to refuse us, and soon it was arranged that she should live in a hutch in the back quarter of the lot while Catherine and I took up the bigger house that now properly belonged to me. The mother never eased her contempt for me, and she was as scurrilous as a dog whenever she caught smell of me, and soon I saw the reason for it. For once she stood with the afternoon light behind her, and I could see them all there, more pestilent than Percy's fleas, a thousand demons covering her, setting her soul against me.

Our happiness was short lived. Catherine's mother's demons were always looking through windows at me. Though I did my best to treat Catherine as my wife it was no use. I entered her with my leather member often and frequently, no matter now it tired me in the effort, for I would not have her complain to the other wives that I had no courage in me. But the soldier's life had ruined me. I worked not, and my tales of weaving and importing also proved untrue. I took my business to the public house and drank ale all hours. When I had no coins left for paying, I went to the house and took some such thing, linens or clothes or what have yous, as they all were now rightly mine, and sold it to one man or another for the price of a drink. Catherine turned a shrew and called me abbeylubber and scolded and complained bitterly how she hadn't any eggs for I had sold everything even the biddies that scratched in the yard. In return I abused her and clapped her ears with my hand and yelled how her mother poisoned her thoughts and set her against me. How she would sit in woeful tears until I went off again to the public house.

So it was, until the night when her hateful mother came after me and sought me in the public house and in front of all present and with her rotten teeth shouted of the womanized nature of me, making a tittle of my affairs before all present. So I approach the spiteful woman with my sheephorn in place and stand and piss a full pint of piss onto her while the men jeer and laugh. "That will learn you for womanizing me," I say, and the carpenter claps me on the back and gives me his jug. But when I leave off my aleing that night I know how much ruin is upon me, and I shun my home for ever and take wandering again in the roads to the south east.

Thus abegging did I feel the full breath of wretchedness for I had become a creature without society, hated by men and women, nor at ease in nature neither, for something in me rebelled against my womanish birth and cursed the form I was born with. Yet, in my mannish state, what had I wrought but grief? If I have ever woven anything, it was a tale of misery, neither man nor woman and neither able to be.

I slept in cow bairths and ditches and asked passers by for a bit of caudle to eat. They called me hateful baggage until one as thin and bedraggled as I and wearing rags for her skirts recognised me where I lay sleeping and spake easily to me and called me Cornelius. This was my own Catherine, returned to me, relating the full tale of her mother's havoc, and she, not wishing to be eternally leashed to so wicked a thing as her mother's tung, did set after me to rightfully be with me. Together, we carried our hunger and begged and walked with hands outstretched.

After we had travelled for many days Catherine woke with a sickness in her that inclined her to vomit, though she had scarce eaten, and greatly weak she became for she spat up the very blood and bile of her. She was so badly that we went to a vicarage and begged sincerely for a bed to lay her in, and after a day of waiting, for God watches even the smallest sparrow fall, a room was given us in an alms house.

Catherine stayed in that bed for near to a week, and I did sit with her, and never did we argue. I pitched the phlegm from her spitting pan daily and held her hand. We needed money for making our way, and once she had some strength returned I went about asking in the streets but the smallest coin made me only think of ale. So I stayed away the whole day with a jug for company, and when I returned to her as drunk as Davey's sow she put the devil upon me with her tung for her strength had returned enough to ballyrag me for taking up my old drunken ways and being a wretch who cares not whether his wife breathes or not, and this riled me. But being drunk I had to piss and fumbled with my sheephorn and while standing above my chamber pot dribbled onto me shoes. "Other men piss without wetting their shoes. What is it in you that you can't even piss like other men?" I threatened her with my fist only to fall drunk asleep before my hand was fully raised. Catherine took a candle then and lit it near me and unfastened my clothing, first my doublets and then my breeches, and felt the soft of my skin and discovered the inanimate nature of my membrum. She was greatly amazed and afraid, for she saw how our natures were identical in every way. Then she took a knife and cut my membrum free and concealed it.

In the morning when I woke I saw clearly what was gone from me, and yet I did not want Catherine to suspect any wrong, so I feigned to have lost a coin in the bed and searched in vain, and soon desperation set upon me for I found it not. Then Catherine looked at me from where she stood and confronted me with my travesty and told me her discovery and how she burned my hateful member in the fire. "Can't you smell the stink of evil burning?" she asked me. I knew that I was ruined and begged her to have the mercy to kill me at once for I deserved not to live and feared a riled mob would come to make mockery of my flesh. For that is what they did with the old couple at the workhouse who were thought to be witches. First they tied the thumbs of the woman to her big toes and flung her in the river, and, once the wife was drown, they tied the husband to her corpse until he also was drown, and the chief tormenter among them collects money for shewing the town such sport.

Except Catherine spake easily to me and called not for my blood. She would abide with me if I mended my ways to live in decency, which I then promised, and this promise I have always kept and not from fear of exposure neither — but upon my honour.

Once Catherine had shown mercy to me, I felt a covenant more binding than with any Lord. Even the Lord who sits beside you in his chair cannot compare with the mercifulness of my Catherine. Of my truer nature we made a pact of secrecy for I still wore my mannish garb and her husband proclaimed to be, and in our lives, where fear might have wreaked evil, only kindness reigned. We stayed at the alms house and kept intimate company, and once Catherine asked me what my name was from birth, but it eluded me and would not come in my thoughts. So Catherine, being learn'd of the alphabet, penned a letter to the parish clerk of the place where I was born and described me in such a way as I was when I was younger and inquired what the Christian name of this maiden might be.

We exchanged work for food at the parsonage and oft' times Catherine took sewing that needed to be done for gentle ladies, and if I had no tasks myself I would sit in the room with Catherine and have her good company. Some days Catherine would feel an itch in her, and we had our intimate ways together again, and I would pleasure her in ways I knew how with my hands and freely caress her teats and lie athwart her and bring her thrill on. One day, in the peak of her pleasure, Catherine reached under the bed and returned my membrum to me, for she had never destroyed it as she said, but put it away thinking she hated it, only to be in the swell of her passion and wish for it once again. So I wore my membrum and mounted her and entered her repeatedly until she shouted with the greatest pleasure imagined.

Then she undressed me, and for the first time I willingly let Catherine take my clothes from me. I stood wearing only the membrum I had fashioned so carefully, and I wondered what it is to be a man, to have arms and legs and a membrum, and what it is to be a woman, to have hands that can express so much. Then Catherine moved gently and knelt before me and fondled my teats to rush my blood and kissed my thighs with her soft lips only to set her lips upon my membrum and take it deep in her mouth. Then the fullest passion swept me such that I could barely stand.

Thereafter I kept my membrum, wearing it always and frequently pleasuring Catherine with it. Soon a letter came from the old parish, and we learned that my name was Catherine the same as she, and there we were, two Catherines, only I was Cornelius compelled to be.

On Saint George's day we woke to a scuffling in our room and discovered a rat the size of a badger thrashing. When Catherine stood to shew it with a broom the rat leapt at her and bit her foot and caused her to bleed. She let out a terrible scream, and I took a stick and brunted the hateful beast to its death, only to see its gut run yellow and its blood run green, and both of us were chilled with fears of the worst. Soon Catherine took all ampery and lay with a fever on the bed. I sought out preparations to help her but without money could not procure any, so I arranged for some travelling marketers to convey Catherine to her mother's home, where she would have money to fetch the physician to her.

I followed a day behind on foot, begging all the way for what I could, crying out of my wife's misery and our great misfortune. I collected a smoked ham and a pot of treakle and was glad to have some nourishment to bring to Catherine, but when I came to her mother's door it was barred against me. Her mother was enraged and stood behind the door calling me scourge and proclaiming the womanly nature of me. Yet I prevailed against her madness and shouted how I had brought food to she who was the rightful wife of me. Beset as she was by so many demons, the mother stank most foul and laughed at my efforts to bang down her door. Her laughter caused me to push all the harder and soon a crowd gathered to watch our dispute. I banged and shouted, and then all of a sudden she opened her door and said, "Amends, amends, enter." I should have known that demons make only a mockery of promises for as soon as I entered she fell upon me with her carvery knife and gashed my thigh and tore open my breeches and seized my masculine emblem from me. She raised it high for all those gathered to see and rushed into the street with it, shrieking to fetch the bailie.

In her shameless frenzy, she left me unattended and free to run away, but 'twas only a rabbit's freedom, for rabbits run free until the tooth of the hound pierces them, and I had no want for such freedom. I longed to see my Catherine and found her in the back room feeling greatly relieved from her ailments. "Catherine, Catherine, 'tis the one who loves you who comes near." And she called me near to her, and together we amended our grief and gave our promise to each other. We kissed and vowed that all that was ever intimate between us be forgotten from Catherine's memory, and our joy as much as our grief be lapsed from her thoughts. The true nature of me, we confirmed for her future and safety, was never by my Catherine known.

Etta James and Your Heart

Ann Decter

"What my Mama told me, an old sayin' is, if there's a will, girl, there's got to be a way; now, Ma-ma, I got the will, but I can't find my way, no-no," Etta sings, rocking everyone round the dance floor; we're rolling Etta's rhythms around a dining room. Liliana passes a beer around dancing hands, her hips in full swing, her full hips in swing, menacing the beat, the music, the room maybe, or maybe it's just a joke, like the way she sticks her tongue out at anyone as soon as their back is turned. Liliana can make herself as big as she wants when she wants to, yet she's a shadow looking for a body to trail in this crowd. She's trailing Noni.

Noni's hugging a tall, thin guy named Michael. Liliana is looking nastily in their direction. Michael's worrying about Jim, a friend who has AIDS and hasn't been able to admit it to himself. I like Jim. I met him at the winter solstice party, this same party, a few years back. He was the only person I did meet, so I liked him. I dance over to Liliana to explain, but even as I speak I know she's in the same position that I was, at the party where I met Jim. Knowing only the person you came with, at a party that's an annual gathering of old, good friends, doesn't leave a lot of options. Especially when it's late and loose, and the party is sliding from room to song to room, and there's a guy in the corner that your date is hugging and

113

comforting. Liliana's had too much to drink and not enough to melt into the flow of music and people; she won't let Noni comforting Michael ride. Strange English country, and she's the stranger. She ignores my explanation and walks over to a small guy with a blond-red beard. He looks like Chuck Norris, except that this is definitely a leftist party.

Etta's crooning about "the jealous kind."

Liliana plants one leg on either side of lefty Chuck, her feet flat on the floor. She swivels and she shakes, her hips teasing him. Chuck doesn't know what to do and what not to do. He looks like he hasn't seen a thrust like that since Elvis died. I haven't.

"Salut." Liliana raises a beer toward Noni, spins on her heels and walks out. You and I laugh. Chuck looks dismayed. Noni drifts off, and you wander over to talk to Michael. I head for the kitchen. Maybe Liliana's found a stash of beer somewhere.

In a minute Chuck is in the kitchen trying to get Liliana to talk to him. She sees Noni across the room, goes over, slides a macho thigh between Noni's legs and pulls her close with a bit of strong arm. Noni goes with it, leans into Liliana for a long kiss. Chuck's watching them neck, rubbing his forehead with his palm.

"She's so sensual," he sighs. "What am I going to do with all this sensual energy?" He asks me, as if I am somehow responsible. Liliana strides by, he reaches toward her — a gesture — she turns and sneers. This party's on overtime. Everybody's forgetting who they are.

"You women are so-o-o sensual," Chuck intones, watching Liliana snap to Etta's R & B through the doorway. You come smokily up the hall, lean against me, and I'm at home again. "But I have all this sensual energy," he repeats earnestly. He seems to be feeling deprived. "That's just the way it is," you say to him, smiling.

Etta says, "Jump — into my fi-ire," howling seductive love. Etta sings love that burns.

"Can I talk to you for a minute?" you ask.

"Sure." Panic. I hear a capital "T" on talk. I know, this is it. The End. I'll never ever lie next to you again, feeling nothing else matters in the whole aching world.

"I, uh, I have to go home tonight."

"Sure." Reprieve. I'm breathing again.

"I don't want to but...."

"It's okay, really, I knew what I was getting into," I say, truth and fiction in equal parts. I knew you lived with her, and I still wanted to know you. A risk isn't a risk if you know exactly how it will work out.

"I really don't want to; it's just that...."

"No, look, it's okay. Honest, it's okay." Your hand feels small in mine. I know this should have come up earlier. It's the opportunist in me that avoids asking questions she might not want to hear the answer to. The head in the sand approach to invisibility. I just keep counting on you to phone me, to be free, to show up soon, and you always do. "Are you all right, though?" I finally ask.

There's a weariness behind your answering smile. You could be wishing you'd be able to be in two places at once. I get brave.

"Um, if, uh, if we can just get through this without anyone getting hurt; that's all I want." I have my hands out in front of me as if I'm holding something back as I speak. Holding something in place.

"Jump!" Etta howls, "Jump into my fire."

We kiss, friends who've just agreed to be kind to each other. Someone calls you to the phone. I'm drifting, combing the tables for unfinished beer. Liliana's doing the same thing. I pick up a can and shake it.

"No," Liliana curls a surly Brando lip. "Bottles only — to see *los cigarios al interior.*"

Cigarette butts, she means, you can't see them in a can. I nod, and she dances, bottle in hand, over to join Noni. They're pointing to a bamboo Star of David on the Christmas tree. I'm dancing again. Women sway and roll, Liliana, Jane, me — a little rhythm, a bit of blues, feet getting heavy on the late-night floor. You're in and out of the room — I'm gone, preoccupied, the music goes right to my limbs. Thinking that the phone call was your ride home, thinking I'll stay until just after you go, then I'll call a cab. I can go with Noni and Liliana; they live nearby. I'm all right. Etta's voice reaches me, "Got no-where to run, tired of be-in' alone, fe-el like breakin' up somebody's home." Achin' up, holding something in place.

Michael's sitting by himself, so far inside he could be anywhere, somewhere near that rock and hard place. Noni and Liliana are hand in glove, dancing physical love in the fickle heart of the late night. Michael's head is fixed at the angle of endurance, neck bent like people who are living a hard, hard thing. And sadder still to come.

I think of a dinner conversation about AIDS a while ago. A woman said, "It's a good thing we're all lesbians," which we weren't, so the conversation stopped there. Her remark stuck with me, because good isn't just the absence of bad. It's the downside of luck, a fool's cold paradise, to be pleased that neither you nor your friends are dying from a disease that's mapping a death tree out of intimacy.

Michael slowly tightens his bootlaces. In the heaviness of his hands there is a warning about how late it is — the night, the year, the decade — late in the life of the world. He drops the other boot by his foot, and this night feels infinite and precarious. Have we been too intimate? Could all this happen again in a few years because lesbians are feeling lucky?

The night is suddenly sore and lonely, could be coming in over the radio at three or four or five in the morning on one of those phone-in shows that people call because it's talk or succumb to the doubt that daytime's ever going to come again.

I can just hear myself, "Well, I'm worried that lesbians just aren't taking AIDS seriously, and I'd really like to say to all the lesbians listening tonight to do some research, take precautions. You know, there're no guarantees, no guarantees at all in this life. Well, that's all I wanted to say. Happy solstice."

I remember hearing a guy who phoned in when I was driving, a long-distance highway run. He wanted the phone number of the woman who had just called and talked about her wedding the next day. He wanted to go to the wedding and talk her into marrying him instead.

Michael puts on his jacket and walks out the door. No one notices.

Liliana walks by, hands me a plastic glass with amber liquid that catches the soft light. She lies down on the floor. Scotch. It's good enough. You and Noni are here somewhere. Everyone else is going or gone. As I dance, leftover Chuck and a big man with dark hair are telling Jane what a great party it was. Then Jane's gone too. I feel your fingers on mine. Noni's leaning over Liliana, who's flat on her back. Noni's slumping. The party's falling asleep. Your hand's asking me to follow you; we slide into an overstuffed chair. You're warm and full of night-time. We're soft and sleepy and close. "Just sit here for a bit, and then I'll go," you say. But I'm just holding you and letting the night come home.

Etta's winding down, winding out, singing "One night,"

and that's all I want, now, one more night with you. One night, every night.

I open my eyes on a room flooded with daylight. Even littered with a party aftermath, it looks great. Daytime, a Sunday morning as normal as normal-could-be. Sunlight reflecting off new snow, been snowing all night.

The room is cold. Liliana and Noni are snoring, high and low. I'm cold where I'm not touching you. My neck is stiff. You look at me.

"Do you want to go?"

You nod. My lips brush your cheek. I go to phone a cab.

With our coats on, the house feels comfortable. I lay Noni's and Liliana's on top of them, for what it's worth. I want badly to go outside. To be where it's light all around.

Year by year I succumb increasingly to the long nights. Into the office just after sunrise and out as the streetlights cast shadows on the pavement, living in a poorly lit setting of cement and glass. And these precious nights with you are a straight trade. Night for day. The cab is quick. I haven't seen eight or nine on a Sunday morning all through the fall. Solstice is past, we're working on daylight now. Maybe next year will be different. A bright, daytime year.

Sitting in the cab as if we've done this a hundred times before, I give your address and then mine. You shake your head. Never mind, I tell the driver, just the second address. I'm too tired to be glad, too glad to be tired. If I was a Christian I might be going to church. Do Christians do that? Take cabs to church? But I'm celebrating the end of solstice, feeling alive.

One easy motion out of the cab, up the stairs, stripping and sliding into bed, your cold skin warmer and warmer.

Liberated and comfortable just to be stretched out full, naked and with you. There's no time at all and all the time in the world, because there's nothing to do now but be loving each other.

Easy, so easy, soft and hard, reaching, finding, leading, following, smooth, warm, careful, coming in and in and in to each other. Here and now. Right now.

Then I'm curled up on you, and I hear your heart beating rapid fire, ripping away. It's the only living thing in the world and I'm inside it. Etta's right. There's blues and there's rhythm, and where there's a will you just got to find a way.

To keep your balance when the night gets too long, to give a lot of room and not let go, to know that morning'll come as long as you just hang in and let it. Come rolling off the tail of the night, rolling off the rhythm and the blues, ripping across your nightmares with enough heartshine to get you through. Morning's always going to come.

Safe Sex

Dorothy Kidd

We were talking in bed, and you asked me if I'd ever been in love. Why I'd never told you anything about her. I lost the questions in a stab of fright
turned over to see her ...

in her apartment. It always seemed dark, oak-panelled, no overhead lights, a small bed lamp pointed away from us. Dark blue sheets covered the mattress on the floor, and she seldom opened the curtains. She was dark too, brown eyes, almost black hair, the creases of her hands held the secrets of people I'd known in past lives.

My worst fear. The void of that bed on the floor, the abyss of longing and loving and never wanting to move in any other way. What was I afraid of, falling into chaos, the entropy of lust? Perhaps it was the patterns of those past lives we shared.

I met a seer later who saw me dancing with a man who had a great deal of power over me. I wondered if she was that person — she had that kind of unknowable force. So strong that I went into hysterics one night
there on the floor

so so strong
my womb in convulsions
laughing at the joy
I felt
so full.

It wasn't as if our souls were joined; more that I found it hard to know the separation. Where my body began and hers ended. Where my body ended and hers began. Perhaps I should tell you that we were exactly the same size and shape even to the speed at which we ran and made love. Our souls had known each other as if for a very long time, me the slightly naïve and she the slightly dangerous one.

We often joked about what we understood of that power — of lust, until she asked me my greatest fantasy, and I couldn't think of anything except what was going on right there and then. Nothing could have been better for me
the colours so bright they sang in sweet staccato.

I caught a glimmer of our difference
and the   gap between us began to
take shape.

Perhaps it was the frustration of forced separation, the long-distance part of the affair that made the contact even more intense. Perhaps it was not a special chemistry, but our mutual craving for intensity that made our bodies feel so fused together.

Then out of that darkness came two different springs.
Here the lush pinks, oranges and reds fill your nostrils with extravagance.
There the brown dirt of a snap prairie spring.
Your lungs choke with dust. Nothing you can dig your feet into, the soil so hard, so frozen still.
One day, no rest on that flat earth from the heat.
The next day blowing snow. We began to step on each other, and it wasn't so much fun anymore. I left and was glad to leave.

We made an ending on the phone, the connection still there but with a new edge,
our voices no longer
so open or so full.
Air had seeped
into the cup
and out
with some bad feelings for the spilling.

There really is a love sickness. I was feverish and delirious for a week, trying to remove the template of her body from my eyeballs, ears and fingertips
searching for my own voice again
to sleep calmly and remake my own dreams.

Slowly I stumbled up from what was no longer the void but
vertigo
feeling my body awakening to my own touch
harkening to my desire for myself
and laughing at the softness of my chest after the rain of
tears....

That's what the melt was like for me, a fusion of energies.
Maybe that's why I feel content and warm to know your
boundaries
to feel the line of your body against me,
to arch my body over you to feel our differences.
When fusion and melt mean the inferno,
not the blending of love between two women,
this is a safer kind of sex.

Salina's Balls

Michele Grace Paulse

for Melissa

Ana was the one who told me Salina had balls. "What kind?"
I asked feeling like it wasn't quite the right response but
hoping it was. I knew there was some kind of rumour going
around about Salina — finally, I was hearing it. But I thought
I could turn the meaning of it around so that it would seem
quite natural for Salina to have balls. She did after all play on
most of the school teams. She was the best volleyball, basket-
ball, grass-hockey, tennis, lacrosse player and runner the
school had seen in years. So, if she had balls, it could have
been volley balls, soccer balls, tennis balls or basket balls.
Who knows. "Who cares," I said, but Ana went on.

"Well, you know how Salina changes in one of the washroom cubicles after P.E.? She must have forgotten to lock the
door last week because Maxine had to go pee and walked in
on her by mistake. Anyway, Maxine said she felt herself turn
red, if you can imagine Maxine turning red, because she said
there they were. Salina's balls.

I thought I was going to die. I shrieked "What?! Are you
crazy!"

My mother yelled from the kitchen, "What's going on?"

"Nothing Mum," I answered, my mind racing for a
reasonable explanation for my excitement. "Ana has this

crazy idea. She thinks if she sleeps with her math books as a pillow she'll absorb more information than if she studies."

"Tell her she's crazy!" Mum yelled back.

"You're crazy!" I said loud enough into the telephone for Mum to hear, then I lowered my voice for the rest of the conversation. "What the hell does Maxine know about what balls look like?" I felt totally exasperated. "It's her parents who complained to Mrs. Blanchard about sex education being taught in schools. Maxine wouldn't know what balls looked like if they rolled in front of her." I laughed at my own wittiness.

"Very funny," Ana said. "I'm just telling it like I heard it. I'm not saying I believe it."

"Well," I said, feeling a little angry, "are you saying anything to stop everyone else from hearing it?" Ana was my best friend in the whole wide world, but sometimes she really bugged me. Especially now because she didn't seem concerned about everyone going around saying and making jokes about Salina having balls.

Ana lived two blocks away from school. I lived eight. I never had time to go over to her place after school so we always went there to eat our lunch. Both our mums worked, and, because both of us were the eldest, we always ended up staying at home doing housework. Even though we saw each other everyday at school, we always had something to say on the telephone later in the evening. We talked endlessly about teachers, homework and what we thought about practically everybody.

I never talked to Ana about Salina. I never talked about how Salina made me feel. I didn't dare. I knew or at least I thought Salina wasn't like Ana and like I pretended to be. Straight. I didn't know what not being straight meant, but I knew or at least hoped it would let me squeeze her gorgeous body next to mine and have her surrender every part of her to my longing lips. Salina kept my mind busy twenty-four hours a day, but I had to watch her out of the corner of my eye. The last thing I wanted was for Ana to catch on that I was looking at Salina all the time. I liked the way Salina walked, talked, moved her hands, turned her head, yelled, jumped, volleyed, kicked, ran, swung at a ball, dressed and twirled her hair behind her left ear when she was listening to a teacher talk in class. I loved it when she wore her jeans, gold chain belt and forest green T-shirt.

Salina was gorgeous. She drove me crazy. I used to go to bed thinking about her kissing me. All over. Her tongue teasing the corners of my craving, wet, warm, sexy mouth. She'd hold me frantically next to her and breathlessly tell me how much she too had been waiting for this moment. My overwhelmed body would go limp in her arms as I begged her to do with me what she wished. And she did.

I wanted her. I wondered, imagined and hoped that some-day I would see what she looked like beneath her jeans, cords, cotton pants, striped pants, chequered pants, black pants, red pants, whatever kind of pants she had on whatever day. I wanted to hold her, squeeze her and pull her tightly against my seventeen-year-old blossoming, lusting body. Put her gorgeous lips smack against mine, never to be separated. Whenever Ana talked about boys and said to me, "Ever wonder what it's like?" I thought about Salina and said, "Ya."

When I noticed Salina going into one of the washroom cubicles to get dressed before and after P.E., I knew someone was going to start a rumour about her soon. I just didn't know what it would be. Having balls was the furthest thing from my mind.

It was spring. Sometimes I didn't know what drove me crazier — Salina or knowing that graduation was just a few months away. Ana must have been going crazy too. I noticed she was talking a lot — all the time — about anything. Passing on the rumour about Salina wasn't unusual because there was always a rumour about someone and something going around, but Ana kept bringing this one up. It was really weird: whenever she brought up Salina, I refused to talk about her. I had to keep thinking of ways to change the subject.

I didn't know how to talk about Salina and defend her without fearing Ana would say that I stuck up for her because I liked Salina. I was sure I'd die if anyone said that. I didn't want to hear myself say that liking Salina was ridiculous because Salina was a girl, because I'd probably choke on my words because I did like her and she is a girl and she's gorgeous and she drives me crazy. When Ana brought up Salina I wanted to throttle her because I was starting to have a really hard time being cool. For a while there I thought Ana believed the rumour, but she couldn't have; it was too ridiculous! Besides, she had to know that anything that came from Maxine's mouth had to be taken with a grain of salt if taken at all.

I didn't see Ana much that summer after graduation. She got a summer job like she did for two summers before, but this time it was way over on the west side of the city, and when she got home she always had a lot of housework and other things to do. We talked a few times on the telephone, and she told me she got into university for September. I had forgotten she had applied. Stuff like university seemed like it belonged in another world to other people. But Ana had gotten in.

I was disappointed. I hadn't gotten a job yet, not even for the summer, and I didn't want to go to university. I wasn't interested, and we wouldn't have had the money even if I was. The whole idea about going to that place so far across town scared me. I stayed home and took care of the apartment and my brothers and sister while my mother was at work. I managed to go to the beach a couple of times and hoped to see Salina there in a bikini, but I didn't. I didn't really think she would be there tanning like all those other people who needed it. I thought maybe, just maybe, she'd be there doing a bold stroke along the bank. She wasn't. I wondered what she was doing for the summer but, since I didn't know her well enough and didn't know anyone who did, there was no way for me to find out. The summer rolled into autumn, and Salina rolled into the back of my mind.

I finally got a job in December in a restaurant downtown. I started at 7:30 a.m. After six months of working in the kitchen I got "promoted" to the front where I served the sandwiches and salads I used to make. I always thought of it as a demotion because now I had to put up with some of the crankiest and snippiest comments ever to come from the mouths of dressed-up office people about how the food was or wasn't. My "promotion" had actually come about when Althea cursed a customer and snapped, "There, maybe its moist enough for you now," as she plopped a heap of mayonnaise, a toothpick and pickle on the woman's egg-salad sandwich. Maybe it wouldn't have been so bad if she had put the mayonnaise between the slices of brown bread so the toothpick and pickle didn't look so much like a miniature ski pole pierced in dung atop a snow-capped muddy mountain.

I started working the front the very next day while Jeannette worked her ass off in the back trying to keep up with orders. I hated it in the front, but the manager thought I was great so she hired a new girl for the back. My shift got changed so now I started work at 11:00 a.m. and ended at 7:00 p.m.

At 6:50 p.m. one Friday, a whole bunch of girls walked in, and Salina was one of them. I felt myself teeter as the usual buzz from customer conversation in the restaurant slowed to a drone and the outline of Salina's still gorgeous body got fuzzy and grey. "You're going into a state of shock," I repeated to myself no less than a million times that second. "Breathe!" I leaned onto the counter for balance, breathed deeply, slowly — and managed to paste a smile on my face in case anyone was watching. I didn't want my sudden state of shock and impending faint to be noticed. I tried to not look at her but my eyes kept sliding over to the table they were now seated at. She kept looking at the menu board. Perhaps at another time and place, in other circumstances, she would have been looking at me. I just stood at the counter gripping onto it and doing my best to regain myself. When my eyes refocused, I peered at Salina between double scoops of tuna salad arranged in a bowl and surrounded by frilly lettuce and carrot sticks.

Salina was having a difficult time deciding what to eat. She heed and hawed. Customers like her drove me crazy because I had to keep an eye on them and not go do something else. The four other girls heed and hawed too. For a moment I thought they were going to go somewhere else. I desperately wanted to talk to Salina and hoped that when that time came my tongue would come back from wherever it had slipped to. I wanted to ask her if she remembered me from school, what she was doing now, what she did last summer, was she glad to be out of school. I wondered if she'd recognize me with the brown scarf around my hair and my matching brown polyester work uniform. I began to wonder if she would even know me. It occurred to me that despite my constant fantasies about Salina I had never spoken to her. I had never sat near her in any classes and was never partners with her for any joint projects. We were sometimes on the same team during P.E., but I wasn't a spectacular player like she was, so she had no reason to notice me.

I suddenly got discouraged and wanted to go home. It was just as well. It was almost 7:00 p.m., and Salina and her friends were still heeing and hawing. As my replacement for the night came on, I heard one of her friends say rather hurriedly, "We have to hurry up. We have to meet Ana in twenty minutes."

"Ana...," I thought. The name reminded me of my friend. During one of the few phone conversations I had had with her last month, she sounded a bit tense about exams and essays. She said she missed me and that a lot had been happening at school. She said she really wanted to see me, and maybe this summer we could hang out a bit together. When she had her hair cut in March, she didn't tell me until a few days later and didn't rush over to show me. Instead, I rushed over to see her. She looked great. I would never have thought it, but short hair really suited her. She looked bolder, and her eyes seemed to bounce right off her face now that they couldn't hide behind strands of hair.

We were supposed to see each other last Saturday night, but she phoned that afternoon and asked to change her coming over until this Sunday. Ana arrived two and a half hours early for supper at my place. "Let's go for a walk," she said quickly with her feet still practically outside the door.

"I can't," I explained. "I'm in the middle of doing the dishes and laundry. Here, have some juice," I said pouring her some. "How were your exams?" I asked sitting across from her. She looked a bit nervous. "Did you do okay?"

"Ya," she said. "When is the laundry going to be done?"

"Soon," I answered, getting up to finish the dishes. "I thought you were going to have supper here." I was feeling a bit annoyed, wondering if Ana had made other plans and was trying to rush our visit.

"I am," she said. "I just want to go for a walk so I came a bit early. I wanted you to come with me."

I finished the dishes and left the laundry in the machine for my brother to do. Ana led the way. We walked up the street, cut through the cemetery and headed in the direction of the park. She noticed a game over at the diamond, and I agreed to go check it out. She quickened her steps saying, "Come on, it might be almost over."

"So what," I thought, as I trailed behind her wondering when she'd become a baseball fan. The game was at an exciting point. The bases were loaded. The pitcher was concentrating on the batter-up; girls were yelling encouragements and good-natured sneers from the stands. The pitcher pitched. The batter's bat met the ball with a whack that sent the ball whizzing into far-left field, way past the last fielder. The runner on third sped towards home and slid in ceremoniously as teammates from first and second and the batter followed in pursuit.

"Way to go Salina," Ana yelled victoriously at the top of her voice. "Way to go!"

"Salina! Salina!" I repeated to my own amazement.

Ana caught herself and said, "Ya, Salina. From school. You remember her?"

My eyes zapped back to the field and cheering spectators. "They're all girls!" I exclaimed terribly excited about the fact.

"Aren't they great?! They're the Diamond Dykes team,"

Ana said looking at me with wonder in her eyes. "I'm going to try out for them next year. I didn't this year because of school and because I wasn't sure...." She paused and looked at me. "What's a dyke?" I asked hesitantly, realizing Ana expected me to know. She looked at me with surprise. "Don't you know? Girls who are gay!" A lump popped into my throat, and I suddenly wanted to cry.

I was about to get all mushy and hug her when someone yelled out, "Ana!" from behind the fence. It was Salina. She was sweaty, dusty and her hair was mussed up. I felt my knees wobble. I wriggled my toes so they wouldn't go numb in my shoes and quickly turned back towards Ana so that I wouldn't go dizzy. Looking back at Ana it occurred to me that she was telling me she was gay — like me.... I wondered if she knew about me, but I couldn't figure out how she possibly could.

Just thinking how much Ana must trust me and our friendship to tell me this about herself brought a big, trembling smile to my face. I wanted to be off somewhere with her — somewhere other than this winding-up softball game because I wanted to get into telling her about me from start to finish and not stop until the last of it was out. I felt overwhelmed, crazy and just darn happy.

"I think you'll be terrific on the team next year," I said. "Because you are."

Great Explanations

Nora D. Randall

I prefer to avoid ridiculous situations, which is why I announced at the breakfast table that I would be out of town when my father and stepmother come to visit in September. "Don't be ridiculous," said Nancy. "They're coming to see you." "We'll charm the pants off them," said Marilyn. "We did last time. They loved us."

I went to the cupboard and got out the peanut butter. The moment seemed to call for action — an amazon who would wield her labrys with both hands and hack away the underbrush of misunderstanding and leave behind her a path of clarity. Which is why I got the peanut butter, a possible alternative.

It's not that I'm inarticulate. In fact I make my living writing reports and speeches for whoever needs a report or a speech written — within a limited political perspective of course. In fact I am a professional explainer.

So why is it that I cannot open my mouth at my own kitchen table and explain to Nancy and Marilyn, both intelligent and supportive women with a sense of humour, my friends, that the reason I shall be out of town for my parents' visit is because my parents think Marilyn and I are a lesbian couple, and I haven't managed to tell them that we are really a couple of lesbians who share a house.

I realize that this is not the typical problem that lesbians have explaining their living arrangements to their parents, which is why I have not bothered to check the advice columns in the gay papers for a solution.

I also have some qualms about soliciting advice from Marilyn or Nancy because I haven't exactly explained to Marilyn that, from the comfortable distance of three thousand miles, my family has embraced her with open arms. Every letter and telephone call they inquire after her health and never fail to say, "Be sure to greet Marilyn for us." Were I to put Marilyn on the phone to speak to them, my parents would not think it strange at all and would chat merrily about the progress of their flower garden. Marilyn on the other hand would feel that such a request from her housemate would be beyond the bounds of propriety. After all, she doesn't ask me to talk to her parents when they call. Marilyn is without pretence in her life, so far as that can be said of anyone.

I, on the other hand, have allowed my parents their misunderstanding for five years now. It started innocently enough. At the time I told them I was a lesbian, I was living alone and had been for several years. Shortly afterwards, Marilyn, a casual friend who was between relationships, asked me if I would consider sharing a house with her. I was beginning to think that perhaps I was terminally single, and, since I don't enjoy living alone, I thought this might be a workable solution. And it has been. We live well together. Not as well as my parents think, but well enough. And we have done so for about six years now.

Marilyn started up with Nancy about two years ago. According to them both this is the big L (love) but they don't want to live together. I like Nancy, and I don't mind having her around a lot. In fact I'd rather the two of them were hanging around our house than over at Nancy's. At least then there are sounds of life in the house as I sit at the computer and explain things.

Anyway, Marilyn hadn't met Nancy when my folks came out that first time. So there were just the two of us and the house. There wasn't any pretence. I had my parents stay in my room, and I slept on the couch in the livingroom — not in Marilyn's double bed. I don't know if they think I did that out of sensitivity for their finer feelings or what. I just know that they loved Marilyn. They took to her right away. I think they had steeled themselves to get along with the devil herself if it came to that, because nothing is worse than a rift in the family. Then to meet Marilyn and find her not only intelligent, charming and competent but also "normal" looking. I think it must have been like an adrenalin rush for them. That's the only thing that would explain what happened. We'd just come back from showing them Queen Elizabeth Park, and we were all sitting around the kitchen table drinking tea. Marilyn and my stepmother, Gert, were exchanging methods of planting bulbs as my father and I listened. Suddenly he leaned toward me and gave me a playful slap on the thigh. I looked at him. He said, "You old son-of-a-gun. I'm really happy for you." I smiled back. Or, more accurately, I had been smiling, and I just continued to do so because nothing else came to mind.

What would you do? Here was a man who had crossed seventy years of religious small-town life to accept his daughter who had not only left town and left the church but had become a lesbian. He was genuinely happy for me, and I was thrilled even though he'd gotten every single detail wrong. I didn't know where to begin to set him straight, and frankly I wasn't sure I wanted to. And also I wasn't sure that he wasn't right. Like a double negative being a positive. I mean, after all the years I had lived in collectives or alone, or had strange jobs, finally I was doing something he understood. I was living with one other person; we enjoyed each other's company; we shared a house and a garden. This is something he could understand. That's what he and Gert did. And to see that smile of approval on his face! That was when I began my life as a closet single person.

The only problem with being in the closet, is that you get to overhear all the things people wouldn't say if they knew you were around. The relief he showed that I had found a nice person to love me orchestrated my feeling of being terminally single. It was just like the time I lived with a gay man. I was amazed at how friendly everyone in our apartment block was as long as they assumed we were a couple — no matter how ill matched.

And what about that time! I had written and told my father, who did not yet know I was gay, that I was moving in with Bill because it was cheaper. He had shocked me by writing back a very stern letter saying he couldn't possibly approve of my living with a man before marriage. I was appalled. I wrote back and said that if I was living with a man I would tell him, and I certainly would not cheapen the relationship by telling him that I was doing it to save money. If I said I was living with a man to save money, that's exactly what I was doing, and nothing more. And now, ten years down the road, I was a lesbian who moved in with another lesbian, and they'd made the same assumption, but given it their blessing, and I had not objected. Is life strange or is it my family? Or is it me?

Surely, if I could tell my pillar-of-the-church father that I am a lesbian, it should be no big deal to say I am not sleeping with the woman I live with. What is the problem?

Loss of status flashes into my mind. I often have these flashes of clarity, where I know things instantly. In fact that's how I realized I was a lesbian. I had applied for a job at a publishing house, and I was taking a word-processing test when I suddenly realized, "My god, I'm gay. I'm a lesbian." Perhaps if I had realized this somewhere else, instead of in front of a computer, my life would be different. Of course many things were going on in my life at the time; it's just that their significance became clear to me at the computer, instead of during those wonderful late-night talks with my best friend Beth. Perhaps it's my sense of timing that has gotten me into this position?

In any case, were I to tell my parents that Marilyn and I are not sleeping together, I would lose status. I had not, in fact, found someone "nice" to love me — for long anyway.

But it's not just loss of status because, if it were, I could concentrate on what that meant and make myself mad enough to tell them I'm really single just to get even. The other thing that stops me is trying to explain to my parents why I would come out of the closet if it wasn't because I loved somebody. Wanting to live with Marilyn and have my family understand the situation and accept us is something they can understand. Telling my parents I realized I was gay sitting in front of a computer is not something they're going to make hide nor hair of. To them it would make as much sense as Edward VIII announcing that he was going to abdicate the throne because he was sexually attracted to foreign divorcees. Why would I pay the high social costs of homosexuality, and make them pay also, if not for a relationship? Why indeed? A question that has occurred to me many times. I had never intended to be a single lesbian, but I am plagued by feelings that I may have arranged it, and then by further feelings that I should flaunt it, and we're off around the circle. Just how much control do we have over our reality? Perhaps I should go out more.

And so my mind wanders down the highways and byways of my twentieth-century lesbian soul until the glorious morning in September when I set off by car to pick up my parents from the airport in Seattle.

In the intervening months I had managed to explain how street kids live with AIDS, how free trade will affect job-entry programs for women and how misuses of pesticides is affecting farmworkers in the Fraser Valley. I had not, however, managed to explain to my parents that Marilyn and I were not lovers; or explain to Marilyn and Nancy that if they continued to act natural that my parents would react to them as an unfaithful spouse and her paramour who are carrying on right under the nose of their wronged daughter; or even managed to arrange things so I could be out of town for the entire event.

I set off for Seattle with a heavy heart. It's a three-hour drive and every minute of it my imagination played little tormenting vignettes — at the airport, "Gert, Dad, good to see you. Marilyn and I are not lovers." Introducing Nancy — "Gert, Dad, this is Nancy ... a friend of the family's...." "How nice. And how do you know Maureen and Marilyn?" The first time Marilyn goes to Nancy's for the night — "I'm spending the night at Nancy's, but I'll see you tomorrow at breakfast." Silence. At breakfast the next morning — Silence. "Oh, no, dear, no toast for me thanks. I don't know why but my stomach feels iffy, and I didn't sleep very well last night." More silence. Finally, "You know dear, your father and I are thinking we'd like to move our plane reservations up to tomorrow. I guess we're not as young as we used to be, but for some reason this trip has just tired your father out terribly." "So long, Cookie. Keep your chin up." I don't know why I didn't drive into an embankment.

Clearly, I had to so something. I picked them up from the airport, and we started the long drive back to Vancouver. We hadn't even hit Everett yet before my father asked, "And how's Marilyn's doing?"

"Marilyn's great," I said. "She has a new lover. You'll meet her tonight. Her name is Nancy. She's a lot of fun. She works as a printer." Silence. "I don't think I ever explained it very clearly," I said. "But Marilyn and I have never been lovers. We're just two lesbian friends who decided to share a house. Everything is fine. We all get along great." Silence.

"How's your job?" my father asked. "It's okay," I said. "But I'm going to start looking around for something different. It's time for a change."

a ritual, purification

Tannis Atkinson

in some ceremonies
people relax, swallow sheeting,
draw it out again (both hands).
here:
shoulders clenched against me you gag
welcome the sharp blows that pass
as remedy for choking.
I don't go down easily.
you will cough me
up and out
scarring yourself as you dislodge me.

Aaaaahhhhh!!!!!

Mimi Azmier

Aaaaahhhhh!!!!! I can't take anymore! That's it!! That's it.... I wanna say something. I'm gonna say something, I've had it up to here ... and there.

I didn't know it until now but I was watching you, yah you! With your surgical masks across your eyes. Opening me up by the crown of my head and then with the rolling up of your sleeves and the ever familiar snap of the rubber (gloves), you reached down through brain, body and soul and very carefully removed my hymen. (It now lies in a satin-lined display case, to be seen by all, in the Hall of Wonders in something resembling the Smithsonian ... but for dykes.)

"Oooooh ... looook ... Harriette! See, I told you ... not once; a virgin; never with a man in her life! Isn't it wonderful!!!"

They then placed my womanhood into a purple box made of impenetrable plastic.

Before they shut my head, they swept and dusted; they filed all my loose papers accordingly with impeccable efficiency; they left a tape in the answering machine of the dos and don'ts of dykedom. (They left wood-fairy dust all over the doorknobs....)

You know what a fourteen-year-old dyke needs when she's just coming out? Well, let me tell you, it ain't no feminist/lesbian group; actually what she needs is to meet this really cool friend of mine; you see she drives this Italian sports car and....

Anyways, so I walk into the community centre and womph!!! tackled in a net of daisy-chains and herbal teas.

"A budding flower," one said.

"Let's nurture her," another screamed.

"Let's water her," two said together.

And in unison, "Let's be the soil for her roots!!"

They fought over who got to be the role-model and gave me lengthy instructions on how to be a woman, what products to use, what books to read and thus what to think.

They handed me sex served on a tea tray, served with lots of saccharine ... saccharine trust; you must learn to see that when a group discusses sensuality it becomes sexuality, and in turn sexuality becomes politics; the last thing anybody is talking about is sex and sensuality, most of all the latter.

Picture it now dear friends; I am fifteen years old, and I am trying to fuck (or make love to, you choose the proper term) this thirty-year-old woman (who I think is my lover but of course she's non-monogamous), who sees my twat as being this honey-wet rose petal. I of course with my Pat Califia/Starhawk instruction book in hand suddenly wonder what I would do if I were to lose my page. All I knew was you couldn't yell "fuck me" because it implied too much penetration.

So where was the undying support from my sisters when I realized I wanted some hot bitch in garters and lipstick to fuck me hard, in a car, with her credit card held tight between my teeth. (... don't get me wrong, I like softball too.)

But nooooo ... gotta be the ultimate super-dyke, gotta be so politically incorrect to be "p.c.," gotta be a member of at least six different support groups, gotta be macro-biotic....

I can see it now.... From the West Coast come a thousand

lesbians in a thousand V.W. vans, running through res-
taurants ordering double orders of alfalfa sprouts to go;
ramming themselves (pardon the expression) into Eastern
cities seeking the role of surrogate mother thinking, "*This* will
further my political career."

The farmers in Southern Ontario become some of the
richest men in the nation; smog increases due to the amount
of bad home-grown smoked. The pool of construction
workers overflows; tofu sells out nation-wide; wooden picnic
tables are boycotted. If the word "sex" is to be used in any
phrase or paragraph it must be explained completely and
concisely, or be completely avoided, and must be used
alongside words such as "celibacy," "watersports," "leather,"
"flog," "mature," "consenting," "Body Politic"....

I wonder? If I was to stand here and say "love-gel ... dildo
... passion ... come ... fuck ... twat ... tits ... lick ... suck ..."
what would you do? What would you say?

"Goodness help us, Harriette! Look, that woman's half
nude!! Stick a label on her; give her a chastity belt; better yet
slap her with a copy of 'Poetry for Women Because I Love
Them but Won't Sleep With Them Because We Are Too Spiritual-
ly Attuned for That,' by Betty Strongtreewithrootsinmother-
soilbrightstarssurroundinggoddessmooninapurplesky.
Put on some Heather Bishop and make her stop speaking
like Carole Pope and screaming like Patti Smith."

A few weeks ago I returned to one of these typical dyke-
night meetings. They (those women), kept referring to the
women who are not visible within the community as not
having come out yet. I wanted to scream; I wanted to grab her
by the lapels of her Lacrosse shirt (a shade of lavender no
doubt), slap her good and hard and yell BIMBO!

Just because they don't like going to shitty bars, to listen
to shitty music, to subject themselves to shitty light shows and

the same god-damn' boring routine and familiar faces; just because they feel like they don't need support from women they don't know and find topics such as "why it is hard to ask another woman to dance" mundane, boring, idiotic and above all else pointless, does not mean that they have not come out and does not mean that they do not exist.

At this particular meeting, of which the topic was "why it is hard to ask another woman to dance," I pointed out that most of my fellow lesbians went on normally with life and felt they had no need to become part of any community, and (furthermore!!) when they came out they came out mostly as women instead of solely as lesbians. They went from pink to blood-red lipstick, cotton undies became silk garters, and they stood taller in their heels. They said bullshit to the politics and indulged themselves in their own sex and sensuality.

After my brief and emotional explanation, one woman approached me and seriously inquired as to where she might find one of these women.

I couldn't believe it.... I just couldn't believe it.

Can you not realize that the woman who just passed you on the street likes walking in heels, enjoys the feeling of her thighs running slick together against her garters and is probably going home to her lover to be fucked hard and in the shower?

Have not one of you hung your head down into the punchbowl and thought, "*A Woman's a Woman but a Good Smoke's a Good Cigar?*" "Why get sober when you're just gonna get drunk again?" Did you buy the Bridgitte Nielson issue of *Playboy*? Do you at least own a copy of *Delta of Venus*?

It seems to be everything has got to be super touch-feely-granola or super leather-whips-grease and chain. Doesn't anybody just get horny? Don't you ever feel hot? Do you know the difference between sex and sensuality? Doesn't anybody fuck their lover, fuck a friend? At least feel like fucking? (Yes, yes, I know, but ladies, we all make love....)

It seems that people think in extremes — Bambi or bondage, leather or home-spun wool, veggies or raw meat. Where is the medium (rare)?

Let's all purse our lips together and repeat after me, "Fuck me ... fuck me hard."

Can you say, "Sometimes I'd like to have sex without commitment..."?

Notice as the two celibate, lesbian, feminist, witch-pagans who have been celibate as lovers for the last twenty years cling to floating baggies of trail-mix and alfalfa, screaming, "I'm melting. I'm melting!!!" (By the way, their names are Juniper and Swampwater.)

Can you admit that you, in fact, hate your V.W. and prefer a Porche or a Mini really...?

Now I want to ask the question that has nagged at me for years, the question that keeps tormenting me, that one that causes me to lay awake at night: Why is it that a lot of dykes want to look like Wayne Gretzky?

The Woes
of Slut Queen

Paradigm

The scene: An opening at a downtown loft apartment. The Time: Shall we place it at early fall? Maybe spring, both times of change, the move from one extreme to another clearly a gay sensibility.

The door is flung open. How this is achieved will be dealt with later, the pursuit of sex need not always cater to realistic details. The murmur of the crowd, the din of party noise gives way to nervous silence. What do we expect? In walks Slut Queen brandishing a sword. She eyes the crowd contemptuously. Tossing back her brushcut she strides towards the bar. Ah, Slut Queen, the mother of the hunt, the age old search for promiscuity. This even in an age where videos must make disclaimers after encouraging the true meaning of the word "rock n' roll." Slut Queen, maker of scores mostly of women, keeper of cheap sex. Her mission? The object of her desire? To get layed, to jump someone's bones, to get her brains fucked out, with anyone ... anyone, that is, who fits the bill of fare. Ah, Slut Queen, guardian of the sacred one-night stand, the kind of woman who gives us all a bad name. Someone who comes on like a ton of bricks and puts you down to another notch on her lipstick case. Slut Queen, defender of other city slut queens and slut queens all over this world and all the other slut princesses and slut maidens and slut duchesses, sleazes and the ever humble hosebag. Slut Queen, the type of girl who gives meaning to the statement: "Your reputation precedes you ..." or "I've heard so much about you...." Slut Queen, she's clean, safe and discreet. She gives throngs their first and best orgasms, she helps women discover their G-spot and all this for the price of a drink ... if that. The neighbourhood girl, Slut Queen, the woman you just love to hate, and if you become jealous and irate with the need to gossip, this only spurs her on. She is the desire of few and the dream of many and certainly not someone you might even try to take home to Mom.

Yes, you might meet her, think she's nice, bright, even respect this woman's so healthy and well-practiced, dare we say talented, approach to sex, but then rumours start flying around, your friends talk. "Do you know that you're keeping company with Slut Queen?" And that can only lead to one thing; few stay past this point to find out what and those that do invariably garner a reputation equal with Slut Queen. This or they are seen as her unfortunate victims. How can you love someone who has slept with so many the number exceeds mandatory retirement age? Is it possible to attend large parties with someone who has known at least half of those there in a more intimate sense? Is this what galls you the most? That she never blinks an eye at all that exposure; sometimes she forgets that she ever did it with them. Is it that, the fear that you too could slip into that blur of sweat and moaning?

But what of Slut Queen, who is to know her woes? The very knife she carries with such grace, has she ever, you ask, fallen on her own sword? Is she ever lonely? Does she like to watch cartoons? What does she do during the day, retire to a coffin filled with fresh singles-bar napkins? Where do Slut Queens go when they grow up, get old, die? Do they go to that place in the sky, the one with the really bad reputation? Do they really spread V.D. and your name with it? But what of Slut Queen, her miseries and accomplishments, what of Slut Queen?

Part Two: Slut Queen Speaks

Definitions: My research revealed the following: that "slut" and all words similar in colloquial meaning, i.e., "strumpet," "trollop," "loose," "sleaze," etc., mean "a bad housekeeper." A woman who is too lazy to do the housework and keeps her surroundings and consequently herself in filthy condition. Gives one pause, no? Those of questionable virtue are not married and therefore have no house as wife to keep and, as we all know, slut queens never have their abode in mind. Well, yes, it is true that we have been known to polish the bathtub in anticipation of sex with someone we particularly want to impress. It wouldn't do to have cocktails, candles and first and best orgasms in a dirty tub. When all is said and done, and they trash slut queens and lay our names to dust under their feet, at least they can never say that we didn't keep our bathrooms in order. By and large slut queens keep good houses. Our bedrooms must be tidy enough to have that extra tube of lube readily available, those handcuffs and ice cubes within reaching distance. Why, we're almost always centrally located, easier to find the bus stop in the morning and, as we all know but won't admit to, slut queens always show their prey to the bus stop. Perhaps, then, we are more gallant than you are led to believe. It's the good girls who dump you unceremoniously on their doorstep, and good girls, as we all know and will readily admit to, live in inaccessible locales.

So now that we have disposed of the myth of bad housekeeping you might ask other questions: "When was it that you first realized you were a slut?" Well, I never went to my best friend and in hushed tones, my palms sweating, hoarsely whispered, "Dora, I … I think I'm a slut…. no, no, I'm not sure, it's just that, well, I like to sleep around a lot…." No. Slut Queens are a product of other's imaginations. Unlike homosexuality, others are always the first to know. It's they who call you a slut. They who snicker and hiss when you walk by, you just thought maybe you had a good time on the weekend. I first realized I was a slut at the age of fourteen. I assume it coincides with puberty. In health class a tough young woman who enjoyed stabbing the Black girls with X-acto knives declared to all present that any girls who were on the pill were sluts. I fell into this category. Those of us who were lucky enough to get information and strong willed enough to seek birth control were the first victims of "reputation." To be completely unsafe and unprepared meant purity. That way you could say it wasn't your fault; you didn't want to do it but he was special. "My guy is different, and I'm really in love with him…."

Later, in my adolescence, I came out to a community where, by all womyn's rhetoric, we had dispensed with these notions. We were non-monogamous, but I soon realized that, as in *Animal Farm*, all women are non-monogamous but some are more non-monogamous than others. Like birth control, one is allowed to slip up, to fall, to sleep around by accident. If I say, I couldn't help myself but … then I am safe. To say I wanted it, planned it, brands you … slut, slut queen. "That chick comes on to everyone/All she cares about is a fuck and a fuck and a fuck." Or as one more political boss I once had put it, "She's a sleazebag."

How then do sluts maintain self-respect in this climate? You might say that we have none given our taste in free sex, but, ah, you have not considered to be a Slut Queen means you must have a head held high. It would make for a bad come-on to sheepishly stumble over to someone, cloaked in a cloud of shame, and beg them to sleep with you. We are a proud breed, like James Dean, rugged at the very least, a cigarette commercial or a threat of some sort, but that is how you see us, want to see us. We may be dumpy or badly dressed. Like the word "slut," we are what you have made us. You might think that you know our story, our intimacies. How can we live with this exposure? But have you ever paused to think that we give the same story to each and everyone of you, but all of yours have different details, secrets, things we know but are too discreet to mention. Discretion in a slut queen, you may ask? Think about it.

This leads us to the most sticky of issues surrounding sluts. Oft times accusations are put forth, usually by those with no intimate knowledge of our kind, that we care not for our paramours. Are they truly just a fuck and another fuck to us? Is this why we often forget that we had sex with them? Ah, a slut never forgets the sex she had — she simply integrates it into the knowledge she has of the person. Unlike you, she is able to stay still in a room with them without stuttering, blushing or running to the bathroom. This is the true test of the slut — how strong is her psyche? Like the man with the x-ray eyes, she simply becomes accustomed to knowing what people look like without their clothes on. Perhaps sluts are the ultimate dreamers of the Freudian nightmare — being naked in a crowd. She knows you, knows what you look like and has probably slept with an ex-lover. Discretion once again enters the picture. Slut Queen never talks, maybe she just mocks, silently. Can you see her eyeing you? What is she thinking? Did your friend tell her in the revealing pose of orgasm, did they cry out your name by mistake and reveal your hidden yearning to dress up like

Virginia Woolf? What is it that woman knows? Most likely she is simply thinking of your watch, trying to see the time. All sluts demonstrate their caring by their forgetfulness — and their art. Not a complete erasure of memory but a selective recall. Yes, slut queens do care about their partners. Would you ever play bridge with someone you didn't like? Think of it like grade school. Who did you pick as a partner in gym? Certainly not the boy whose voice irritated the very lining of your stomach. You choose your best friend or someone you thought nice — bar that you were thrown together by the teacher. Fate joins you in the game of foursquare. See we're back to safety; you had no choice; you just fell into it.

Perhaps then you think that sex should not be the central focus of our lives. The word "oversexed" might now come, if you'll excuse the pun, to mind. What then is sex if not central? Do we see it as an issue or simply as an act? Not a thing to be thrust forward in times of want, accusation and danger. Is it really the code by which we live? If it is you who creates the word "slut" and who judge these degrees of morality, then it is in your mind and yours alone. Oversexed is then like overzealous, trying to preach to the unenlightened. Too much of a good thing and you're bound to want to share it. But no, we slut queens do not rise and sleep by our genitals alone. Our desire to go down on you waxes and wanes like your very own. Sluts are people too; we're just more upfront about the material aspects of life. Body.

By this time, those of you who haven't been won over to our cause or stopped listening after the third paragraph must surely be asking yourself: "A bad family background, is that what's responsible?" Perhaps you've read enough exposés on runaway teens to think you know the answer; all that sluts really want is love. Hmmm, perhaps you could form a home for wayward women and with enough prayer to the great crystal mother in the sky, enough busy political work and enough readings from *Against Sado-Masochism,* we could be cured, saved. Tone ourselves down, settle for an affair in Michigan once a year, followed by the necessary tears and admonishments. Lengthy conversations with your friends on how you and your lover are non-monogamous all the while remaining completely inactive and guilty, trying to work it out. But no, we sluts refuse to be taken, held down, constrained, wed to a code of morality our parents lived with, that we lived with. To be told that we were, in the hellfire and brimstone of female sexuality, sluts.

As for bad family, who doesn't have one, tinker, tailor, soldier, trollop.

On reading
Sexual Politics

Carolyn Gammon

How to explain
to Kate Millett
to myself

while reading
a Norman Mailer extract
where a woman gets fucked
to a pulp

How to explain
while reading
I reached down
into my pants and stroked my clitoris
wet fingers and probed inside

How to explain
I went back to his words
and working faster
jammed my cunt on the corner of the chair

came gloriously
head on the open book

"The prevailing culture ...
is saturated with sexuality ...
that simultaneously
tantalizes and repels"

Thank-you Adrienne Rich

Evolution

Carol Camper

I know we must come from the sea
because my lover tastes of salty pools.
I know woman is tied to this earth
because she quakes beneath my hand.
Evolution makes me dream of women's thighs
like the foothills of heaven.
Evolution makes my tongue dart like silver fishes
into the living coral.
Evolution ties me to women with eyes of obsidian
flashing with lightning;
women who are moving, grand, engulfing currents,
who pulse with life like the sea.

Iron

Tari Akpodiete

I work out in the school gym at night, pumping iron to stay strong and keep in top competitive shape for the varsity fencing squad. Since Canadian schools don't give out massive athletic scholarships, I'm working my way through.

I practise sword-play and foot-work with the rest of the team, but I strength-train on my own time. It's just as well anyway; I don't follow the program laid out for me by the coaching staff.

They put together a powder-puff workout to be done on the universal, no free weights at all, which I prefer. They don't believe that a woman should have muscles. They think that she should be all smooth slinkiness. I don't agree, and what they don't know won't hurt them. Since starting, I've been to them twice for new uniform articles; once for a new jacket because my old one was too tight around my arms, and I had split it across the back, and once because I needed new protective cups because my chest had expanded.

I win almost all the time. And that's what they are looking for, no matter what they say about winning not being everything and the fun of competition being what's important. I don't do it for them; I do it for myself, for my own enjoyment.

Special arrangements were made so that I could use the gym's facilities after regular hours. One of the attendants, usually a senior Kinesiology student on work-term, stays until midnight so I can work out. At first, I was worried about someone hanging around, watching me pump and burn. Sometimes, I feel self-conscious if someone watches me working out, but this one was never in sight. I was given a little gadget and shown how to activate it if I got into trouble — a life-line of sorts. I wore it around my neck. In the seven months since I'd started, I'd never needed to use it; I hoped I never would.

One night, while bench pressing, I was startled by a voice behind me saying, "You're cheating." My deep concentration broken, I felt the weight start to slip. Before I could panic, whoever it was leaned over and raised it smoothly and easily, bringing it to rest on the uprights. Anger surging through me, I sat up quickly, intending to blast, and was hit by a wave of dizziness so strong that I felt myself passing out. Helplessly, I started to slip to the floor and was promptly caught in a well-muscled pair of arms.

"Easy. I've got you," murmured the voice. "Relax. It'll pass in a moment. You were pumping to exhaustion, and then you sat up too fast." I tried, unsuccessfully, to steady the whirling; my empty stomach started to heave. "Oh no, not here," said the voice. I was gathered up then, and I must have passed out because all I remember next is waking up with a cool cloth on my face. I reached up to remove it, tried to sit up. A hand stopped me, pushed me back. "Lie down. You'll just get dizzy again. Give yourself a few moments." The cloth was removed, and my face was gently wiped.

"Okay. Open your eyes now." Everything was blurred. Something was swimming in front of me, and, as my eyes came into focus, I saw the face of one of the most attractive women I had ever seen, concern etched on her features. Although I couldn't recall her name, I recognized her immediately. She was a grad student in the Health Sciences Department. I'd seen her around campus and had followed her hungrily with my eyes. Once, mistaking a classroom, I had accidentally walked in on a lecture she was delivering and had stayed to listen — mesmerized. I'd often fantasized being in her arms and in her bed.

"Feeling better?" she asked.

"Oh … yeah. I'm fine." I felt a bit confused.

"I'm sorry. I didn't mean to startle you like that. Are you sure you're all right?"

"Fine. Was I … uh, sick?" All anger forgotten now, I was embarrassed.

"No, you weren't. And if you had, it would have been entirely my fault."

She was so close to me that I could smell her scent. It was a mixture of sweat and musk and something undefined. I could see her heartbeat throbbing in her throat. Her breath was gentle and warm on my face. I looked up into her eyes and was caught in their cornflower-blue depths. I saw desire written there, blunt and undisguised. A wild surge ripped through me. I watched her eyes widen in recognition and understanding.

She pulled back a bit, smiled slightly. Her hand came up and gently caressed my cheek before sliding on to cup the back of my head. She did not pull me forward; I leaned to her. Eyes closed, our lips met in the barest of kisses. I stopped and opened my eyes to find her looking at me. As much as I wanted her, I was afraid that someone would walk in.

Noticing my inadvertent glance toward the door, she answered my unasked question. "We're alone. The co-op student was sick tonight. That's why I'm here. I've locked up already. Don't worry." Her other hand came up to rest on my bicep. I felt a gentle pressure as she kneaded the muscle, and, looking down at her own well-developed arm, I was glad of the care that I had taken.

I've always admired women with muscles. Unlike some people, my coaches for example, I don't think that it's obscene. Watching the strength and grace of muscled women had made me want to be the same. And here was this woman, practically a pin-up of my sexual desires, looking at me, wanting me, touching me.

We kissed again, this time letting some of the want come through. Our lips met and parted. She pulled me to her and held me tightly. I wrapped my arms around her, moaning as she took my mouth with thrusts of her tongue. I'd been with several women, but this was something else. Somehow I knew that this was going to be more than just a regular fuck.

I had some hidden needs. I'd tried talking about them with other partners only to be met with combinations of shock, disgust and pity. After the first few rejections, I'd learned not to bring them up unless I wanted to be humiliated. Tired of rejection and vanilla sex, I had been celibate for a while.

The way this woman had pulled me to her, the way that she was holding me and kissing me told me that I had found what I was looking for. There was something else too, something very stirring and a little frightening. I didn't stop to ask myself about afterwards; I just decided to enjoy the now.

In an agony of desire, I ran my hands down her arms, squeezing and kneading as I went. I found her waist, narrow and defined, and slowly pulled her workout top up until I could reach the bare flesh of her back. Stroking and rubbing her back, I continued to kiss her deeply. She responded by pushing herself harder into me and moaning into my mouth.

A few months ago, the grip she had on the back of my neck and forearm might have been painful, but muscle protected them now, and I wasn't worried about bruising. Her fingers found and caressed my abdominals, raking their washboard length. All those thousands of boring crunches were paying off now. In her ardent response, I recognized something that I suffered from myself, a severe case of skin hunger.

Breaking off the kiss, she looked deeply into my eyes before pulling on my hair and tilting my head back. I gasped as I felt her lips and then her teeth on my throat. She lavished my throat, alternating between kisses and bites until, no longer able to bear it, I pulled her away forcibly. A small space between us, we sat panting and holding each other. Gently stroking her cheek, I saw her eyes close slowly and her head fall back as she exposed her own throat to me and asked a silent question. Needing no encouragement, I kissed it very gently and slowly ran my tongue up and down over the rings. I felt her breath rush out, and, feeling her shudder, I drew her close sensing her trust.

As we sat holding each other and rocking back and forth, I was startled by a hot wetness on my cheek. I opened my eyes to find hers swimming. Clearly embarrassed, she tried to turn away, but I wouldn't let her; she tried unsuccessfully to stand up, but I held her to me even more tightly. As we stared at each other, I felt my own tears welling up. I knew why she had started crying because I felt it too, had felt it as we had started kissing, had been frightened by it.

She tried to talk and couldn't, cleared her throat and tried again. "I think we'd better talk before we go any further." There was a tremour in her voice, and, not trusting my own, I simply nodded in agreement. She thought for a moment. "I know it's late but have you eaten yet?"

"I was planning to eat after working out." I couldn't suppress a smile. "I'm famished."

"Yeah, me too." She nodded and stood, drawing me up with her, my hand nestled in hers, our fingers interlaced.

"Come on," she said invitingly, "I'll buy you dinner."

Ends of Desire

Elaine J. Auerbach

Last fall, I split up the irises. The bulbs were close together, and Mrs. O'Neil didn't approve of their intimate swooning.

"So glad you did something about those irises, Denny," she says now that spring has arrived and the buds are lusting to bloom. "They were positively lewd last spring. Awful the way they were falling all over each other."

Mrs. O'Neil loves a proper garden. Hedges and shrubs pruned of all stragglers, pansies positioned in rows like soldiers on parade. Forget-me-nots are forbidden to self-seed in her garden beds.

Now she wants the irises staked. I hate to practise bondage with plants who have no safe words, but I profess myself a gardener so there are compromises I must make. I've slashed and burned my way through waves of Morning Glory, conquered many a rhizome with my trusty spade. A weed, as any gardener since Eden will tell you, is nothing more than an undesirable. I'm not the only one who works very hard for those intent on eliminating undesirables.

Every plant is purposeful, but some plants are, according to customs nobody questions or understands, more desirable than others. I've heard of noxious gases and noxious weeds, never of noxious tulips. But Mona has. I've talked with Mona about tulips. She quoted poetry at me, some suicidal poet writing about a miscarriage, who thought tulips should be behind bars like dangerous animals. I told her what I thought about garden beds being zoos for plants, but she wouldn't agree with me, saying I was taking things too far. Mona and I are always disagreeing about something intrinsic, yet I can't help desiring her more than anyone else in the entire world. This I don't understand. What I do understand is that I've never learned how to fight with those I love because no sooner was I in love than I began to know who I loved and ended up knowing more than loving. I've known far more than I've loved. It's easy to know. And it's easy to mistake knowledge, especially carnal knowledge, for love. You really begin to discover what love is by what it takes out of you rather than what you get out of it, factual or otherwise.

I have many thoughts about being. With my hands in roots, I'm always alert to silent states of interior existence. Being takes a lot of effort. You have to work at being who you are, and when you are a less-being like myself, there's more to do every day. Identity doesn't end. There're no endings, just continuities. Ceaseless experiments.

Sometimes I imagine I've reached an ending. A happy ending where I trail off into the sunset, blissfully content, with Mona experiencing a similar ecstasy. My mother, Santa Pallans, told me that Jehovah's Witnesses have it right — the world is flat — and if you go to the end of the earth, toward that brilliant burst of sun, you'll be turned to cinders. Some of a mother's wisdom is more expedient than wise.

Many years ago, when I recognized I was a less-being according to customs nobody questions or understands, I led a 3-D life with Darla. I danced, I drank, and I didn't give a damn. Add another D to that—make it a 4-D life—D for my darling, dearest Darla. And maybe another D for the dole because that was how I made a living then. Seeing life in 5-D can be truly amazing. You'll have to take my word for it.

I met Darla at the Woolworth's lunch counter, a place my mother had led me to as soon as I could walk. (Another place Santa led me to was Our Lady of Grace school where I came under the tutelage of Sister Ruth of the Flowering Cross. From my convent-school days I learned the necessity of choosing between loving women and knowing them, with no middle course to take. Since I could never know Sister Ruth, shrouded as she was in layers of black cloth and a legal alias, I loved her. I never loved Darla, but mistook her at first for a profane version of Sister Ruth. It was a well-intentioned mistake, the intention being that I wanted to run my hands all up and down her body, something I would never have dared with Sister Ruth.) Darla and I ate steamed hot dogs and talked.

"Are you married?" she asked.

"No. Are you?"

She gritted her teeth. Her thick, black eyebrows arched like the backs of two cats ready for combat. She whipped off her silver-studded black leather jacket and thrust her elbow onto the counter, her hand forming a tight fist in the air. At first I thought she wanted to have a go at arm wrestling. I didn't know what I had said to provoke her. Then I saw it. On her massive left forearm, upside down so that I could barely make out the image, was a tattoo of an exploded atom bomb. I asked her to put down her arm so I could see her stigmata better.

"Bye Bye Dick Heads" was written beneath the mushroom cloud.

"This was my husband who thought he could shoot me up with dope and use me for a punching bag," she said, pointing to a tiny black speck at the bottom of the cloud. "And this," she continued, pointing to a trail of dots that ran down to her wrist, "is my father who tried to do the same to my mother and killed her in the end. And the rest are all those cocksuckers who've tried to make my life a hell-hole. I've nuked them all. They're charcoal now, the pricks."

According to Darla, patriarchy was not just a philosophy, it was all men, everywhere and for all time, who through the mystery of birth were pitifully deprived of being women. She needed very little to carry out her attacks on men and could always count on the support of women in transition houses and rape-relief centres. Odd though it may seem, Darla had an unbounded love — expressed exclusively in the company of women — that came from a life of being fucked over, literally and figuratively. I fell in love with her experiences of abuse and torture, which were only a part of Darla and not her entire self. I fell in love with an idea that led me to have other ideas, which, I discovered quite by accident, weren't at all bad to have, such as my strict vegetarianism.

All women are not victims. But some women are victims and some are witnesses. Victims are always looking for a witness. The one who saw as they saw. The one who, by admitting she was a witness, will set the victim free from the frozen death-trap of her past.

Witnesses are always eluding detection. They don't come forward easily with their testimony. Some remain dumb forever, having forgotten what they witnessed or finding it too painful to relive and retell.

It's not unusual to know at least one story where a witness lingers at a safe distance, clinging to her fragile security.

For instance, a long time ago, before mega malls, when chain stores and plastic wrap were just beginning to wind their way into daily life, there lived two girls who were the best of friends. When Lorna looked out her bedroom window toward her friend Jenny's house, she could see the black, tar-papered chicken coop at the back of Chester's Butcher Shop. Every morning at dawn Chester's rooster would begin his crowing followed by Henry Kuchinski's cock shortly thereafter. Henry kept his own brood of chickens one block away from Chester's. There were very few of these backyard poultry farms left in the town. People went to the A&P where they could choose from more than a dozen plucked, cleaned birds, pre-packaged and labelled like a jar of preserves. The antiseptic atmosphere of the chain-store meat department made it very difficult to get near the feathers or the feed or the general mess that chickens can't help but make in their short, cooped-up lives.

Lorna and Jenny were intrigued by the coop in Chester's yard and by its inhabitants. Since Jenny lived next door to the butcher shop, Lorna usually took the long way when she visited Jenny at her house by cutting through the fence of hedges, around past the coop and up to Jenny's side door. Occasionally she and Jenny would see Wanda, Chester's sister, sauntering across the back lot of the butcher shop with an axe swinging from her hand. The children would watch from the stoop as Wanda entered the coop, closing the bright red door behind her. There would be an awful commotion of cackling and squawking that would subside when Wanda emerged triumphant from the door, dangling a white chicken by the legs. She would sashay over to the chopping block beneath the tall, overhanging elm tree, and in one swoop, the chicken would lose its head, Wanda's stained apron would collect a few splashes of blood and the cleaning would begin.

Jenny and Lorna would approach cautiously to where Wanda was sitting on the steps of the coop, plucking her latest contribution to the meat case. They would avoid looking at the limp head with a roving eye that lay on the chopping block and would become absorbed in Wanda's swift and agile movements. After no more than fifteen minutes, the cleaning process completed, Wanda and the girls would gather up the feathers and toss them, like confetti, into the fire Wanda had made in the rusted oil drum.

Lorna was big — some would say fat. Others, thinking they were polite, would call her big boned. She had long, black wavy hair that sometimes was very greasy and looked as if she'd doused her head in olive oil. Jenny was small — half the size of Lorna though they were born minutes apart from each other — and she had a very wide mouth, lots of teeth and a yellow complexion that the neighbour children called "green." Chester the butcher liked to tease Jenny. He picked on her because she was small and less obstinate than Lorna, who let it be known that she abhorred such tasteless familiarities.

Lorna would watch as Chester dragged Jenny into the back room of the store. With Wanda holding her sides and crying tears of laughter, massive, crimson-faced Chester would take some old packing string and wrap it around the squealing Jenny's wrists, threatening to lock her up in the freezer with the carcasses or in the basement with the spiders and supplies.

Lorna watched, always watched. Saying nothing as she nibbled her red licorice, waiting for the game — for it was a game, wasn't it? — to end.

What was Jenny thinking while she thrashed away at

Chester's big belly, fighting to free herself from hands as big as baseball mitts? What was going through her mind and into her memory during these seizures of time in the back room of the butcher shop?

She was thinking that she would never give her love to one person, or vow allegiance to a waiting sentinel of pain such as her best friend Lorna. She would travel light all her life, a butterfly of many selves, equal to all, fettered by none. She would die in a blaze of colours when she died, and when life became difficult, she would close upon herself a veil of threads woven from the world surrounding her and re-emerge, in different colours, when *she* was ready. She learned the lesson that every less-being on planet earth learns, the lesson that Ishmael learned before he took the voyage to find the monstrous white whale, Moby Dick — it's well to be on friendly terms with all the inmates of the place one lodges in.

I thought at first that Darla was my witness, but she could only be a victim like myself and sometimes, the victimizer. I wondered when I would ever find my silent, watchful Lorna, my open-eyed witness.

Though Darla liked to use leather and chains, she was always sweet and gentle with her habits. Darla awakened me to customs, those things nobody understands and everybody practises, and I'll always be grateful to her for that. She also introduced me to Flip, Anita, Carlene, Rosa, Latina, Josie and Flo, all of whom I got to know intimately but never loved. I didn't think I have chosen knowing over loving, but when I discovered I had it was no surprise. I have chosen now to love Mona, hating everything I know about her, but deeply, very deeply controlled by my loving of her in spite of what I know.

For she is my Lorna. The best witness, the only witness willing to admit to the crimes committed against me.

Everyone's heard of love at first sight, but this was not how I became Mona's lover. I infiltrated her presence as if I had a sixth sense operating somewhere. Of course, it isn't un-usual for me to exercise capabilities outside of the recog-nized norm. As a person who's lived in five dimensions, I'm capable of many things. I guess I owe much of my talent to my mother, Santa Pallans. She's an ornithoscopist now, or so I've heard. An ornithoscopist, in case you're wonder-ing, tells fortunes by the flights of birds. With all the time Santa spends at the seaside, watching endless sky meeting endless water, it's no wonder she's tuned to the patterns of creatures seeking to flee the earth. She's done time in sub-ways and bus stations preaching against materialism. She's loitered along beach-fronts — in penny arcades — telling lost souls that their hard luck is about to change. She's saved many a one from drowning in a storm of sorrows. I recently saw her picture in the paper with a woman from the Plastic Terrorist Association. The PTA has one purpose: to do away with the manufacture of poisonous plastic by dumping used yogurt containers, plastic shopping bags, and other forms of plastic packaging in supermarkets and malls. My mother is a lot like Darla, I'm discovering, al-ways trying to get at the customs nobody understands and everybody practises. It took me a while to recognize the maternal erotic in my affair with Darla.

But what about Mona? What kind of feelings has she awakened in me? As I've already said, I hate everything about her. But is hate too strong a word? No. As Darla hates men because they can never become women, I hate Mona for the woman she has become. It is a hatred that arises from an overflow in the well of my pity. Mona lives always on the lip-edge of less-beingism. A margin of a margin of a margin, always edging. She is an inactive participant who will never go beyond the artificial boundaries she constructs, while I've already fallen off the page. I'll have to go back to beginnings again, to how I met Mona, since first impressions always tell a different tale.

It was the autumn before this spring. The month was October; it was the middle of the afternoon. I was raking leaves for old Countess Radomska when I found the wallet. It was a worn cowhide Buxton with a change purse in the middle, heavy with pennies. Someone's been collecting lots of thoughts, I imagined, and saving pennies to pay for them. I told myself it was ludicrous to think such things, but the wallet bulged in such a peculiar way, a swollen vulva, tumescent before coming, and as I groped through its folds, I knew the powerful truth of my own intuitions.

It was crammed with a collection of letters. No credit cards, fourteen dollars in bills, twenty library cards — some expired — a social insurance card, lots of business cards and a poem scrawled in a pinched and excited hand.

Nowhere in the mass of material could I find an address or phone number, and though I easily forgot the contents of the wallet, the name of Mona Lautner, the woman without an address, lingered and wouldn't go away, wiping from my mind any interest in other people. She became the filter through which I began to view the world. I ceased visiting the Lily and the Rose, my favourite bar. When I met my friends, I had nothing to say, and my mind would wander to the image I had constructed of Mona. I took photographs of women on the street, sure that one or all of them was Mona Lautner, present though I'd never seen her.

It was early November. I had finished up with the Countess for the season and was on my way to John's nursery with a load of leaves for his compost heap. Crossing the street ahead of my pick-up was a woman I'd never seen before. As she walked, there didn't seem to be any ground beneath her. I pulled over to the curb to watch her as I was doing every day with strange women who caught my attention. She was at least six-feet tall. I was transfixed by her large, heavily lidded eyes, baby smooth complexion, black hair with twists of grey scattered throughout. But it was her legs. Those legs. Those thighs. Long and taut inside a pair of tight black slacks. Legs perfect for less-being lovemaking. All my imaginings were incarnated in her body.

I jumped out of my truck and confronted her.

"Excuse me," I said, trembling all over. "I found this wallet the other day, and I was wondering if it belonged to you?"

She stopped abruptly, as if in shock, then she looked down at me and smiled.

"Wherever did you find it?"

"I work for the Countess Radomska," my tremulous voice announced. "I was raking leaves, and it was under the bushes."

"How strange! I can't imagine how it got there."

My heart was signalling but I didn't have an inkling what the message was about, my breasts were swelling, the sidewalk was shifting, and I was captured in the air like a bubble, moving in a sphere with Mona that was travelling to eternity in the forever-moment of our first encounter.

Mona was uninvolved, imperceptive of my desires. Yet she answered my need without hesitation.

"Well, this has never happened to me before. I guess you deserve a reward. How about coming for lunch?"

Of course I lept at her invitation and suffered my first disappointment. Mona served nothing but cold meats.

"Mona, we have to talk about this. I'm a vegetarian. I don't eat meat."

"Nonsense!" she said. "Everybody eats meat."

"Not me," I said, proceeding to lecture her on the sickening details of carnivorous behaviour.

"I talk to vegetables before I boil them," she explained, adding, "Aren't we forcing vegetables to be something they might not want to be?"

"I agree. We've enslaved them in greenhouses all over the world, feeding them chemicals. But to console carrots and cucumbers before you slice them up, well, I really think that's being sadistic."

These encounters are not very pleasant, for Mona begins to cry and calls me cruel. She can never make up her mind about the world she inhabits. She is someone who doesn't partake of tellurian existence — and I end up in space, a deserted moon attracted to a planet spinning out of control, revolving in an orbit against my will.

So we go, round in circles. She is changeable by the minute. Last week she was a vegetarian after reading her father's D-Day journal where he described skinning a live pig. Then she read about Blacks who pick vegetables in the southern United States, living in sub-human conditions, treated just like the animals who wait in misery until they're slaughtered. She is terribly confused about human cruelty. As confused as I am about human love. Love and cruelty, for anybody's information, are not the same. It is a unique occasion when a victim and a witness can learn together to distinguish between the two.

This is supposed to be a love story. Can there be just one? Does it only happen once? I don't think so. But in my case, where my being and my love have been so intertwined, I would have to say for now, for me, there's only one love, only one story, and this is it, the story I have tried to tell.

This isn't Mona's love story. Mona is just beginning to know me. I'm her threshold to experience. We've had no carnal knowledge of each other. Yet. Maybe when Mona loses her superior beingness and becomes a less-being she will tell her own love story, her knowing being over, my loving becoming whatever it will become.

And isn't this what I've been dreaming of — an ending? Maybe. But I also dream of a garden of nettles, a field of rampant dandelions, a towering city of Morning Glory and Mona's black, liquid hair filling the gap in my breasts. One of these things is bound to come true.

Take note, Mrs. O'Neil. My days in your garden are definitely numbered.

the loss of gynæ

Ellen Quigley

skin touches skin
reveals the body's outer cover
one on the beach
inscribes words in sand
the trappings of language
move up her body
cover her skin
in opalescent liquid
she is female/a woman
knows she was not born
in male parthenogenesis
knows she is not
an overgrown rib
a homunculi
senses her inherent difference
but cannot articulate this
dives in to see
and scrubs herself hard
the connections do not split
she is still woman/female
though the blood of gynæ
pulses strong under cover
gushes between her legs

she has been talking about a women's building
for as long as she can remember
always trying to get some space
to define who she is
what she wants

she remembers leaving her husband
the difficult separation
of woman from man
she remembers the gynæ the gyne
the gin she threshed cotton with
and begins to thrash out
to separate
the weaker
feminine rhyme
the double
wo   manish
wo   manly
fe   male's dependence
from her self
her   his story
to separate kern
from environment
a study of erasure
and substitution

who named us
            claimed us
                  stole our power?

she finds gyne and feme
base word women
but no reason

in the dictionary
for the male addition
she finds gynæceum
a women's building
and O
now gynœcium
for the andro form

wife-man woman
fee male man
what are the rhymes
the ill allusions of order?
was there a debt to pay
for autonomy?
were they *fées*
to men?

Gyne on the beach
names her sounds
shapes signs with lesbian rule
                    a pliant alphabet
aouei
to root muscle blood ligament
lavender gynæ in language
♀ as ♀ æ

Purple Thistle

Deena Nelson

One day Mrs. McNaughton started to talk. Not that she was normally mute, but most of her conversations ranged from the laconic to the terse and, like her kitchen, were full of children, laundry and baking.

This particular day started the way most others did with the alarm at four-thirty. Shortly after her husband, John, left the bed, there was a bang on the door down the hall to wake the most recent in a succession of hired men.

Mrs. McNaughton lay in bed, quite still, till she heard the screen door slam, twice, with a thirty-second interval between. She rolled over on her side to face the window where it was still quite dark. Another ten minutes and she heard the machinery start up. Farms were quieter once, but at least this way she knew that the men were safely at work and that she would have the house to herself. Mrs. McNaughton swung herself out of bed. Now down to the bathroom and back upstairs to dress.

At five o'clock Mrs. McNaughton was at the kitchen table, cigarettes and tea in front of her, staring out the south window toward the lake she could just barely catch sight of. Every day it was her habit to sit like this and plan her day. First she searched through her body for the signs of any physical problems that would have to be gotten around in the course of her work. No incipient migraine, no ache in legs or toes that could lead to cramp. Her back, like always, was fine. She had a strong back.

Next came the weather. The sky was lightening up, a haze rising off the south field. There was still a dawn chill but the day would be hot. To avoid sunstroke she decided to do the weeding in the morning and the laundry in the afternoon.

"First things first," came the firm statement from Mrs. McNaughton as she arose from the table. She talked to herself a bit, but only when no one else was about. It was like a bit of company, and she found it kept her moving along. It had the feel of a ritual about it — trace memories of numberless child-mother dialogues that had ended, finally, when Mrs. McNaughton's youngest boy had moved into the city the previous year. Even her children's visits with all the grandchildren didn't quite recapture the way it had been. Her oldest daughter's family was down this week, the first of summer vacation, and there was more talking and more cooking but that was really all the difference that Mrs. McNaughton could see.

Down to the cellar she went, for two jars of peaches. As she finished setting the bread and butter by the toaster she could hear the others stirring upstairs and, startled, dashed with unusual haste into the bathroom. Swinging the door closed Mrs. McNaughton turned, catching her reflection in the mirror. There was a feeling of unreality about the face in the mirror. The features were hers, the dimming eyes and the wrinkles. She'd watched them coming and knew when they'd arrived. But somehow, today the fit wasn't right, the proportions were a little bit off.

At the sound of water running in the kitchen Mrs. McNaughton pulled her eyes from the mirror. "God, what foolishness." With a certain amount of maliciousness Mrs. McNaughton tugged a brush through her hair. "Rushing around like this. You'd think your own daughter hadn't seen you a bit of a mess before."

Smoothing her dress, she cast another glance at the mirror and turned away, relieved to see that her face was her own once more. Re-entering the kitchen Mrs. McNaughton found her daughter Marg, mouth pursed, a slight frown about her eyes filling the kettle.

"Girls still asleep?"

"Yes. Will too. I don't understand how anyone can sleep as much as those three."

"Well, you were always an early riser but you grew up in the country. Will and the girls come from town and just never had to get used to mornings."

The compressor at the barn gave a rumble and stopped. Alerted by the sudden silence Mrs. McNaughton started breakfast.

Will and the two granddaughters, still sleep-jumbled, appeared in the hallway as the screen door slammed.

"Breakfast ready yet." Statement rather than a question, the half-growl came from the figure slapping dust off his pants by the door. A smaller man moved around John and into the bathroom as Mrs. McNaughton began ladelling out the porridge and putting food on the table. Marg fussed with the youngest girl's hair while Will and Sue, the oldest granddaughter, looked on.

Breakfast was a quiet meal, and food disappeared quickly as the adults and Sue ate in silence. The radio was on, and its only competition was presented by Ellen, the youngest granddaughter.

"Sue, can you take me swimming today? You promised. Please? There's nothing to do around here."

There was no time for a reply, which was just as well because none was forthcoming. Sue's head was down, and her total concentration centred on blocking out the nasal twang of the farm-report man.

"Grandma, did you used to make your own bread? Mum says you did. Sue didn't believe her, but I did. Can you show me how?"

"Marg, for christsake make the kid be quiet. With all her nonsense I can't hear myself think."

John's voice, while still nowhere near full capacity, called forth the usual reactions from his family. Marg's hand found Will's forearm, Sue left the table and found a book, and Ellen shrank into her chair, frozen, till Mrs. McNaughton turned to her.

"All right, dear, after I've done the dishes. Now you run along upstairs and make your bed."

"But Sue slept...."

"Ellen just GO." This, from Marg in a tone remarkably like her father's, sent the little girl running.

The radio announced the Dominion Observatory Time Signal. At the sound of the tone it was nine o'clock and time to get back to work. The men went back outside. While she and Marg cleared the dishes, Mrs. McNaughton hoped that Ellen would just forget about the bread making. There was just so much a person could do in one day.

Will read the papers he had brought in his briefcase, Sue her book. It was beginning to warm up with the late Spring sun hitting the house full force, unprotected on the top of the hill.

Mrs. McNaughton and Marg had finished the dishes and were just starting to tidy up when Ellen reappeared.

"Now can we do the bread? I did our bed and Mummy's bed and your bed too. So can we? Please?"

Mrs. McNaughton consigned the day to the rubbish heap where all the other days, days of perfect labour, spoiled by the vagaries of children or weather or John, lay. The weeding would have to wait, wash too, probably.

"Well, I was going to do the garden and...."

Ellen, seeing another summer vacation day about to dissolve into an endless stream of chores wailed, "But you Promised!"

Will looked up from his papers.

"Go on now, Betsy, the garden will be there tomorrow. Maybe we can get Marg and the girls to help you then."

Mrs. McNaughton turned to the window and fumed quietly. The child was understandable, and she really didn't mind the idea of doing something for her, but that son-in-law was another story. Some nerve he had, calling her by name — like a child, telling her to take it easy. Making bread! Take it easy? Mrs. McNaughton fought down her incredulity at Will's arrogant stupidity. God, how she hated making bread. And those three — help her in the garden — she'd have to spend the whole time keeping them from pulling out the plants and stomping all over the beds.

Mrs. McNaughton put down the broom.

"All right then. Let's get started dear."

The yeast had risen. Mrs. McNaughton had mixed in the flour and sugar and salt. The first sour smells of the budding yeast were filling the kitchen. The dough was clammy to the touch and had a dead feel. Mrs. McNaughton showed the little girl how to knead and left her to the task, turning away to look out the window toward the barn. Will came in, Sue trailing him; both restless with the weight of leisure upon them. Will tried, for possibly the millionth time, to engage his mother-in-law in conversation.

"That house down the hill. It was left to you wasn't it? I always wondered why you didn't sell. The market's probably not good but I'm sure you could get something for it. I know

John wanted to a few years back when he had that problem with the baler. Money would have come in handy then."

Mrs. McNaughton's hands tightened a little on the counter edge. Try as she might she could not seem to make herself like Marg's husband.

"I mean it's not as though any of the kids are ever going to want to move back here now. They all have their own lives. When John retires the two of you will probably just sell it and the farm too and move into town. There's not likely anyone in the family who would want to take over either one."

Mrs. McNaughton turned to face Will. She had to make some sort of reply. After all it wasn't really his fault he was such a fool.

"I really don't know, Will. There just never seems to be a good time to let go of some things."

Mrs. McNaughton's vague note of dismissal, peevish but far too mild to be a recognizable rebuke, achieved its desired effect. Will headed for the back door.

"Guess I'll go see what the men are up to."

Mrs. McNaughton turned to check Ellen's progress. Sweat was beginning to show at the girl's temples, and she looked tired.

"Well dear, you see what making bread is like. It's a lot easier to just buy some things at the store."

She moved over beside Ellen and took over the kneading. The dough was coming to life now, gaining a resiliency that seemed to actively resist Mrs. McNaughton's hands. It had been a very long while since she had done this but it took only a few seconds for her hands to recall that particular pushing and rolling rhythm from the past. Ellen and Sue looked on as Mrs. McNaughton pursued the dough around the baking board with a subtle violence. For a moment the only sounds were the pounding of the breadboard against the wall and the faintly obscene popping of yeast bubbles. The humidity was rising now. All three were pulled into their own separate worlds by the swelling scent of the dough.

Sue broke the spell.

"Gram, I can't believe you actually own that house down there. It's such a nice house. I don't see why Dad doesn't think anybody would want it. All those big nice trees out back. I bet it's even got a fireplace. The yard's all prickly weeds and flowers and things. I used to go down there and hide on Ellen when she was bugging me."

Ellen glared, considered a retort but, lacking the energy, subsided into a lazy pout instead. Ignoring her sister, Sue crossed the kitchen to the window opposite the one facing the barn. About halfway down the hill the tip of a chimney was visible, silhouetted against a stand of tall pine. The house supporting it was obscured by a tangle of overgrown orchard trees and wild undergrowth. Staring out at it Sue tried to penetrate the shadows and continued in a quieter, intense tone.

"Was that your house when you were little?"

Sue was normally a silent child, a reader more involved with the characters in her books than with daily life. Mrs. McNaughton, surprised at this sudden energy and interest in her life, looked up from the bread and stared at Sue as if she had never really seen her before. Then she began to talk.

"No, I never lived in that house, dear. It belonged to two old ladies when I was a girl. I don't really know why they left it to me. I was off at teacher's college when I received a letter from a lawyer telling me I'd inherited the house. He didn't seem to have any more idea than I did. I guess they died without family and since my father used to do them a few favours like ploughing the lane and hauling wood they just decided to leave it to our family. When they moved away my brother was still alive. I guess they naturally assumed that he would get the farm, so they left the little house to me. As it happened, with Donny dying in that car crash, I ended up with both.

"They moved away when I was, oh, around thirteen or so. I can't say I ever really knew the two ladies. They never went to any of the church things that we went to and pretty much stayed to themselves; but I could see them when I sat up on the veranda roof, by the north bedroom. That one used to be my brother's. I used to like that rooftop.

"No one would bother me there. The sun was hot, and the flies would crawl on my legs when I got too lazy to wave them away. I went up there when things got to be just too much: too many adults, too many chores, too many thoughts. I'd take some lemonade, if we had any, and a book. I'd sit up there and read till I lost myself in someone else's life; someone who never existed, written about by people long dead and so far away. Once I got far enough away from the farm and the cows and my family, I'd look down from my vantage point and watch the ladies while they gardened.

"They didn't grow anything flashy or showy or big. My mother raised gladioli, a big garden of them that people would come and have her arrange for the church. I helped her with those, but I didn't really want to. Then there was this man in the village that had a beautiful rose garden. At least that's what everyone else said. But I was never all that impressed.

"But the ladies down the hill didn't have that kind of garden. They had a lot of little flowers; those tiny snapdragons — weeds really but we called them butter and eggs — pansies, johnny-jump-ups, lupins and all kinds of other things I really don't remember the names of. Right in the middle though, every year, they left a great huge Scotch thistle — just the one mind you, they weeded out all the rest. I think it was that Scotch thistle that started their reputation for being odd."

Mrs. McNaughton stopped and pushed the hair back from where it had slipped down over one temple. Her face was flushed from the heat and the exertion, and she thought the bread must surely have reached the right stage by now. She spread butter on the inside of a large bowl and turned the dough into it, then covered it with waxpaper and a not-too-dirty tea-towel. She looked up at the girls, then out the window, as she continued.

"I don't really know all that much about them. They were already living there when I was born, so how they came to be there I never heard. They'd both been married because on the mailbox their names were listed as Mrs. Luanna Evans and Mrs. Evelyn Shaugnessy. No children or anybody ever came to visit though. I'm not sure how old they were but when I was a child they looked pretty old to me.

"That garden was something, though. There was never any real pattern to it. I watched them while they were planting, and they'd just arrive home with a box or two of flowers and put them in whatever empty space was handy. Sometimes I'd go sit in the trees where they couldn't see me so I could hear them better. I suppose it was wrong of me, but it didn't do them any harm. And they'd get in such silly arguments it was hard to resist."

Mrs. McNaughton's voice changed in unconscious imitation. Her tone became more lively and artificial giving an arch quality to her normally subdued manner.

" 'Mrs. Evans.'

"Mrs. Shaugnessy would always start it off. I always thought it was funny the way they called each other by their old-lady names when they argued.

" 'Mrs. Evans, I wish you wouldn't put the marigolds next to the irises. I think they would do much better next to the white peonies.'

" 'Well you may be of that opinion, Mrs. Shaugnessy, but I think in this case I'm really going to have to insist on having my way.'

"I know this sounds a bit strange but they would put on such airs when they were carrying on like this. Another thing that struck me was the expression of their faces. They didn't look like old ladies at all then. They looked more the way children do when they catch each other doing something silly.

" 'There are all those ants on the peonies, and I want to use the marigolds for cut flowers, and you KNOW how much I hate ants in the house.'

" 'There is only one thing, my dear, that you've forgotten. Marigolds and peonies don't bloom at the same time — bloody, silly woman you are sometimes.'

"At this point, when the mock politeness broke down, and it always did sooner or later, they'd start calling each other names. No one from home would ever have believed this because they never, ever, acted like this when they knew someone was around. They just never noticed me.

"Anyway that's when things would really get good, and they'd start making faces or spraying each other with the garden hose. It always ended up with one of them chasing the other through the flowerbed, round the crab-apple tree and right into the house. I generally went in then too, because I'd discovered that the ladies rarely came out again afterwards."

Handing Sue a cloth, Mrs. McNaughton began cleaning the kitchen. Ellen left quietly before anyone could notice she wasn't helping.

"There were other times when I watched them — generally it was in the early evening. You know, when the sun's gone down, and there's that soft light that blends in with the shadows. And they'd be different. Sometimes they'd walk around, just bending over and touching their flowers once in a while, touching each other on the shoulder or back when they passed. Other times they'd sit on lawn chairs, heads close together, talking so softly I couldn't hear them."

Mrs. McNaughton straightened up from the table she'd been wiping, looked down at the handful of crumbs she had amassed and sighed.

"That always made me feel odd. It was like reading a book you like so much you want it to be real and to go on forever. But the two ladies were real, and I still couldn't touch them.

"The summer when I was twelve I really thought about them a lot. It seemed to me like we shared something since I knew about their secret life, even though they never realized it. For a while I tried to catch their attention; popping out of the woods or playing in the field by their house. I even went so far as to borrow my brother's binoculars and pretend to be bird-watching. But none of that worked. The ladies were just there for each other, and I guess I grew up a little when I finally realized that."

Sue and Mrs. McNaughton caught each other's eye. The kitchen was clean. In a moment of wordless conspiracy Mrs. McNaughton went to the refrigerator and got lemonade while Sue fetched the glasses and some cookies. Both sat down at the table, Mrs. McNaughton lighting a cigarette.

"So I got tired of mooning around on the roof by myself and started spending more time at the library, hoping to impress the assistant librarian. She seemed to me to have scaled the heights of cultivation when I saw her struggling through *War and Peace*. After a while I got bored. I didn't seem to be getting anywhere impressing her, and she didn't seem to be doing any better with that book. Seemed like she'd be reading that one forever.

"By the time school started that year I could hardly wait. I was bored and restless somehow. I'd never paid much attention to the kids in school before. I guess I probably seemed a bit stuck-up, but the main reason I hadn't tried too hard to make friends is just because I figured I'd be bad at it. But since my books and the roof-top didn't seem enough anymore, I decided maybe it was time to try.

"I don't remember actually liking any of the kids I went to school with particularly. Children of that age aren't terribly nice. And they're not stupid either. I think most of them know the things they do aren't nice but they can't seem to help it anyway. It's just the way they are. I remember all they seemed interested in was the way different people's socks smelled, and that they like to point and snicker at people that didn't fit in.

"I didn't like them much, but I guess I just decided that they were supposed to like me so I set to work to make myself popular. I began to act just like the big shots. I made fun of anyone who didn't act that way. I was pretty smart too so I helped the lazy ones with their homework."

Sue looked hard at her grandmother. Her voice was picking up speed and rising as though she were angry at something. It was rare for Mrs. McNaughton to talk this much let alone to become upset about anything.

"So I became part of the 'in group.' It was more like a herd. By mid-October I was in the thick of it. It seemed like everybody wanted to be my class partner; some of the girls even started to ask me over to their house after school.

"Every once in a while I'd check on the ladies. They were still the same — hadn't even noticed that I wasn't around. That bothered me a little."

Mrs. McNaughton stopped with an audible sigh, took a long sip and continued in a voice of long-past remembrance.

"Then Hallowe'en came. Back then it was still fun; better than birthdays, better than any holiday except Christmas because it was ours. It was just for kids. The grown-ups didn't go out to parties the way they do now. They had to stay home to give out candies and protect their property. There weren't the poison scares then either. The only thing to be afraid of was us."

Mrs. McNaughton hesitated. Continuing, her voice became harder and colder than Sue had ever heard a voice go.

"I don't know if the whispers were around before I started hearing them, but the word had been out for some time that Mrs. Evans and Mrs. Shaugnessy were ... 'different' was the best thing that I heard. They were called 'unnatural,' 'queer in the head.' I don't recall hearing the word 'Lesbian' — that's what they were of course. Now almost everyone knows what that means but, back then, I don't think most people knew the word and, if they did, would never dare use it in case it seemed they knew too much about that sort of thing. I had this sense that they were dangerous — somehow to me in particular — though when I think of them now I can't see how two people so happy with just their own company could have been thought dangerous to anybody.

"Anyway we were a herd — a vicious twelve-year-old herd with all the conscience of your typical mob, and, like a dog that's gone wild, we were terribly good at picking out the weak and unprotected. We all knew the ladies were a safe target and somehow, God help me, an appropriate one."

Mrs. McNaughton stood up and moved to the window facing down the hill. Sue stared, seeing a woman she'd never expected her grandmother to be.

"That night.... Even though it's forty-three years ago I'd

give anything to take back that night. Anyway, I still don't remember how it started, who said the word that really set us off. I can't lay a finger on anyone because I just don't remember. Maybe it was the shock of the whole thing or maybe guilt, but so much of it is gone.

"I can remember getting dressed in my costume. I went as a troubadour; black, crushed-velvet pants, red frilly shirt. It was really quite ugly when I think about it, but at the time I thought it was just wonderful. And I had a big black hat and a beat-up old guitar I'd found in the attic. Nobody else could figure out what I was supposed to be but I know I had something vaguely Shakespearean in mind.

"That night all of us, the ones who had notions of our own importance and some sort of corner on the popularity market at school, met by the church. At first we just did the usual things — hit all the good houses for candy, eat ourselves sick, set tires on fire in the middle of the road and torment the little kids. Then — I don't know who gave the word, it might just as well have been me — we were at the ladies' house."

Mrs. McNaughton's voice deepened and softened as if it were being weighted down by all the years that had passed.

"It had been a mild fall that year, and I remember the marigolds and zinnias were still blooming. And that thistle was standing there. All the purple gone, nothing but dry brown now, but standing there just the same. The ladies were in their house, in the kitchen having tea or maybe something just a bit stronger.

"Everything was so quiet. Clean fall smells were all around in the cooling air; maple and pine from the woods, strange spice smells from flower-heads turning to seed, all the hot heaviness of late summer washed away. I can still feel that silence. I thought it would last forever.

"Then John and some other boys let the air out of the tires

in the car. That hissing was so loud in the night. Someone started to giggle. The others joined in, and then I was laughing too."

She lit a cigarette and continued, tapping the ashes into a plant on the window sill. Sue was forgotten now. Mrs. Mc-Naughton wasn't talking to anyone anymore. She was just talking.

"What happened next was strange. It was like there was a long string running down my spine, and someone was slowly pulling it out and tearing it away from me, and then it was as though I was on the veranda roof again, looking down the hill, watching as the children ripped apart that garden, watching that one red shirt battling that old brown thorn bush.

"The ladies heard us then, and I was suddenly back in the garden, watching Mrs. Evans come to the door with her tray. When she opened the door, the light was so bright I turned away for a second. Everyone went quiet, and then there was a sickening wet sound, and I turned back to see the simple, surprised 'Oh' on her face.

"I watched it all after that from the veranda roof. I don't know whether it was cowardice or some slightly demented guardian angel that allowed me to, but I looked down that hill as I had so many times before, and I watched the ladies. And I watched the children. And I saw all the nice things turning bad. I saw the tomatoes they'd spent all summer raising hitting Mrs. Evans. Then I saw her fall. And I saw Mrs. Shaugnessy holding her, kneeling on the kitchen floor, in a housedress like Mrs. Evans', in a housedress like my mother's. And I saw her look up and stare at the children as their arms slowed, then dropped down. Not saying a word she stared, and the children slowly backed off and finally turned away till there was just the one red shirt standing alone in the garden.

"God how I willed that red shirt to go away, to follow the rest back down the road to the corner where I could see the others, quiet, then giggling, gaining in bravado till they could face the walk back to their houses and bed. But there it stayed. My shirt, covering my back. Undeniable evidence.

"I can't recall her voice; it was like I couldn't hear anymore; but I swear in that weird light — moonlight and kitchen light combined — I saw Mrs. Shaugnessy's mouth saying 'Go home Betsy. Just go home.'

"Then the red shirt turned finally and walked up my hill."

Mrs. McNaughton glanced at the cigarette in her hand and crushed it out in the geranium. She turned, catching Sue's surreptitious swipe at her eyes.

"Well, look at the time. We'd better get dinner."

"Funny, I don't know how she knew my name."

odds and ends

Christina Mills

rummaging through feelings,
more and more frantic
to find the one i can take and wear,
and that will finally allow me to sleep,
i come across an odd sock
— the jealousy when she called
(the night before i hid beneath a pillow,
not wanting to hear even the tone of your voice
as you murmured and laughed
that intimate laughter).

a pair of pants
full of holes
— the loneliness
watching your even breathing
as you slip
so easily
away.

here's something promising.
an old red shirt,
faded but serviceable
— the memory of your hands and tongue
begins to warm me.

i touch myself
tenta
tively
then urgently,
arching to release
my body only.
then am swept by desolation,
fierce as nausea
— it doesn't fit!

face wet, arms aching
i scrabble through love's debris,
unable to toss it all out.
still unwilling
to slam that drawer shut
once and for all.

Raven's Long-Distance Love Affair

Two Feathers

The black 1977 Monte Carlo whizzed down Interstate 75 at eighty miles per hour. Raven's heart palpitated wildly inside her chest and butterflies danced in her stomach, as she anxiously peered out of the passenger-side window at the road sign that told her, Tennessee 3 miles. Soon, she and four other Native women musicians would cross the state line from Kentucky into Tennessee. Two years prior, she had met Marianne, Missy, Karen and Debbie, through a mutual acquaintance, at a house party in Hamilton, Ontario. The core of their conversation centred around music. Raven learned that Debbie played lead guitar; electric bass guitar was Marianne's specialty; Karen possessed adeptness on the drums; and Missy was talented on the piano and keyboard. Twenty-one-year-old Raven sang and played percussion. All five women expressed a desire to play live. None of them had done that before, except for some jamming sessions at a few house parties. A week after their first meeting, Raven suggested that they jam together in the basement of a friend's home on Burlington Street. It was there that she called them The Red Skin Sisters. After six months of rehearsing cover songs, they had proclaimed themselves confident enough to book some gigs in the United States. Now, they were returning for the second time in two years, to perform in Kentucky and Tennessee. They had also become very close friends. This tour would be for the entire month of July. Raven wasn't feeling anxious because of the fast car ride. She was nervous about seeing her long-distance lover, Mary Louise. They had met after a show, the year before. Mary Louise had been in the audience when the band played in a parking lot near the main intersection, in Jellico, Tennessee. One sultry night a few weeks later, their relationship was consummated. Raven was besotted and mesmerized with her lover. But she was also frightened because she had never dated another woman before, yet Mary Louise had some previous "experiences." After Raven returned home to Canada, her heart pined for her mate's intimacy and warmth. She occasionally travelled to the United States to be with the one she truly cared for. When that wasn't possible, they had kept in touch with each other, via Ma Bell. Raven had always told her the truth — that she was an honest woman and that her heart belonged to Mary Louise. Harassing thoughts of her heterosexual friends and family back home discovering her sexual preference plagued her relentlessly. In her mind, she rationalized that a same-gender relationship isn't a sin in her Longhouse religion because it is never mentioned during ceremonial festivities. But, in all certainty, if the members of her community found out, they would ostracize her, and she would be the subject of their cruel jokes. She also had no guarantee that her family wouldn't treat her with indifference and perhaps disown her if they knew about her secret life.

Raven turned around to see if the van carrying Karen, Marianne and the musical equipment was still trailing them. Satisfied that Karen, the driver, was able to keep up, Raven turned back around and stretched out in the front seat of the spacious, new car. It had been a long, tiresome journey from Hamilton, Ontario, punctuated intermittently with stops along the way to allow the crew to sleep, eat and relieve themselves. She told Debbie, "Hey, I think you best slow down some. We're very close to the state line, and I can see a state trooper's patrol car near the toll booth. I want to be with Mary Louise, instead of spending time in a jail cell." Debbie laughed and reassured her. "Okay, don't worry. You'll soon see Mary Louise." Missy, who had been riding in the back seat had mostly been quiet up to now. She remarked, "Lucky you, Raven." Debbie wisecracked, "Sure, if she gets lucky tonight." Raven responded, "Hey, Debbie, what about you? You haven't been with anyone in a long time. If you don't use it, you'll lose it!" All three women laughed in unison as their car snaked it's way up to the toll booth. Raven's heart was beating so much faster now. Soon she would be with the love of her life. Two state troopers, a female and a male, emerged from their patrol car and eyed the car's occupants suspiciously, just as Debbie was about to throw some change into the collector. "Where y'all from?" the male officer asked in a Southern drawl. "Hamilton, Ontario, Canada. Why are you stopping us?" Debbie queried. "We have information that occupants of a car with Ontario license plates have committed a crime in this state. Can I see your driver's license?" Debbie complied. After checking her license, he handed it back to her. He asked, "Okay, what reason do you have for being in the United States?" She answered, "We're here to work as entertainers in night clubs. The two occupants inside the black van behind us are members of our band." He then inquired, "Do you have a work permit?" "No. We are treaty Indians, and we don't need one. We can work and visit any time in this country. It is our birthright," she informed him. Undaunted, she showed him her certificate of Indian status card. He then told everyone to step out of the car while the female officer searched the car's trunk and the inside for contraband. The male officer trudged back to the patrol car to radio his command post for information from his superiors. Finding none, the female officer smiled at Raven, who had been busy mentally undressing her six-foot frame and admiring her curves. The male state trooper came back and barked, "You're all right. You can go now. Enjoy your visit!" With a glint in her eyes, the female officer stared deeply into Raven's dark brown eyes for what seemed like a lengthy period of time. Guiltily, Raven sat back in the car, but did not take her eyes off of her. Raven thought, "Oh my god, what am I doing? I'm already with someone else, and here I am looking at another woman." Her eyes swept over the officer's body one last time. When their eyes met, they exchanged warm smiles before turning away from each other. Raven whispered, "I wouldn't mind getting to know her." Debbie mildly reproved, "Hey, I saw you admiring her. I think she liked you too. You old smoothy you." Raven responded, "I guess it's okay to look, just as long as I don't touch. Mary Louise would kill me if she ever found out about this." Debbie threw some change into the collector and proceeded across the state border into Tennessee. Raven exclaimed, "Finally, we're in Jellico! I wonder if Mary Louise is working the afternoon shift at the hospital? Hey Debbie, hurry! Let's find a telephone!" Debbie smiled and said, "Settle down, you'll be with her soon." Missy added, "Aren't you going to be romantic? I mean, like, buying her roses and all?" "Oh hell! I never thought of that. Thank you," Raven replied. The Monte Carlo pulled up to a telephone booth at a roadside restaurant, and the van parked behind it. Karen shouted at Raven, "What's happening now, girl?" Raven was fumbling nervously with a piece of paper with Mary Louise's telephone number on it. She answered, "I'm calling my woman!" Cheers could be heard from both vehicles. Raven knew that the people who were with her now could be trusted not to reveal to anyone back home about her secret life, and she was grateful for that. Debbie, a bisexual, was the closest to her. Missy's door swung both ways too, and Raven loved her like a sister. Karen and Marianne were casual lovers. The sensation of butterflies dancing in Raven's stomach was more pronounced when she began dialing Mary Louise's number. The phone rang once, twice, and then, "Hello." "Baby, it's me," Raven heard herself say. "Oh, hi honey. Oh god! Are you here? I've missed you so much," came the sweet voice from the other end of the line. "I've missed you too. Yes, I'm here. I want to be with you as soon as possible." Mary Louise asked, "How long will it take for you to get to my house?" "I have to help set up camp first, then I'll have Debbie drive me over to your place. I should be over there in about an hour," came the answer. Her lover said, "Great, I'll be waiting. I love you." Stunned by her last comment, Raven simply said, "Thank you. I'll be there soon." Her hands were shaking with excitement as she put the receiver back in it's place. She darted out of the telephone booth to tell her entourage the good news. She didn't have to say anything. The broad smile across her face said it all.

Raven whistled happily at the campground while assisting Debbie and Missy to set up their tent. She would be sleeping with them during their stay. Marianne and Karen would have the privacy of their own tent. Raven was really looking forward to the night. Her band didn't have a gig scheduled, and she would be able to spend it with Mary Louise. It was beginning to get dark outside by the time their chores were completed. The stars shone brightly in the dark sky. They could feel the warm, southern night wind's invisible hands lifting away the city's tension and sense of enclosure. They chided Raven about the female state trooper, and said they would tell Mary Louise about it. Finally, Raven stood up and announced, "Well, we made it here in one piece, and I'm really grateful to all of you, my dear friends. I love you, but not as much as I love that blonde who is waiting for me in the next county." Her pals smiled warmly at her. "Hey Debbie, can you take me into town so I can pick up some flowers?" "Maybe I can pick up some flowers too," Debbie quipped. Raven roared with laughter, knowing that she meant picking up women. Raven's eyes glinted with love for Mary Louise as she paid for her card and flowers in Canadian funds. "Where y'all from?" asked the cute, petite store clerk. "Canada," supplied Debbie. Debbie and Raven heard the clerk say to another customer, "They're from Canada!" "Where's that?" the customer asked. Both Natives shook their heads in amazement and walked out. Once outside, Raven questioned, "I wonder if the clerk is gay?" Her companion rebuked, "Oh, Raven, why don't you go and ask her! Besides, you're already spoken for!" Their eyes danced with laughter as they jumped into the car and sped away to the next county.

Raven was certain that her heart skipped a few beats when they rode into Mary Louise's laneway. The thought of being in her arms excited her to such abandonment and ecstatic joy that she did not hear Debbie confess her sexual feelings for her. She tripped over reality when she heard her say, "Raven, go to her now. She is waiting for you at the doorway. God, she's so lucky to have someone like you." Ignoring the last comment, she told her, "Okay, pal, I'll probably get her to drive me back to camp. But don't worry if I don't come back tonight. Goodbye for now, babe." Debbie winked at her and drove away.

Mary Louise's outstretched arms enveloped Raven's neck

and shoulders. When their bodies made contact, the familiar sexual excitement surged to the forefront. Raven handed her the card and flowers. She said, "Thank you." Between kisses, Mary Louise revealed, "Oh darling, I missed you so much. I was so afraid that you lost interest in me and had found someone else." Raven's mind flashed back to the female officer at the state line and reassured her, "I'm here baby. I could hardly wait to be with you again." The two women walked in the house and sat down on the couch, hungrily kissing and caressing each other. After a while, they got up and took a shower together. Raven felt sexual excitement in her groin as she was being led by the hand to the bedroom. Mary Louise's blonde hair flowed in soft curls just past her shoulders. Her beautiful, blue eyes spoke of love for Raven. She said, "Honey, take me. I'm yours." They lay down on the bed naked, attentional energy focused on foreplay. Raven wasn't sure if she had been in love before, and she wasn't sure how one was supposed to feel if they really loved someone. Was this lust or love she was feeling for her? Raven gently stroked Mary Louise's warm, firm breasts with both hands and kissed her lips lightly. The nipples stood up and became hard with each caress. Raven took her mate's left breast in her hand and kissed it, then the other. Mary Louise let out a low moan. Raven's hands moved up and down her body slowly, then to the inner thighs and back up to the breasts. Her partner's fingers ran through her dark, shiny hair, alternately caressing her back and behind. Mary Louise's moans became louder. Her respiration was so much faster now. She pulled Raven on top and in between her legs. Their place of power connected, white heat began centring them. Raven moved her body slowly at first. Then faster ... faster ... so much faster now. She kissed her hot lips passionately. Mary Louise let out a loud cry, and their night exploded in fireworks. Their sweet juices flowed, combined and streamed downwards. Satisfied, they held each other and kissed softly. Three hours had gone by since Raven had arrived at Mary Louise's place. They fell asleep in each other's arms until the morning light peeked past the partially opened curtains of the bedroom window. When they awoke, they repeated the same performance like the night before. Finally, they showered together, got dressed and had breakfast. Mary Louise told her that she would be working the afternoon shift for the entire week, but she would try to make it to the bar to hear her sing. She knew that Mary Louise was really dedicated to her job as a registered nurse at the local hospital. For a few fleeting seconds, she thought of asking her to steal some narcotics from the Emergency Ward. Then she dismissed that notion as an element of danger to their relationship. She had a feeling that Mary Louise would end their affair if she ever found out about her drug use. "Best to hide it from her for now. Cut it out altogether before it becomes a problem! What about Mary Louise? Hell, she would be fired and charged if she were caught by her co-workers."

It was two-thirty in the afternoon when Mary Louise kissed Raven good-bye and let her off at the campground. Debbie, Missy, Karen and Marianne welcomed her back with hugs and kisses. Debbie remarked, "I hope you didn't use up all of your energy for this afternoon's rehearsal and tonight's gig." Raven laughed and told her that she had enough stamina to go a few rounds in bed with her and still would be able to go on stage. Everyone chuckled wholeheartedly. In preparation for their four o'clock rehearsal at a local bar, Raven changed her clothes from a burgundy, short-sleeved shirt and beige slacks to blue jeans and a T-shirt. Everyone else was dressed similarly. "Okay people, let's go and do it!" Missy called. They took their places in the car and van and drove to the local watering hole. When they arrived, there were only two male patrons sitting on stools near the bar. They were drinking shots of whiskey and conversing with a female bartender. Marianne approached her and announced, "We are members of The Red Skin Sisters Band, and we are here to practice a few sets for tonight's show." "Great. The manager told me you'd be coming here this afternoon. Y'all make yourselves at home. Let me know if you need anything." "Thank-you," Marianne responded, before walking to the stage area. Raven was busy checking out the sound system. She noted that there were enough vocal and percussion microphones for the entire band. "A great working sound system," Raven proclaimed. "Good, now let's go outside and help unload the equipment," Marianne said. They walked out the back entrance to the parking lot where the van was parked and helped the others unload the drums, guitars and keyboard. Raven helped Karen bring in the drum kit, while Debbie carried her own guitar and assisted Missy with the keyboard. Marianne brought her own bass guitar in. The women took their places on the platform and began their warm-up of cover songs. It lasted three hours, and everyone felt satisfied with the workout. The crew left the bar to go for supper at a restaurant down the street. An hour later, they returned to camp to prepare for their nine o'clock engagement. During their hour long preparation, Raven consumed four bottles of beer and two shots of rum. Debbie had been watching her drink. She questioned, "Are you going to be able to sing for us tonight?" Raven replied, "Oh hell yes! What is this? You think I can't handle it?" "Just checking," Debbie answered. She had seen Raven this way now for about six months, and each time it seemed to her that Raven's intake of alcohol and drugs was increasing. Debbie worried that Raven was becoming addicted to those substances. She was certainly becoming defensive about it. She sadly shook her head and walked away. "It's time to do our sound check now!" Marianne yelled at the others. "Routine!" Missy called back. The band members drove the half mile back to the bar.

Raven paced nervously in the dressing room and waited for the Talwin and Valium tablets to take effect. She had obtained a prescription for forty Talwins and sixty Valiums from her doctor about a week earlier. The narcotics were to control the pain in her broken finger, which she received in a fight with a fellow on a street in Hamilton. The tranquilizers were used to help her sleep. She had been experiencing insomnia for about six months. Raven heard the manager introduce the band to the bar patrons. The drugs and alcohol were beginning to take effect by the time she went on stage. "Hello there! How you all doing?" She greeted the large crowd. "All right!" they responded. "Okay, we're going to start off this set with a Peter Frampton song. It's called *Show Me the Way*, and it goes something like this." The audience cheered in anticipation. Debbie was the lead-off for the musicians. Karen, Marianne and Missy followed simultaneously. Raven sang the song. After it was over, she went into the next number, amid wild cheers from the audience. She was able to get through the first set without a problem. During their half-hour break, Raven consumed two more beers and two painkillers. Half-way through their second set, her speech was becoming slurred. It was eleven-thirty when they completed the second set. Raven rushed to the dressing room and drank another beer. She also ingested some more pain pills and tranquilizers. She had just put them in her mouth when the dressing room door opened and Mary Louise walked in. She said, "Darling, how are you? I got down here as soon as I could, after my shift." Raven gulped down some water with the medicine before she staggered up to her feet to give her partner a kiss. "Oh hell, I'm doing fine. Glad you could make it," she answered. "How much longer do you have to go before finishing for the night?" Mary Louise wanted to know. "Just one more set. It's almost time to go back on." "Okay honey, I'll wait for you at the table nearest to the stage," Mary Louise informed her. Raven hugged her before dashing towards the microphone on stage. A strong alcohol odour wafted up to Mary Louise's nostrils. "Whew! She reeks of alcohol. She's been drinking a lot. Will I be able to talk to her about it?" Mary Louise pondered. Raven's slurred speech became more acute near the end of their last set. The people in the audience were apparently intoxicated. They were boisterous and rowdy. Some men were trying to climb on-stage, but were taken away and told to leave by the nightclub's bouncers. It was one o'clock in the morning when the five women finished for the night and dashed to the dressing room. Mary Louise walked into the dressing room to congratulate the band on a fine performance. She asked Raven to go home with her. "Wait. I want to have a shot of whiskey before we go," Raven told her. Mary Louise looked at her and said, "No, honey. I think you've had enough. Let's go now." Missy said, "I think you've had enough, too. So go with her. We're going to stay for a while. We'll get the money for tonight's work from the manager, and we'll give it to you tomorrow." Mary Louise was pulling Raven past the table where the others sat down to order their first drink of the night. Raven called, "Okay, I'll see you tomorrow." They waved good-bye to her. On the three-mile ride to Mary Louise's house, Raven put her hand on Mary Louise's thigh and stroked it. "Stop that. You're going to make me put this car into the ditch!" Mary Louise teased her. After brushing her teeth and taking a shower, Raven climbed into bed with the lovely Mary Louise. Their lovemaking that night was hot and passionate.

The morning came too soon for Raven. She was feeling the ill-effects of her over-indulgence in pills and alcohol from the night before. "Come and have some breakfast, dear," Mary Louise called. "No. I'm too dizzy and nauseous," Raven said. "That'll teach you!" rebuked her lover. They spent the rest of the morning and part of the afternoon talking about their relationship. Raven wasn't too happy that it was long-distance. Mary Louise told her that she was concerned about her alcohol intake. Raven became defensive and said it wasn't an issue. They dropped that part of the conversation and continued to talk about their affair. "I can't move to Canada right now. My family and friends are here. You don't want to move here because you have family and friends back home too. I'm sure you don't want to be uprooted any more than I do." "That much is true. I just find it so hard being away from you. What is it? A month here with you, three months there?" Raven asked. "I know; it's true. I miss you too. I guess that's the way it's got to be if we want to continue to see each other." "I wish it were different. I mean, I wish we could be together more often," Raven continued. Mary Louise held her hand and said, "Let's not worry about that right now." Raven agreed to drop the subject. While Raven's girlfriend showered and got ready for work, she sat on the couch to think about her drug use. She didn't think alcohol was the main problem. She wondered. "Has she seen the needle tracks on my arms? I don't think so, or else she would have said something." The needle tracks were from injections of Demerol, Talwin and Valium, that she paid for in cash from a friend, who stole it from a hospital where she works in Canada. She hadn't used intravenous drugs for over a month. "No. Drugs aren't a problem with me. I haven't injected myself in a long time. I've only taken them orally," she reassured herself. Mary Louise opened the bathroom door and called, "Sweetheart, I'm ready to go. Are you?" "Yes, I am," Raven replied. On the drive to the camp, Mary Louise told her that she would only be able to see her every other night. She said that she was becoming exhausted from work. Raven told her that it was fine with her. At the camp, the lovers kissed goodbye. The band members were busy getting ready for another rehearsal and another night of performing. They greeted Raven warmly.

For almost two weeks, Mary Louise and Raven spent every other night together, making love and discussing their lives. On the last night of their tenure in Jellico, Raven informed her that they would be entertaining in a nightclub near the Smokey Mountains. This would be their last two weeks of working in the United States, before returning home. Mary Louise sadly told her that she probably wouldn't be able to make it down for the first week because she was going on the night shift at the hospital. Raven held her tight and said that they had to go look for a motel room near the Smokey Mountains. Raven spent two hours with her before returning to the camp at about four-thirty on a Sunday morning. The other women were asleep. Not wanting to disturb them, she slept in the Monte Carlo. They had breakfast in the morning and began packing their camping gear for the trip to find a motel near their next workplace. When they were ready, it was agreed that Missy would drive the car. Debbie and Raven would be her passengers. Marianne jumped in the driver's seat of the van, with Karen as her passenger. When the vehicles began pulling away, Raven felt sad that she wouldn't be able to see Mary Louise for another week. But, she would be seeing her for the whole last week of July. This was when her lover would get time off from her job. Raven turned around to Debbie in the back seat and confessed, "I'm worried that Mary Louise has discovered my drug use or maybe she is interested in someone else." Debbie counselled, "No, she doesn't seem the type to go fooling around on you. Babe, when you see her again, you've got to be up front with her. I worry about you abusing alcohol and drugs. I'm really afraid for you. I don't want you to die from it." "I worry about you too, Raven. Everyone here worries," Missy told her. Raven agreed, "Yes, I know I've got to quit using those poisons. Look at all of you. You don't need to resort to them before you go on stage. Hell, I'm so chicken! I get so frightened of the crowd that I take pills and booze to overcome that fear." Debbie said, "If you're willing to stop using, then we'll give you emotional support. It's up to you." Raven felt caged in by them. Nevertheless, she said she would give it a try. The women sang for the entire, two-hour ride to the Smokey Mountains and discussed their last show. When their vehicles pulled into the parking lot, an old grey-haired man came out to greet them. "We're looking to rent four rooms for two weeks," Missy informed him. "We have four rooms for y'all right here." Karen asked, "Can we view them?" The old man nodded and motioned for them to follow him. Everybody followed him into the motel. After viewing the rooms they asked what it would cost. He said, "Thirty dollars a week for each room." They agreed to rent the rooms. He said, "My wife at the front desk will write out receipts." Marianne and Karen paid the gray-haired woman sixty dollars for two weeks, as did Debbie and Missy. Raven obtained a receipt for a single room. When the lodging issue was settled, they unpacked and went to their beds to relax. Raven tried to go to sleep, but could not calm down. After a while, she jumped up and went to her friends' rooms to see if anyone wanted to accompany her to the bar they had seen on their way in. Debbie was the only one who felt like going for a walk. They stayed at the bar for two hours and drank a few beers. This time, Raven did not get intoxicated. They returned to their rooms around ten in the evening. Soon, they were fast asleep.

It was two-thirty in the afternoon when the band members arrived for a rehearsal, at a small bar near the mountains. The times for rehearsals and performances were about the same as it was in Jellico. The routine was pretty much the same as before, and so were their audiences. The crowds consisted of local townspeople and visitors from the surrounding states. The first night of their performance was on a Monday. There weren't too many people in attendance, but Raven was back to her old habits of consuming too much drugs and alcohol. Debbie and the other women felt disappointed. During mid-week, the attendance picked up. Towards the end of the week, the nightclub was filled to capacity. Raven was beginning to remember these events in sequences and so was experiencing alcohol and drug induced "black-outs." She felt frightened that she could not remember singing some of the songs from the night before when she awoke the next day. She often asked, "How do you think we did last night?" Debbie would tell her, impatiently, "Fine. Except you slurred your words a lot. You should know; you were there too."

The subject of Raven's affection came to see her mid-way through the last week of July. Mary Louise entered Raven's room with a suitcase in her hand. She stated, "Hi darling. If it's all right, I'd like to spend the rest of the week with you." Raven had been recovering from yet another alcohol and narcotic binge. Not bothering to get up off the bed, she disinterestedly motioned for her to come in. She said, "Oh sure. Whatever." The people in Raven's band were acutely aware of her increasing inattentiveness towards them and the non-caring attitude she held in regard to life in general. They surmised that it was related to her chemical dependency. "What the hell's wrong with you, Raven? You don't seem to give a damn about anything anymore, except maybe when you're stoned," Karen had berated her the night before. "Otherwise, you just brood in your room and don't really communicate with us that much anymore. I think you're addicted to booze and those damned pills! You need help. What about your girlfriend? Don't you care about her anymore? You haven't even mentioned her in the last week and a half." "Get out of my face! Let's just get this show over with and return to Canada!" Raven had retaliated. Mary Louise was taken aback by Raven's coolness. She also observed her physical appearance as being nothing short of tired-looking, with dark circles under her eyes and a puffy face. She had made up her mind to try to find out what was wrong with her and would help her if she could.

Drunk and stoned, Raven had somehow managed to complete the last week of work. The next day, three hours before she and the crew were to leave for Canada, Mary Louise confronted her. "Darling, I can't handle his long-distance relationship, and I know about your drug abuse. I've seen the needle tracks on your arms. You've been treating me with indifference ever since I got here. When you made love to me last night, you didn't show me any affection. You were like a stranger to me. You've changed from a fun-loving, caring and affectionate person." Raven's face expressed horror and indignation, as she waited to hear what she would say next. "Honey, I think we shouldn't see each other anymore. I'm sorry," said Mary Louise. Raven exploded in anger, "You're sorry, for what? It's my own damned fault! I'm no damned good for you. I've become a druggie and a lush!"

Her girlfriend tried to console her. She wrapped her arms around her and coaxed, "Sweetheart, there's help out there for you. Alcoholics Anonymous has a good program with a high success rate, and then there's Narcotics Anonymous, with a similar program." Out of pride, Raven held back her tears. She looked deep into Mary Louise's eyes and responded, "My drug use and alcohol consumption is really out of control. It has changed my personality. When I am ready, I will seek help, not before. Just leave me the hell alone! Damn you...." Raven edited her thoughts and continued, "I said I'll go when I'm good and ready!" Mary Louise counselled, "You best do it right away before it costs you your life." Raven did not respond. Later, out of love and desire, Mary Louise began caressing her and lay down on the bed. "Come lie beside me. Please make love to me one last time," she pleaded. Raven agreed, but it just wasn't the same as before. The feeling was gone. She felt so empty now. She felt like she just went through the motions. Exhausted, her soon-to-be former lover fell fast asleep. She showered, got dressed and kissed the lovely Mary Louise on the lips gently. She whispered, "Good-bye darling. I'll always love you." She fetched her suitcases and quietly walked out.

The Monte Carlo and van weaved along interstate 75 at a snail's pace through a heavy rainstorm and traffic jam. Raven sat in the front seat, with Debbie at the driver's wheel. Missy sat in the back seat. Raven had told both women and the others, earlier, that her affair with Mary Louise had ended. Everyone was sympathetic and urged her to seek help for her problems. "We're behind you all the way," they had said. Teardrops flowed down Raven's face. The windshield wipers slapped back and forth, beating out her pain. The driver held her hand while she cried a mournful dialogue. Debbie knew that Raven would talk about it when she was ready. Missy tried to soothe her. She put her hand on her shoulder. They were now three miles into Kentucky, travelling eastward, bound for Hamilton, Ontario. "Oh God. What am I going to do?" Raven called out to no one in particular. Compassion was evident in her friends' eyes, but they remained silent. After a while, Raven regained her composure. Her eyes were puffy and bloodshot when she joined her friends for coffee at a roadside café. "I know it's going to take time for me to get over her. I also know that I have to make a clean break, where my chemical dependency is concerned. I have to try," she said, sounding sincere. Marianne agreed, "Yes, you can do it. We'll help you in anyway we can." The others nodded in agreement. When they finished their coffees, they continued the journey. About one mile from the roadside café, the car and van had to negotiate around a two-car collision. Two state troopers were directing traffic. Missy exclaimed, "Hey Raven! There's that woman state trooper at the side of the road!" Raven visually examined the officer and declared, "Forget it. I don't need anymore long-distance lovers." Laughter rang out, as Debbie eased the car around the tangled wreckage of the two cars and drove on. Raven turned around in her seat to watch the woman officer, until her vision became obscured by the rain and distance between them.

heart to let

Christina Mills

so she waltzes right in as if she owns the place,
sits herself down with nary a by-your-leave.
frankly, i m a little miffed.
i don t recall putting out a sign, i sez,
i really wasn t thinking of letting it.
she just looks at me
and sweeps away a cobweb.
all at once i m embarrassed.
well, it *is* a mite dusty, i sez,
been empty for years,
i haven t kept it up.
she don t seem to care,
just looks around
taking her sweet time, mind you,
as if it s already hers.
don t take her long though
— she knows what she wants, that one —
no haggling.
just that smile like you wouldn t believe.
i like it, she sez,
i think i ll stay

Sometimes Virgil Hates Toad

Sarah Louise

TODAY is one of those times.

Toad, Virgil's affectionate name for her chinless old friend, has been drinking since Virgil left for work at 8:00 a.m. Budweiser in a chilled mug and Crown Royal in her favourite tumbler sit on the kitchen table in front of Toad. She keeps her eyes on the brown liquid, especially the warm whiskey, and forgets for a long minute that the door behind her has just opened and Virgil is back.

Still? Virgil's voice penetrates Toad like a wrong note in the middle of a tune. It reminds her of the Irish dyke singing off key in the pub last night. Her peacock blue jeans, her dazzling blue ass nearly fill the room.

See that? Toad asks, as though Virgil is blessed with the same vision. *Sure is pretty.*

Unlike yourself, says Virgil. *How many times you going to quit before you quit?*

TODAY is Tuesday, a bad day in anyone's book. It's so close to half way through the week that it hurts, but so far from the end that it hurts more. Toad, who is very sensitive to facts like these, has made a decision she thinks will help. She is going to drink from one end of the week to the other so that the in-between part isn't so noticeable. This seems as reasonable to her now as it did last night in the pub. It is also certain not to get Virgil's approval, but Toad seldom considers her friend when it comes to such personal matters.

Hey Virg, says Toad, her chunky torso forming an acute angle with the table, *here's to smoother sailing*. She drains the whiskey and winks at Virgil through the thick bottom of the glass. She can see, in spite of the distortion, that Virg is not amused.

Rain rain go away, says Toad in a nursery tone, *come back again some other day*.

VIRGIL is making dinner. Tall Toad, who has been losing her shape over the past five years or so, isn't interested in the food, only in the idea that Virgil's cooking is responsible for the fat around her waist.

If we gave up eating, she says, *we could take life more seriously*.

We'd have to, says Virgil, still unused to having her feelings hurt by a drunken Toad. *Forty days and forty nights and it would be all over. Can't have much fun with that*.

Faced with a spoonful of ratatouille at the end of Virgil's extended arm, Toad lights an English Oval and blows smoke rings in Virgil's direction. If only I could hook one on her nose, she thinks. That'd finish her.

You're too stuck on dignity, Toad says. *One of these days your noble nostrils'll catch a wind and over you'll go, down on your ear among the ants*.

Virgil retracts the spoon and continues to stir. Toad goes to the fridge for a fresh mug and a beer. Her swagger betrays the pride she takes in what she just said. I can still put a sentence together, she thinks, regardless of the circumstances.

Bet a nickel you can't remember your last line, says Virgil, who often knows Toad too well for her own good.

Have a drink, says Toad, emptying a beer into Virgil's stew.

CONVERSATION is not a favourite of Toad's, even though she may have a talent for it. This puts her at odds with Virgil, particularly when she requires an explanation for one of Toad's periodic relapses. AM radio, however, gives Toad a real kick, and she likes to turn it on when she knows she should be talking. It puts her in mind of a plate of fried potatoes topped by a poached egg and chased by a few beers. In Toad's culinary book, there is nothing more soothing to the palate — another thing she has against Virgil. No deep-frying allowed in her kitchen.

You'll never stop, says Virgil, trying to control the disdainful set of her mouth. *You've got about as much self-discipline as a birthday kid in front of a chocolate cake.*

Toad has turned on the radio, just after wrecking the ratatouille. She really puts her shoulders into the music so that she looks, from Virgil's point of view, like an ex-bodybuilder flexing her muscles for a long-ago judge.

I'm hungry for you, I'm hungry for you, I'm hungry for you. It's the repetition that fixes Toad's attention, makes her feel timeless, immortal, out of reach of all the terrible Tuesdays in store for everyone else. It's what drives Virgil crazy.

Mindless, says Virgil. *Why do you want to be that way?*

Toad runs her road-map eyes over Virgil's mystified face. *The trouble with you Virg, you're too mired in reality to appreciate the finer things in life.*

Virgil is buffaloed, but not for long. The ups and downs of cohabitation with Toad have taught her to recover her balance quickly.

Thus saith the Toad, says Virgil, with a flourish and a bow.

TOAD tears the cellophane from a box of Black Russians. She removes one of the cigarettes and admires the gold filter tip. A hand she recognizes as her own strikes a match against the table. She inhales, the aroma reminds her of something — she has a curious feeling that she's left everything, including Virgil, behind at some bend in the road. She's light, like a feather or a balloon, and doesn't need bones to hold her up anymore.

Drunks aren't allowed to smoke in bed in this hotel, says Virgil, as she grabs up Toad's cigarette from the floor.

This, madam, is a table, not a bed, says a smirky Toad, not certain to whom she is speaking.

For you, all the world's a bed, says Virgil, *and I'm just the friendly chambermaid.*

VIRGIL and Toad are no longer lovers, though Toad would like them to be, whenever it's convenient for her. Virgil's occasional urges in that direction are nearly always foiled by an episode like today's, which leads her to believe that Toad is confused.

You're oozing Crown Royal from every flooded pore, says Virgil, throwing open the kitchen window.

God damn it, says Toad, *you're always right. It's the world. If it wasn't for that we'd all be better off.*

Virgil is sorry she used the word, even though it was an hour ago. Toad's references to the world are in fact references to the two of them, since Toad hasn't gone further than the local pub in years.

I'm always right? yells Virgil. *It's like you go under water everytime I open my mouth. I've been talking to myself for years.*
Keep your pants on, Virg, you know what drunks are like.
Yeah. Oblivious, irrational, egotistical....
That's the spirit, Virg, get right in there and shoot.
Out of sync, impervious, offensive to nasal as well as other passages....
Shit, shit, shit, says a wincing Toad, *I love you Virg.*
Sounds like AM *radio,* concludes a winded Virgil.

THE sky is cloudy and not quite dark. Toad sits on the back step examining her short fingers, her baby thumbs, for warts. I'm Virgil's Toad alright, she says to her hands, but she's just Virgil and she never stops. Always, for all eternity, for longer than we can be friends, she'll be Virgil. Fortress Virgil, that's her.

IN the livingroom, Toad is hanging signs. She finishes as the toilet flushes and Virgil emerges from the john.
What'll I do, says the first sign, flanked on both sides by musical notes.
Virgil looks sternly around the room and sees at least six other sheets of white paper taped to the walls, interspersed with arrows for her to follow.
When you
Are far
Away
And I'm
So blue
What'll I do.

The last sign is decorated with a broken cigarette hung over an empty champagne glass. Toad is sitting under it, her face a benign full moon level with Virgil's belt.

Going somewhere? asks Virgil.

If you say so, says Toad, a tear on each cheek.

I take it I'm supposed to be Gatsby, says Virgil, *waiting around for Daisy 'till I get shot.*

Everything's a joke, says Toad.

Of course we don't have a pool, says Virgil, *but the tub'll do I guess.*

Christ, Virg, give a drunk a break. Toad peels the picture of the empty glass from the sign above her head. *I quit again, Virg, after tonight, I quit.* She gives Virgil a determined look to show how serious she is.

I suppose it wasn't all Daisy's fault, though, Gatsby's getting shot.

TROUBLE *with this particular finer thing,* says Toad, holding her whiskey against the light, *is it gives me palpitations. I don't like my ticker going off like an alarm. I don't like knowing it's even there, know what I mean Virg?*

I hate to be banal at a time like this, says Virgil, *but time's running out, my friend, and so's my patience.* Virgil paces, runs a hand through her thick hair, looks around for her reading glasses. *I'm going to bed,* she says, coming to a halt in front of the pale Toad.

You won't get a rise out me, says Toad. *Too many threats and they lose their punch — Psychology 101.*

Virgil, who rarely has a violent urge, wants to hit Toad in the belly or pull her hair or better yet, arrange it so her eyelids won't close for a full twenty-four hours. *If I wanted to counsel*

drunks whose brains are beginning to fizz, says Virgil, *I'd offer my services downtown.*
Oh shit, Virg, I didn't volunteer for this job either.

TOAD sits alone in the kitchen, a pot of coffee on the stove. Caffeine, Virgil has informed her, does nothing to counteract all that booze, but still, Toad feels like it's her tip of the hat to sobriety, and besides, she likes it.

Rain hits the window behind her. A tune comes back to her, something about a cake in the rain and never having that recipe again. Imagine, she thinks, fifteen or twenty years ago. I'm not there anymore, the spaces I used to occupy don't have me in them anymore. Somebody else lives in my old place, shops in the corner store, goes to the laundromat patrolled by that little blonde. And whoever it is has no idea I was ever there, no feeling for history. It's like being dead, for Chrissake.

Toad pours herself more coffee. She leaves room for half an inch of cream, wondering about arteriosclerosis as she adds it to the coffee. Seems, she says to her reflection in the silver creamer, there are more opportunities in this life to do yourself in than anything else. I mean, everything I like is lethal. No wonder Virgil is Virgil, says Toad in a burst of clarity, it's a lot safer than being me.

VIRGIL comes in out of the rain and kicks off her rubber boots. Toad is still at the table, her last Black Russian on the edge of the ashtray, sending a thin blue stream of smoke toward the ceiling. It's oldies but goodies hour on the radio.

One of these days, says Virgil, who wants Toad to mind her absence even after all these years, *you'll be sorry I'm not around.*

Toad looks at Virgil's feet. The high arches make her uncomfortable. They remind her that Virgil is always ready for take-off, though she never goes very far. *Shit Virg, you know I don't want us to part company. One of us is no good without the other.*

Speak for yourself, says Virgil, eyeing Toad's cigarette with distaste, *and stop calling me Virg as though we were, at this very moment, bosom buddies or something.* She strides into the livingroom, followed by Toad.

God damn it, says Toad, who stops dead along with Virgil in front of the radio, *it's the Everley Brothers, remember them?*

With regret, says Virgil, reaching for the off-switch.

Wait, says Toad, her hand on Virgil's, *this is nostalgia.* Toad sings along, her voice low and stringy. *Whenever I want you all I have to do is dre-e-e-eam, dream, dream, dream…. Just think Virg, we didn't even know each other then. I didn't even know you existed.*

Isn't it funny? says Toad after awhile, forgetting to let go of Virgil.

Truth and Circumstance

Megan Hutton

We wondered if there was an end to this dusty prairie road. The map clearly showed it as a much better route. We were beginning to wonder if we had made a mistake. "Are you sure he lives out here?" My companion and life-mate is struggling with the well-worn map, ragged now from being folded many times over in so many different directions. "I haven't seen a building for over an hour." She is right. I'm having some doubts now too, but have decided to keep them to myself. It is July, and the heat has been relentless. Instead, I say, "I'm almost certain we're going in the right direction." Just then another rock flew under the car, reminding us we might have been better off if we'd stayed on the main road. "It isn't that I mind the adventure, but this is getting ridiculous." I can see her eyes searching the horizon for some sign of life. Mine were searching for a gas station, but I didn't think this was a good time to bring attention to the gas gauge, the needle flicking back and forth across the empty signal.

This was only the beginning of our relaxing trip across Canada. Our first stop was my uncle's. The last time I saw him I was about ten. I'd taken the bus to Prince George from Vancouver, and my Aunt Helen put me on a train from there. I was going to see where I was born. My uncle picked me up from the train on a horse. We went everywhere that summer on horseback or walked. We picked wild berries and watched for the bears. How could anyone forget a holiday like that. There were no fences, cars, or tall buildings, just miles of rolling hills dotted with the bright yellow buttercups surrounded by the Rocky Mountains. My deep yearning for the solitude of that simple life began long ago. We finally did find a gas station, and, with rural familiarity, they directed us to my uncle's farmhouse. As we got closer, I was hoping I would recognize him after thirty years. "There he is. See? He's waving his arms." I pointed down the road to a small figure in the distance obviously as excited as we were about the visit. I recognized him immediately. I hoped I'd changed more than he had. We had barely stopped the car when he gave me a big hug, "I didn't think I'd ever see you again old girl." "Old Girl" was what he'd called me when I was young. I'd never asked why, but decided it was a compliment because I was applauded by some members of my family for being wise beyond my age as a child. Of course, there were others who had no comment.

The week went by quickly. My uncle was the perfect host except for his breakfast hour. Every morning about five we could depend on him to poke his head out of his back door and call to us in our motorhome. "It's daylight in the swamp. Get up. You're missing the best part of the day." He wanted as much of our company as possible, and we weren't looking forward to saying goodbye to him either. The last evening we spent sitting on the back porch. A prairie storm had just broken across the late afternoon sky, and the sunset went from ochroid to hyacinth red. There was a clear peace in this place we were in. Words weren't always necessary, and my uncle did not mind we were two women in love.

"Don't suppose anyone's told you the truth?" My uncle

was heading towards us with two mugs filled with hot home-brewed coffee. I was startled. This past week had been so peaceful, so void of stress. Last night we had talked about family, and I guessed this was just a continuation of that conversation. My uncle did that. Somehow you just caught on. The word truth triggered something inside me that made my stomach tighten. We weren't sure we were ready for too many more bouts of realism around family. For us, at this moment, the words truth and family did not go together. We had vowed together to be cautious from now on about who we would choose to be part of "our family." My mate, Autumn, reached over and took my hand.

"There wasn't much to you," my uncle said as he stopped for a minute and picked up his rifle, which was always close by. I was relieved. This was safe; I knew this story. I'd heard many times before how my grandfather helped to deliver me in the old log house by the Fraser River. How I weighed about two pounds, was warmed on the oven door and slept in a doll's cradle. My uncle took a red handkerchief from his shirt pocket and ran it over the barrel of his gun. He stood up and pointed it towards the cornfield where the birds were beginning to carouse the tall stalks. "Of course, we didn't expect you to be much of anything." The birds weren't frightened by the stuffed scarecrow whose arms were reaching up to the sky. The crack of the gun broke through the layers of heat built up from the summer storm. "The way she went at it, trying to get rid of you." The crows flew off in all directions, flying for their lives. Then he added, "Course, she didn't see much of a future for any of you then." My uncle was slipping another round of ammunition into the cartridge. I thought of my mother. My mother who was to labour twelve times. Twelve times alone. My body didn't move. A deep pain gnawed it's way to my womb. "I have feeders all over but these damn' birds want my corn." My uncle was intent on keeping his concentration there. "Just thought I'd let you know you don't owe anyone a damn' thing." With that he mumbled something about having things to do inside. Autumn and I sat and watched the birds feed on the ripe corn.

I thought about my uncle's words. Truth or circumstance. I was clearly realizing the difference between the two. My mother represented a strong woman to me. From her I got my independence, my inner strength for survival. For whatever reason she had, it didn't matter. I was here. What else was there. I loved her more at that moment for the pain she had endured alone, and for what she was now. I didn't need to know anymore.

We make our way east. We talk about our lives, our sisters, our mothers, how we became who we are today. We are thankful for where we are. We know we have come a long way. We stop in Winnipeg. We spend some time with Carole, an old friend from high school. Autumn gets to show off her talent at fixing things and repairs the dishwasher. The three of us ride around too fast in Carole's beat up Volkswagen and go for a swing in the park. Too soon again we are on the road.

It is January. Aunty Olga has more than made us feel welcome in Toronto. The weather is bitterly cold, and we stand with a small group of women outside the Morgentaler abortion clinic. Beside us, the Pro-Lifers are raucous and persistent as they wave their placards in our direction. "Murderers, murderers," their words appear to freeze in mid-air as they meet the harsh winter wind. "Killers of innocent babies." A very poor artist has drawn a crude picture of a fetus and chosen my face to flaunt it in. "Sinners, you'll all burn in hell," their wild eyes and glazed looks try to penetrate our senses. I look away from their tormented faces and pull all my fragmented thoughts together. They try to prevent a woman from entering the clinic, and we go to her aid.

I am momentarily suspended in time. I remember how my mother looked at this woman's age — a small attractive woman, not five-feet tall, her dark hair curling around a heart-shaped face, a smile that gave her eyes life. The photograph of her on my dresser is a misrepresentation. The anguish and isolation are well hidden. I understand how that part of my pain must converge with my mother's before I can experience who she was. At that moment, two parts of me have merged. I want more for her. The woman we walk through the doors with gives me a nervous smile and a barely audible "Thank you." Our eyes meet, and for an instant my mother is looking out at me. I am, at once, where I began, and who I am now.

You Have the Right to Remain Silent

Gabriela Sebastian

It's summer. Maria and Karen are having a picnic in a public park. They have two bicycles, two helmets, a softball bat, two softball gloves, a softball, and a soccer ball. There are sandwiches and some fruit on the ground. There are also the elements to prepare a Latin American drink called mate.

Maria is a refugee from a Latin American country who came to Canada by herself about two years ago. She is very involved in political matters. She speaks English well but has a noticeable Spanish accent. Maria is twenty-four years old, short, has dark hair, a healthy appearance and has a very intensive look in her eyes. She is never totally relaxed, and there is something in her look that reminds one of sadness, pain, tiredness ... a mix of feelings. Sometimes she seems to be very far away; maybe in her country with her people.

Karen was born in Canada and comes from an upper-middle-class family. She is tall, white, has blonde or light-brown short hair, and a strong appearance. She is twenty-one years old. Karen is almost a yuppie even though she doesn't have much money. She believes in the "American way of life," but she reads the NOW *Magazine*, is vegetarian, and goes to Pro-Choice demonstrations.

Maria and Karen met in a gay bar and have been lovers

for eleven months. When the lights come up Maria and Karen
are playing soccer. Karen wears fashionable green military
shorts and a T-shirt. Maria wears black shorts and a red
T-shirt.

MARIA: *(commentating on her own game at great speed.)* Maria
lleva la pelota, esquiva a un jugador por la derecha, otro por
la izquierda, avanza hacia el arco, el arquero sale a su en-
cuentro, Maria patea.... Gooooooool!!!!! Gooool!!!!! GOL!!!
GOL!!! *(runs around the stage as if it were a stadium and kneels with
her fist closed and up in the air yelling.)* Goooooool!!!!!
KAREN: What the hell are you saying?
MARIA: It doesn't matter. I'm winning anyways.
KAREN: I'm tired. *(lies on the ground. Maria plays alone.)* So
you won't talk to me, right?
MARIA: I don't want to talk about it. Let's play. *(Karen
doesn't move. Maria keeps playing for a while.)*
KAREN: I don't understand.
MARIA: *I* don't understand.
KAREN: Just because I want to be a cop you want to throw
away everything we have?!!
MARIA: What do we have, Karen?
KAREN: I love you.
MARIA: Let's play.
KAREN: *(upset)* Did you listen to me?
MARIA: *(serious)* Yes, I did. I love you too, but I don't think
we know each other.
KAREN: What do you mean? We've been together for
eleven months!! *(Maria sits and starts preparing mate. She
remains silent.)*
KAREN: Are you gonna drink *that* stuff, again?
MARIA: *This* stuff has a name: MATE, M - A - T - E, MATE! Can't
you remember?
KAREN: I do remember, I just like teasing you. *(gets closer*

from behind and hugging her says) I know that poor people drink
it in your country because it keeps them awake and not
hungry....

MARIA: Wow! I'm impressed!

(Karen starts kissing her, Maria pushes her away.)

KAREN: ... and it's also a kind of ceremony among friends
where everybody drinks from the same ... *mate....* *(Maria
smiles at her.)* Could you say "threatened" for me?

MARIA: Get out of here!

KAREN: *(begging)* Please, please, please, just once....

MARIA: *(with difficulty)* th ... th ... threatened!

KAREN: *(very excited)* Every time you say that with that
accent it turns me on.

(Maria blushes and shakes her head no. They drink mate.)

KAREN: I don't understand why it's so terrible for you. I
know you are from Latin America, but this is Canada.

MARIA: Police are the same everywhere.

KAREN: You're being prejudiced.

MARIA: I am not. Why do you want to become a cop?

KAREN: *(standing up)* I want to take care of people. I want
to protect them.

*(Maria stands up and starts walking around Karen as if they
were in the army and Maria were the superior. Later on during this
"game" she will grab the softball bat.)*

MARIA: "To serve and protect."

KAREN: Exactly.

MARIA: You must say: "Yes, sir!"

KAREN: Yes, sir!

MARIA: To keep the peace!

KAREN: Yes, sir!

MARIA: To kill criminals!

KAREN: Yes, sir!

MARIA: To arrest people in gay bars!

KAREN: ....

MARIA: To arrest people in gay bars!

KAREN: *(doubting)* Yes, sir....

MARIA: You don't seem very convinced. I want a clear answer, now. To arrest people in gay bars!

KAREN: *(angry)* Yes, sir!

MARIA: *(has been increasing the volume of her voice, now she is yelling at Karen)* To keep the poor people poor and the rich people rich; to serve and protect property; to kill anybody who wants to be different!

KAREN: *(not following the "game" anymore and sitting down)* Police don't kill that many people in Canada!

MARIA: I haven't told you to sit down. Stand up! *(seriously)* You want to be in the police force you gotta learn to respect authority. Stand UP! *(Karen stands up.)* Good girl! *(Maria has been using the bat as a gun and touches Karen's bum with it.)* *(sarcastic)* You are made to obey.

KAREN: Can we stop here?

MARIA: Why? Aren't you having fun? This is nothing compared with what you'll have to go through at the police school.

KAREN: You're wrong! There are some good people there. We'll change the bad things. You'll see.

MARIA: Can I laugh?

KAREN: Fuck off!!

MARIA: That's nice of you. I can see you're already taking out that violence that the police force needs.

KAREN: *(trying to change the subject)* Can I have some *mate*?

MARIA: Trying to be nice? Don't waste your energy.... *(noticing that Karen is about to cry)* I'm sorry, baby. I'm really sorry. *(making her sit down)* But you have to understand that it's scary that my own lover wants.... I'm a refugee. You know that I had to leave my country.

KAREN: Well.... What did you do?

MARIA: What did *I* do? I asked for justice, and I ended up here. *(very tense and standing up. It seems that she told Karen this a thousand times. She grabs the bat and keeps talking.)* What did *you* do?

KAREN: I haven't done anything.

MARIA: Are you sure? Who do you think is paying the training of the military in the Third World? *YOU! (At the same time she uses the bat as a gun.)*

KAREN: *(very upset)* Me??!! I wouldn't give a fucking cent to those murderers!!!!!

MARIA: *(acting like in a war, jumping and protecting herself)* I'm sorry to tell you but you give more than "a fucking cent" since *you* put *your money* in a bank that has investments in Third World countries. Since *you* pay taxes, and the government has business with dictatorships. Since *you* are having a good life because police and military men are killing thousands of people down there every day....

KAREN: *(drinking mate)* I know. I know that, but here is different. You have a naïve way of seeing police in Canada.

MARIA: They rape women; they kill people out there; and I have a naïve way of seeing them?

KAREN: Yes! You only see the bad part. I'll do good things on the streets. I'll be helping people.

MARIA: If you get to work on the street.

KAREN: What do you mean?

MARIA: Well, you're a woman, and you're not even straight. Don't try to come out because you'll be just coming out of the police force.

KAREN: Yeah, yeah, yeah, but discrimination is everywhere.

MARIA: *(sarcastic)* And you wanna help to keep it.

KAREN: Oh, shut up!

(*They both remain silent for a minute. They would like to say something to convince each other but they also feel that something has broken between them.*)

KAREN: (*gets closer and says sweetly*) I would like you to understand why I'm....

MARIA: (*interrupting furiously*) I'm gonna tell you why. You want the power. You like it. You've been discriminated against since you were born, and you are tired. You're sick of being treated like shit. And you know what? You're right. I'm tired too, but becoming part of the oppressor doesn't help. You don't know what to do with yourself. You've been changing jobs, going back to school and dropping out many times. You just want someone bossing you around while keeping the illusion that you have the power and are helping the community. I have to admit it's an easier way to survive if you can forget about everything and let them brainwash you. They will — believe me — they know exactly how. You won't recognize yourself after a year of training. (*She has been putting everything away while talking.*) Put it on. (*handing Karen's helmet to Karen. This helmet should remind the audience of a military helmet.*)

KAREN: (*sarcastic*) Are we leaving? You haven't finished your speech.

MARIA: Put it on, please, and get the bat. (*Karen obeys curiously.*) Let's say that it's two years from now and a new abortion law has come out: Abortion now is illegal; it's a crime. Pro-Choice people are very angrily going to Queen's Park. You've been assigned to keep them away. You are Pro-Choice, aren't you?

KAREN: Yes. I think women should have the right to....

MARIA: (*interrupting*) Yeah, yeah, yeah. That's your side. (*She has put the bikes like a barricade between them.*) What do we want?!! CHOICE!! When do we want it?!! NOW!! Choice!! Now!!

Choice, now!! Choice, now!!!! (*Sounds start to come out as if from a demonstration from Latin America. Karen has taken her "police" position. Maria seems to be a hundred people at the same time.*) Shame! Shame! (*Karen doesn't move, trying to stay away from this "game" but she is getting nervous.*) Come on, Karen you gotta stop me or you'll be in big shit! (*Sounds from demonstration get louder.*) Policia federal la verquenza nacional! (*Federal police national shame!*) Shame! Shame! Ole, ole, ole, ola, a los asesinos la carcel ya, a los companeros la libertad! (*Jail to murderers, freedom to political prisoners!*) (*Maria pushes Karen. Karen reacts right away, pushes Maria to the ground and pins her down. The sound of the demonstration stops. Maria starts crying but keeps screaming at Karen.*) Are you proud of yourself?! C'mon beat me up!!!! It would be so easy for you!! C'mon!! (*Maria spits at Karen.*) You're the power! You're the authority! Go for it!! Do it!!! (*Karen is about to hit Maria but stops.*)

KAREN: (*like coming back from a trance*) I'm sorry, Maria, please, stop crying. I love you, please. I won't be a cop. I promise you…. (*Maria calms down.*) I love you. (*They hug each other for a few seconds, and Karen tries to kiss Maria.*)

MARIA: Please don't. There are two cops over there.

BLACK OUT

Two and a half years later. It's winter. There is a futon on the floor, clothes all over the place, two or three milk crates full of books. The radio is on. Maria is rushing around, grabbing some clothes and putting them in a small knapsack. She seems very scared.

The radio says: "After many years of waiting refugees are finally having an answer to their futures. Among the 85,000 cases from the backlog only 40,000 are allowed to stay. The other 45,000 refugees are facing deportation within the next 72 hours unless they leave the country on their own. A list of 50 names of those who have already refused to leave the country has been given to the press, and police are looking for them. Human Rights Organizations...."

Maria turns off the radio, grabs her coat and her knapsack and goes to the door. Knocks on the door are heard. Maria freezes.

VOICE OFF STAGE: Open the door! The area is surrounded! Open the door!

MARIA: *(runs to the audience, jumps off the stage and grabs hands of the audience people.)* You gotta help me, please, if they send me back I'll die. Please, please!!

(A shot is heard on the door and Karen comes in dressed in a police uniform. She has a gun in her hand and looks for Maria. Maria is hidden in the audience.)

KAREN: Maria! Maria! You have no choice, no place to go. C'mon. *(Karen doesn't see Maria so with her arms extended and the gun between her hands points into the audience scanning. There are 30 seconds of complete silence. Finally she reaches Maria among the audience, her arms fall slowly. She is obviously shocked by Maria's presence.)*

KAREN: I wish you weren't here.

MARIA: I am here, and I need you.

KAREN: I can't.

(Maria tries to escape going to the other side of the audience.)

KAREN: They won't help you. You taught me that. We like our life-style, and we'll keep it no matter how many people have to die. They say they care *(pointing at the audience)*, but it's just a lie. I am honest. I like what I do, and if I have to kill I have no doubts about it. *I* cared for you once but that was a long time ago.

(Maria runs. Karen jumps off the stage and catches her. They fight but Karen is well trained, and it's easy for her to overpower Maria and put the handcuffs on her. Karen takes Maria to the backstage while Maria is looking towards the audience.)

BLACK OUT

The actresses are never seen again.

Home Safe Home Free

Leleti Tamu Bigwomon

Lately it seems I want to stay home, keep the phone plugged
out keep the blinds drawn and order out, even have someone
come pick up my dirty laundry.

Because in my home I'm home safe home free
safe from racist remarks written graffiti style on city walls
I'm free from homophobic people who tell me I'm sick and
use verbal abuse and physical threats hoping I will go away.
But am I ever really safe, even at home?
Sometimes I get up late at night to check the windows and
doors I know I've already locked but still feel the need to go
through this process again.

Home safe home free

Not with my social insurance number my OHIP number in
their computers giving easy access to my name age and phone
number don't they know I pay extra to have it unlisted, so
much for privacy

Home safe home free

On that piece of land that was willed to me as the only living grandchild of Gertina Matilda Thomas. I was planning to save a little money no particular amount since I can get 7 Jamaican dollars for 1 Canadian. This was a good plan until I came out you see there is no culture for lesbians in the parish of Trelawny.

Home safe home free

Where is safe? What is free? I just need a space where I can smoke a doobie if I have one, a space where I can make love if I feel to

Home safe home free

At a place where I can kiss her an hold her without having to look behind me to see if it's safe.

Home safe home free

Where is safe what is free
living in this tenement on Dixon Rd., on this land of no milk an little honey, struggling to feel home safe home free.

Swimming Upstream

Beth Brant

Anna May spent the first night in a motel off Highway 8. She arrived about ten at night, exhausted from her long drive — the drive through farmland, autumn-coloured leaves, the glimpse of blue lake. She saw none of this, only the grey highway stretching out before her. When she saw the signs of a motel, she stopped, feeling the need for rest; it didn't matter where.

She took a shower, lay in bed and fell asleep, the dream beginning again. Her son — drowning in the water, his skinny little arms flailing the waves, his mouth opening to scream, but no sound coming forth. She, Anna May, moving in slow motion, running into the waves, her hands grabbing for the boy and only feeling water run through her fingers. She grabbed and grabbed, but nothing held to her hands. She dove and opened her eyes under water and saw nothing. He was gone. She dove and grabbed, her hands connecting with sand, with seaweed, but not her son. He was gone. Simon was gone.

Anna May woke. The dream was not a nightmare anymore. It had become a companion to her. A friend, almost a lover, reaching for her as she slept; making pictures of her son for her to see, keeping him alive while recording his death. In the first days after Simon left her, the dream made her wake screaming, sobbing, her arms hitting at the air, her legs kicking the sheets, becoming tangled in the material. Her bed was a straightjacket, pinning her down, holding her until the dream ended. She would fight the dream then. Now — she welcomed it.

During the day she had other memories of Simon. His birth, his first pair of shoes, his first steps, his first word, "Mama," his first book, his first attempt at eating with a spoon, his first day of school. His first were also his last. So she invented a future for him during the day. His first skating lessons, his first hockey game, his first reading aloud from a book. His first.... But she couldn't invent beyond that. His six-year-old face and body wouldn't change in her mind. She couldn't invent what she couldn't imagine. So the dream became a final video of her imagining.

She hadn't been there when Simon drowned. Simon had been given to her ex-husband by the courts of law. She was unfit because she lived with a woman, because a woman slept beside her, because she had a history of alcoholism. The history was old. Anna May had stopped drinking when she became pregnant with Simon, and she had stayed dry all those years. She couldn't imagine what alcohol tasted like after Simon came. He was so lovely, so new — the desire for drink evaporated every time Simon took hold of her finger, or nursed from her breast, or opened his mouth in a toothless smile. She had marvelled at his every moment of being. This gift that had come from her own body. This beautiful being that had formed himself inside her, had come with speed through the birth canal to welcome life outside her; his face red with anticipation, his black hair sticking straight up as if electric with hope. His little fists grabbing, his pink mouth finding her nipple and holding on for dear life. She had no need for alcohol — there was Simon.

But the old history was extra ammunition in the war that was played out in the courts of law. Anna May knew it was really about the fact that she loved a woman, and a woman, Catherine, loved her.

Simon was taken away from them. But they saw him on weekends, her ex-husband delivering him on Friday night, Catherine discreetly finding someplace else to be when his car drove up. They still saw Simon, grateful for the two days out of the week they could play with him, they could delight in him, they could pretend with him. They saw Simon, but the call came that changed all that. The call from Tony saying that Simon had drowned when he fell out of the boat as they were fishing. Tony sobbing, "I'm sorry. I didn't mean for this to happen. I tried to save him. I'm sorry. Please Anna, please forgive me. I'm sorry."

So Anna May dreamed of those final moments of a six-year-old life. And it amazed her that she wasn't there to see him die when she had been there to see him born. This life. This gift.

Anna May stayed dry, but she found herself looking in cupboards at odd times. Looking for something. She knew. She was looking for something to drink. She thought of ways to buy wine and hide it, taking a drink when she needed it. But there was Catherine. Catherine would know, and Catherine's face, already so lined and tired and old, would become more so. Anna May looked at her face in the mirror. She was thirty-six and looked twenty years older. Her black hair had grey streaks she had not noticed before. Her forehead had deep lines carved into the flesh. Her eyes had cried so many tears, the blue was faded and washed-out. Her mouth was wrinkled, the lips parched and chapped. She and

Catherine, aged and ghost-like figures walking through a dead house.

Anna May thought about the bottle of wine. It took on large proportions in her mind. A bottle of wine, just one bottle that she could drink from, but never empty. A bottle of wine — that sweet, red kind that would take away the dryness, the wrinkled insides of her, the dead insides of her. She went to meetings but never spoke, only saying her name and, "I'll pass tonight." Catherine wanted to talk, but Anna May had nothing to say to this woman she loved, who slept beside her, who had the same dream. Anna May thought about the bottle of wine. The bottle, the red liquid inside, the sweet taste gathering in her mouth, moving down her throat, hitting her bloodstream, warming her inside, killing the deadness.

She arranged time off work. She told Catherine she was going away for a few days — she needed to think, to be alone. Catherine watched her face, the framing of the words out of her mouth, her washed-out eyes. Catherine said, "I understand," and helped to pack a bag. She helped to pack a basket of food, a thermos filled with hot coffee. "Will you be all right?" Anna May asked. "I'll be fine. I'll see friends. We haven't seen our friends in so long. They are concerned about us. I'll be waiting when you get back. I love you so much." Anna May got in the car and drove. She drove along 401, up 19, and over to 8 and the motel, the shower, the dream.

Anna May smoked her cigarettes and drank coffee until daylight. She made her plans to buy the bottle of wine. After that, she had no plans, other than the first drink and how it would taste and feel.

She found a meeting in Goderich and sat there, angered at herself to sit in a meeting and listen to the stories and plot her backslide. She thought of speaking, of telling what was on her mind, but she was afraid they would stop her, or say something to her to make her stop. "My name is Anna May, and I'll just pass." Later, she hung around for coffee, feeling like an infiltrator, a spy, and a woman took hold of her arm. "Let's go out for a talk. I know what you're planning. Don't do it. Let's talk." Anna May shrugged off the woman's hand and left. She drove to a liquor outlet. "Don't do it." She found the wine, one bottle, that was all she'd buy. "Don't do it." One bottle, that was all. She paid and left the store, the familiar curve of the bottle wrapped in brown paper. "Don't do it." Only one bottle. It wouldn't hurt, and she laughed at herself, at the old excuses bubbling up in her mouth like wine. Just one. She smoked a cigarette, sitting in the parking lot, wondering where to go, wondering when to stop and turn the cap that would release the red sweet smell of the wine before the taste would overpower her, and she didn't have to wonder anymore.

She drove north on 21, heading for the Bruce Peninsula, Lake Huron on her left; passing the little resort towns, the cottages by the lake. She stopped for a hamburger and, without thinking, got her thermos filled with coffee. This made her laugh again, the bottle sitting next to her, almost a living thing reaching out of the paper bag. She drank the coffee, driving north on 21, thinking not of Simon, not of Catherine, thinking of her father. Charles, her mother had called him. Everyone else called him Charley. Good old Charley. Good time Charley. Injun Charley. Only her mother's *Charles* gave him dignity. Charles was a hard worker. He worked at almost anything, construction being his best and favourite. He worked hard, he drank hard. He attempted to be a father, a husband, but the work and the drink took his attempts away. Anna May's mother never complained, never left him. She cooked and kept house and raised the children and always called him Charles. And when Anna May grew up, she taunted her mother with the fact that *her* Charles was a drunk, and why didn't she care more about her kids than her drunken husband? Didn't her mother know how ashamed they were to have such a father, to hear people talk about him, to laugh at him, to laugh at them — the half-breeds of good-old good-time-Injun-Charley?

Anna May laughed again, the sound harsh and ugly inside the car. Her father was long dead, and, she supposed, forgiven in some way by her. He was a handsome man back then, and her mother a skinny, pale girl; an orphan girl, something unheard of by her father. A girl with no family, no relations, no history. How it must have appealed to the romantic that was her father. He could give her everything she didn't have. Anna May thought that her mother was probably satisfied with her life, but, then, they had never talked about it together. Her mother, who sobbed and moaned at Simon's death as she never had at Charles's. Charles was never mean. He just went away when he drank. Not like his daughter, who'd fight anything in her way when she was drunk. Anna May laughed again, the bottle bouncing beside her as she drove.

Anna May drove north, and her eyes began to see the colours of the trees. They were on fire. The reds and oranges competing with the yellows and golds. Every tree alive with colour. She smoked her cigarettes and drank from the thermos and remembered this was her favourite season. She and Catherine would be cleaning out the garden, harvesting the beets, turnips and cabbage. They would be digging up the gladioli and letting them dry before packing the bulbs away. They would be planting more tulip bulbs. Catherine could never get enough of tulips. It was because they had met in the spring, Catherine always said. "The tulips were blooming in that little park, and you looked so beautiful against the tulips, Simon on your lap. I knew I loved you."

Last autumn Simon had been five and had raked leaves and dug holes for the tulip bulbs. Catherine had made cocoa and cinnamon toast, and Simon had declared that he liked cinnamon toast better than pie.

Anna May tasted the salt tears running on her lips. She licked the wet salt imagining it was sweet wine on her tongue. "It's my fault," she said out loud. She thought of all the things she should have done to prevent Simon's leaving. She should have placated Tony; she should have lived alone; she should have pretended to be straight; she should have never become an alcoholic; she should have never loved; she should have never been born. "Let go," she cried somewhere inside her. "Let go!" Isn't that what she learned? But how could she let go of Simon? And the hate she had for herself, for Tony. How could she let go of that? If she let go, she'd have to forgive — the forgiveness he begged now that Simon was gone. Even Catherine, even the woman she loved, asked her to forgive Tony. "It could have happened when he was with us," Catherine cried at her. "Forgive him, then you can forgive yourself." But Catherine didn't know what it was to feel the baby inside her, to feel him pushing his way out of her, to feel his mouth on her breast, to feel the sharp pain in her womb every time his name was mentioned. Forgiveness was for people who could afford to forgive. Anna May was poverty struck.

The highway turned into a road, the trees crowding in on both sides of her. The flames of the trees almost blinding her. She was entering the Bruce, a sign informed her. She pulled off the road, consulting the map. Yes, she would drive to the very tip of the peninsula, and there she would open the bottle and drink her way to whatever she imagined was there. The bottle rested beside her. She touched the brown paper, feeling soothed, feeling a quick hunger in her stomach.

She saw another sign — Sauble Falls. Anna May thought this would be a good place to stop, to drink the last of the coffee, to smoke another cigarette. Her legs were getting cramped, and she needed a break from the car. She pulled over onto the gravel lot. There was a small path leading down onto the rocks. Another sign — *Absolutely No Fishing. Watch Your Step Rocks Are Slippery.* She could hear the water before she saw it.

She stepped out of the covering of trees and onto the rock shelf. The falls were narrow, spilling out on various layers of rock. She could see the edges of Lake Huron below her. She could see movement in the water going away from the lake and moving towards the rocks and the falls. Fish tails flashing and catching lights from the sun. Hundreds of fish tails moving upstream. She walked across a flat slab of rock and there, beneath her in the shallow water, salmon slowly moving their bodies, their gills expanding and closing as they rested. She looked up toward another rock slab and saw a dozen fish congregating at the bottom of a water spill, waiting. Her mind barely grasped the fact that the fish were migrating, swimming upstream, when a salmon leapt and hurled itself over the rushing water above it. Anna May stepped up to another ledge and watched the salmon's companions waiting their turn to jump the flowing water and reach the next plateau. She looked down towards the mouth of the lake. There were others, like her, standing and silently watching the struggle of the fish. No one spoke, as if to speak would be blasphemous in the presence of this. She looked again into the water, the fish crowding each resting place before resuming the leaps, the jumps. Here and there on the rocks, dead fish, a testimony to the long and desperate struggle that had taken place. They lay, eyes glazed, sides open and bleeding, food for the gulls that hovered over her head. Another one jumped, its flesh torn and gaping, its whole body spinning and hurtling until it made it over the falls. Another one, its dorsal fin torn, leapt and was washed back by the power of the water. Anna May watched the fish rest, its open mouth like another wound. The fish was large, the dark body undulating in the water. She watched it begin a movement of tail. Churning the water, it shot into the air, twisting its body, shaking and spinning itself. She saw the underbelly, pale yellow and bleeding from the battering against the rocks, the water. He made it. Anna May felt elation in her body. She wanted to clap, to shout at the sheer power of such a thing happening before her. She looked around again. The other people had left. She was alone with the fish, the only sound besides the water, was her breath against the air. She walked further upstream, her tennis shoes getting wet from the splashing of the fish. She didn't feel the wet; she only waited and watched for the salmon to move. She had no idea of time, of how long she stood waiting for the movement, waiting for the jumps, the leaps, the flight. She watched for Torn Fin, wanted to see him move against the current in his phenomenal swim of faith.

Anna May reached a small dam, the last hurdle before the calm waters and the blessed rest. She sat on a rock, her heart beating fast, the adrenaline pouring through her at each leap and twist of the fish. There he was, Torn Fin, his last jump ahead of him. She watched him, then closed her eyes, almost ashamed to be watching this act of faith, this primal movement to get to the place of all beginning. Only knowing he had to get there. He had to push his bleeding body forward, believing in his magic to get him there. Believing, believing he would get there. No thoughts of death, no thoughts of food, no thoughts of rest, no thoughts but the great urging and wanting to get there, get *there*. Anna May opened her eyes and saw him, another jump, before being pushed back. She held her hands together, her body willing Torn Fin to move, to push, to jump, to fly. Her body rocked forward and back, her heart beating madly inside her breast. She rocked, she shouted, "Make it, damn it. Make it!" The fish gathered at the dam. She rocked and held her hands tight, her fingers twisting together, nails scratching her palms. She whispered, "Simon, Mama's boy, my boy, my boy, my baby. Simon." She rocked. She rocked and watched Torn Fin fight to reach his home. She rocked and whispered the name of her son into the water. Like a chant — "Simon, Simon, Simon," into the water, as if the very name of her son was magic and could move the salmon to their final place. She rocked. She whispered — "Simon. Simon. Simon." Anna May rocked. She put her hands in the water, wanting to lift the fish over the dam and to life, and just as the thought flickered through her brain, Torn Fin slapped his tail against the water and jumped. He battled the current. He twisted and arced into the air, his great mouth gaping and gasping, his wounds standing out in relief against his dark body, the fin discoloured and shredded. He turned a complete circle and made it over the dam.

"Simon! Simon!" Torn Fin gave one more slap of his tail and was gone, the dark body swimming home. She thought ... she thought she saw her son's face, his black hair streaming behind him, a look of joy transfixed on his little face before the image disappeared.

Anna May stood on the rock, hands limp at her sides, watching the water, watching the salmon, watching for her son. She watched as the sun fell behind the lake and night came closer to her. She walked to the path and back to her car. She looked at the bottle sitting next to her, the brown paper rustling as she put the car in gear. She drove for a while, stopping at a telephone booth.

"It's me. I'm coming home. I love you."

She threw the bottle into a trash bin and drove south towards home.

She could still hear the water in her ears.

Contributors' Notes

TARI AKPODIETE was born in England and is now a Canadian citizen. She has lived and worked all over Canada but most enjoyed the time she spent in Labrador. Currently, she lives in Toronto and works in media.

TANNIS ATKINSON has read her work at A Space Gallery, in Toronto, and at two Strange Sisters events organized by Buddies in Bad Times Theatre. She has written for *RITES* and *Canadian Women's Studies/les cahiers de la femme,* among other publications. Since 1982, she has worked in adult literacy, encouraging writing and publishing by adult new readers. She now lives and works in Toronto.

ELAINE J. AUERBACH was born in Passaic, New Jersey. She was named by a nun and raised in Nutley by a second-generation working-class immigrant family. She has lived in New York, San Juan, San Francisco, Fredericton, Vancouver and Edmonton. With the love of her life, she has put down roots in Waterloo, Ontario, where she is a freelance writer and custodian of wildflowers and herbs. She has written fiction, poetry, reviews and articles for various publications.

MIMI AZMIER: "I'm 22, born in 1967. I am now studying my third martial art and will be studying Interior Design in September 1990. I left school in grade 9 as I became disappointed in the system. Afterwards I joined an all-women's punk band, "Unwarranted Trust." We appear on an album and several tapes. I went to college for a year and studied construction. I am a certified general labourer and a carpenter's apprentice. I came out when I had just turned 15 and became very involved in the women's community, from which I now disassociate myself. I believe it lacks a sense of the 'human.' When I meet a woman or anyone for that matter I want to know the person, having coffee with a compilation of political dogmas does not make for a 'fun'-filled evening. I like shaving my legs; I like my corset as much as I like my cowboy boots, silk as much as denim. I believe that we as women must loosen the bondage of our own rules before we attempt to tackle the rules of others."

LELETI TAMU BIGWOMON is a Black womon lesbian feminist mother poet dreadlocks fusing different parts of me and lovin' wimmin Globally.

MARUSIA BOCIURKIW: "I'm a video artist, writer, and feminist activist, born in Alberta in the late 1950s, eking out a living in Toronto in the 1990s, fighting poverty and right-wing back-lash, trying to maintain community and a sense of humour. My videos include *Playing with Fire* (1986) and *Night Visions* (1989) and my articles and short stories have appeared in *RITES, Kinesis, Fireweed,* and *Fuse.* 'Blue Video Night' is about finding a lesbian/feminist/activist voice, and then creating the theoretical and social spaces to make that/those voice/s heard, which, these days, is what much of my life is about, too."

DIONNE BRAND was born in the Caribbean and has lived in Toronto for the past eighteen years. She has published fiction, poetry, and nonfiction prose. Her most recent work of fiction is *Sans Souci and other stories.*

BETH BRANT is a Bay of Quinte Mohawk from Theyindenaga Mohawk Territory in Ontario. She is the editor of *A Gathering* of *Spirit*, a collection by North American Indian women (Women's Press). She is the author of *Mohawk Trail* (Women's Press). She is currently working on a collection of short stories, *Food & Spirits*, to be published by Press Gang Publishers. She has appeared in numerous feminist, lesbian and Native anthologies and journals. She sometimes teaches creative writing for women and will soon start work on editing an anthology of Native lesbian literature and art. She is a mother and grandmother.

CAROL CAMPER: "I am a Black lesbian feminist, 35 years old and the mother of 2 teenagers. I am Toronto-born, an artist, a shelter worker. I also work in community radio. I am a member of the Black Women's Collective. I am an incest survivor. I am a communicator. I must communicate whether it be via visual arts, the written word or the spoken. The word is part of who I am — part of my life — my journey. Part of my journey is also to explore my connectedness to the earth and the parallel evolution that forever ties our identities and our fates to this planet. Hence the earth and ocean imagery that recurs in my poetry."

ANN DECTER grew up in Winnipeg, Manitoba. Her published work includes the short prose book, *Insister* (Gynergy, 1989). She currently lives in Toronto and works as a writer and editor.

BETH FOLLETT is a writer and counsellor living in Montreal. She works with women who are survivors of child sexual abuse.

CAROLYN GAMMON, a red-headed, red-pubed dyke, lives and writes in Montreal. She is currently battling for the right to receive a Mistress of Arts degree from Concordia University. Since writing "On reading *Sexual Politics*," Carolyn has found better materials than a Norman Mailer excerpt for her masturbation recreation.

CANDIS J. GRAHAM: "I started taking my writing seriously in 1976 and, since then, I have worked part-time in traditionally women's jobs (mostly office work) to support myself and my writing. My short fiction has appeared in various anthologies and periodicals, most recently in *By Word of Mouth* (Gynergy) and *Finding the Lesbians* (Crossing). "Primrose Path" is dedicated to Margaret Telegdi."

PINELOPI GRAMATIKOPOULOS likes to crochet on the bus to pass the time, but especially to invite the conversation of other ethnic women.

MEGAN HUTTON: "I was born in Northern British Columbia in 1946. I work and write in Toronto but my heart is in British Columbia. I have been a poet from my 'Bunkhouse' days in the 1960s. I am currently working on a collection of poetry. This story is for 'Annie.' "

KATHRYN ANN lives and works in Kingston both as a writer and a counsellor for young women who are recovering from sexual abuse. She draws cartoons as an antidote to what appears, at times, to be a rather grim reality.

DOROTHY KIDD lives in Vancouver. She works as a writer designing educational programs for community groups and producing community radio and television programs. Every once in a while she writes for herself.

SARAH LOUISE: "I came to Canada from New York State in 1972 and have lived on the West Coast for half of the last eighteen years. My poems and stories have appeared in *Quarry, CVII, Fiddlehead, Prism international, Descant,* and *The Indian P.E.N.* The story that appears in this collection is based on my own experience, and reflects my concern with the relatively high incidence of alcoholism in the lesbian community."

INGRID E. MACDONALD is the author of articles and short stories, including "Polished and Perfect" in the Women's Press anthology *Dykeversions: Lesbian Short Fiction.* A regular contributor to *RITES,* Ingrid also works as the assistant production coordinator of Toronto's *NOW Magazine.* "Catherine, Catherine" is based on incidents in the life of Catharina Linck, a German executed in 1721.

CHRISTINA MILLS: "I am a mother, community activist, translator, songwriter, feminist, runner (okay, jogger), procrastinator and dreamer studying community medicine at the University of Ottawa. I celebrated the beginning of my fifth decade by submitting my poems for publication and starting to work on a third language.

DEENA NELSON is a writer, a sculptor, among other things, who makes a living beating around the bush. Currently she is involved in an alternative housing project in Toronto. After work she retreats to a country house she shares with two dogs, eleven cats and her lover, Sue. She believes the development of lesbian writing is dependent more on the volume of voices heard than on the artificial creation of a secondary language.

PARADIGM, known to her friends as T.O.'s coolest Marxist witch, has recently finished her first year of a very remedial education. Despite this background in law she hopes to be employed as a pirate this summer working the Georgian Bay area.

A. PARPILLÉE cannot appear in print as herself. There's no place yet for who she really is.

MICHELE GRACE PAULSE currently lives in Toronto with Rosamund, her sweetie. They recently published *Asha's Mums*, a children's book about a young girl whose two mums become an issue for Asha's teacher and the curiosity of classmates.

ELLEN QUIGLEY is a poet, critic, anarcha-feminist, and freelance editor. She lives on a farm outside Kingston with her life-partner of eight years, their one-year-old son, another woman, three cats, and a dog. Her poems, articles, and reviews have appeared in *Canadian Literature, CVII, Essays on Canadian Writing, Fiddlehead, Fireweed, pink ink, rune*, and *Studies in Canadian Literature*, among other places. She has also co-edited a multivolume series of critical articles entitled *Canadian Authors and Their Works*.

NORA D. RANDALL is a writer who has taken to performing. She and Jackie Crossland have formed a company, Random Acts, for the purpose of performing stories. They have done *Mavis Tells the Story of Marlene and the Chicken Yard, Postcards from Hawaii, Great Explanations: 4 Lesbian Stories*, and *The Fairy Princess and the Princess Fool* in festivals in British Columbia and Ontario.

GABRIELA SEBASTIAN: "I am twenty-five years old, and I live in Toronto. 'You Have the Right to Remain Silent' is my first work, and it was born when I realized that not every dyke is a feminist, non-racist activist."

NALINI SINGH: "I was born in Guyana and have lived in Toronto for the past seventeen years. I work at Nellie's Hostel for Women in Toronto."

TWO FEATHERS is a Lower Cayuga/Onondaga of the Iroquois Confederacy and a band member of the Six Nations of the Grand River Reserve near Brantford, Ontario. She resides in Toronto and is currently writing her first book.